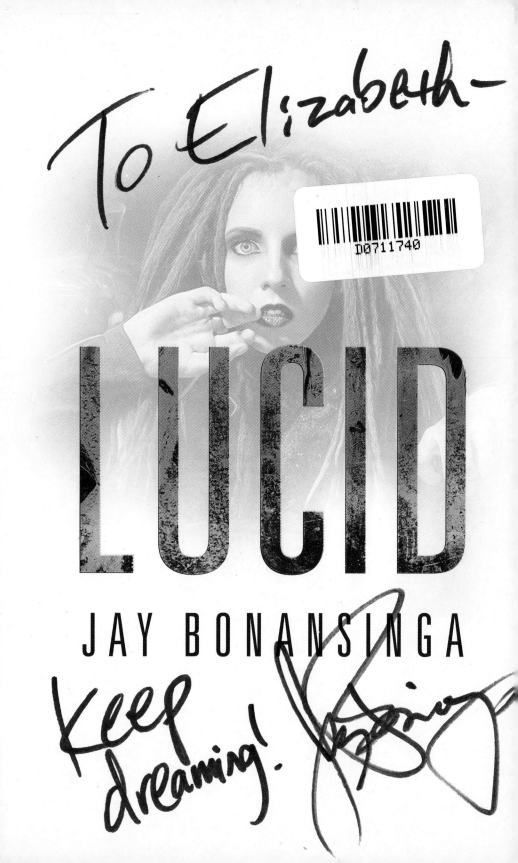

To Elizabeth—

LUCID

JAY BONANSINGA

Keep
dreaming!

Lucid

Published by Permuted Press

109 International Drive, Suite 300
Franklin, TN 37067

www.permutedpress.com

For Jilly, my muse, my world

First and foremost, a huge thank you to MacKenzie Fraser-Bub, without whom this book would have not reached you and would not exist in its present form. Many thanks, as well, to my manager and spirit guide Andy Cohen of Grade A Entertainment, Stephen Emery of Circle of Confusion, Michael, Anthony, and Katie at Permuted Press, John Ford, Brendan Deneen, Jeff Siegel, and Dave Johnson.

PART ONE

THE OTHER SIDE OF THE DOOR

"All that we see or seem / Is but a dream within a dream."
—E. A. Poe

ONE

"Have a seat, Lori."

The school shrink motioned to an armchair next to a coffee table. A balding man in his fifties, he wore John Lennon glasses and a non-threatening sweater vest, and he spoke in the soft, encouraging tones of a camp counselor. His office was a small nest of cozy furniture at the end of Faculty Row. The room was filled with potted plants and framed slogans on the walls such as HANG IN THERE and ONE DAY AT A TIME. The morning sun shone through the blinds.

Lori Blaine slumped down into the armchair across from him with a weary sigh. She was dog-tired, and over the last couple of days had been considering propping her eyelids open with toothpicks. Three weeks away from her eighteenth birthday, she was a tall, lanky, butterscotch-skinned girl of mixed race—a Jamaican dad and an Irish mom—which gave her narrow, sculpted face an ageless look. She had long, tawny-brown hair that she wore in Medusa-like cascades of dreadlocks that resembled a fireworks display on her head. Gold hoops pierced her left eyebrow and right nostril. Today she wore one of her trademark outfits: combat boots, ripped jeans, and a black leather vest over a sports bra that clung to her flat chest. She was constantly being reprimanded by the school's etiquette Nazis for inappropriate attire—a badge of honor among the misfits in her social circle.

"So . . ." The shrink offered a syrupy smile from behind his desk, the grin of a camp counselor with some prepackaged learning activity planned. "What's going on?"

"Oh . . . you know," Lori muttered with a yawn, looking down into her lap and yearning to be anywhere else but here. "The usual. Endless days of quiet desperation . . . searching for a reason to go on in our imploding society." She looked up and gave the man a sheepish look. "Sorry . . . just trying to lighten things up a little."

The shrink chuckled at her feeble attempt at humor and then glanced down at a manila file folder open on his desk blotter. "Says here you're suddenly ignoring Mr. Gibbons' calculus assignments." The shrink took off his glasses and looked up. "You want to talk about that?"

Lori wondered if the shrink had any idea how fixated the math teacher had become on the use of infinitesimals, which had never satisfied the Archimedean property and were now so passé in the scientific community that they might as well be cave paintings—even when applied to nonstandard analysis—but Lori was in no mood to plunge into a treatise on the mathematical limits of infinitesimals, not to mention the limits of the balding, officious little math teacher, Harlan Gibbons, so she maintained noncommittal silence. It was a defense mechanism that she had developed over the years of being pegged as freakishly intelligent. She didn't want to be freakishly *anything*—but especially not something as geeky as supersmart. Maybe that was why she always held back, didn't raise her hand in class, degraded her own performances on tests, and engineered mediocre grades on purpose to ensure that she would never be shunned by the hipsters for being such an annoying brainiac.

After thinking it over for a second, Lori just shrugged again and told the man, "My mom's in the process of hiring a tutor for me, so no worries there."

"That's outstanding, Lori." The shrink gave her a big, encouraging smile. "That's an excellent plan. Is there anything else you want to talk about?"

Another shrug. "Actually . . . uh . . . no. Not really."

"You know you can talk about anything in here," the shrink prodded. "Anything at all. What happens in Vegas stays in Vegas."

Lori gazed into her lap and didn't say anything. Her eyelids felt as though they each weighed a thousand pounds. If she stared long enough at the beaded seams of her worn jeans, she could easily drift off. She clenched her hands into fists in an attempt to keep herself awake and attentive, but it was a losing battle.

"Or we can just hang out," the shrink went on. "Just hang and shoot the shizzle."

"Whatever you think . . . I'm in your capable hands," Lori mumbled, trying to stifle a sleepy giggle. Lori almost felt sorry for the man. The shrink didn't really mean any harm. He was only trying to help.

"You know I spoke with your mom," the shrink was saying now, standing up. He came around the front of the desk and sat down on a second armchair across from Lori. Folding his glasses and slipping them inside his vest, the shrink had a thoughtful expression on his face all of a sudden, as though he were getting down to the crux of the matter. "She said something about a sleep issue?"

Lori sighed. Her mother was another example of an adult with the best intentions but no clue as to how to relate to Lori. Divorced when Lori was eleven, Allison Blaine had struggled to keep her two-bedroom bungalow on Monterey Court (and keep her job at the advertising agency) so that her only child could have all the advantages of the supposedly superior school system in Valesburg, Illinois, as well as all the gifted programs that she had tried unsuccessfully to get Lori to embrace. But Lori wanted to be in a gifted program about as much as she wanted a liver transplant.

"It's really not that significant," Lori said at last, gazing into her lap. Her dreads dangled across her face like ropy brown streamers.

"You want to talk about it?" The shrink was staring at her.

"In all honesty . . . not really."

"Are we talking nightmares and that kind of thing?"

Lori wondered if she should mention the door. Over the course of the last year she had only told two other human beings in the universe about the door: her mother and her best friend, Hugo. And neither had much to say about it. Nor *was* there much to say. It was just one of those odd little dream-details that had been nagging Lori for a few months now, ever since she had noticed its constant presence in her dreams. "Okay, yes," Lori mumbled finally, "sometimes they wake me up."

"Your nightmares wake you up?"

"Yes, basically."

"Does this happen every night?"

"Not every night . . . but lately, I guess, *nearly* every night. I haven't really been keeping track."

The shrink looked like a dog that had found a bone. "Can you tell me about them? The nightmares?"

Lori looked up at the man and shrugged. "What would you like to know?"

"Can you describe them? What they're about?"

A shrug. "There's really nothing special about them, they're just . . . typical nightmares."

The shrink reached over to his desk and grabbed his little shrink's notebook. He opened it and clicked his pen. "Are they all different?"

Lori looked at him. "Define different."

"Well, for instance, is there a recurring nightmare? One you have over and over?"

Lori shrugged. "Not really. Except . . ."

The shrink leaned forward in his chair. "Except what?"

Lori decided right then. What the hell? Why not? The door seemed like a good way to avoid talking about anything substantive with this hopelessly nerdy therapist. "There's a door," she said.

"Go on."

"That's it. For a few months now, I've been seeing this door. No matter what the dream is about."

"Is it familiar?"

"Not really. It's just a door. It's always on the edge of the dream."

"Is it open or shut?"

"It's . . . shut."

"Is it locked?"

Lori thought about it. "I guess so. I'm not absolutely certain."

The shrink made a note and then looked up. "You're not sure?"

"The thing of it is, I always wake up."

"The door wakes you up?"

"I don't know . . . yeah."

"Is it always the same door?"

"Yes, basically."

"Can you describe it?"

"What do you mean?"

The shrink closed the notebook. "What I mean is, is it wooden? Is it metal? Is it scary . . . or plain . . . or *unique* in any way?"

Lori thought about it. "It's a door I've never seen before. I can tell you that much. In the real world, I'm talking about."

The shrink nodded. "Okay."

"It's fairly . . . plain, I guess you would say." Lori gazed off into the corner of the room, thinking about the door. She did not like thinking about it. "It's not wooden," she muttered noncommittally. "But it's not . . . it's not really . . . it's kinda hard to . . . um." Her eyes glazed over, and her stare settled into a sleepy stupor. "It's . . . you know . . . a door."

"When you see this door, Lori, how does it make you feel?"

Lori looked down. She was starting to regret talking about this. "Not exactly terrific," she murmured. "I can say without reservation that it does not fill me with delight when I see it."

"It makes you feel bad, this door, when you see it?"

Lori nodded. "You could say that, yeah. I usually see it out of the corner of my eye. No matter what I'm doing in the dream. Or where I am. It's like . . . *peripheral*. But it's also very disturbing."

The shrink nodded sympathetically, then opened the notebook and wrote another note. Then he looked up. His eyes gleamed with an idea as he measured his words. "And you've never thought of maybe opening the door? Seeing what's on the other side?"

Lori looked at the dust motes floating, luminous in the rays of early morning sun. She was starting to regret dredging this whole thing up. "Like I said, it does not fill me with glee every time it makes an appearance. The door just feels wrong. Creepy. I know they're just dreams but the strange thing is, I also know—"

Lori stopped herself again. She couldn't help it. Her gut was tingling with dread.

"Go on, Lori, it's okay," the shrink urged. He was gnawing at that bone.

Lori gave him another shrug. "Okay . . . full disclosure? I've never shared this with anybody."

Pause.

The shrink closed his notes. "It's okay, Lori. Whatever it is. We'll tackle it together."

After another long pause Lori finally said, "When I'm having a dream . . . at some point . . . I realize I'm in a dream. In other words, I know I'm dreaming while I'm in the dream."

The shrink stared. It was obvious his mental circuits were humming as he processed all this. He blinked. "Lori, you do realize what this means, don't you?"

"Okay, let me stop you right there." She raised her slender hands as though she were about to surrender. "Before you go into a whole dissertation on lucid dreaming, just let me say . . . I'm familiar with the concept. I understand it means one can, you know, be in the driver's seat of one's dreams. Dictate what happens in them . . . that kind of thing."

"It also means you are one of only 13.5 percent of all human beings on this planet." The shrink grinned at her—a grin that was vaguely disturbing to Lori. The doctor went on to explain that studies have shown lucid dreamers to be generally healthier, happier people than ordinary dreamers. Once they develop their skills, lucid dreamers have the power to go anywhere in their dreams, do anything, address any issue. Fly. Travel. Slay dragons. Work out any intractable problem that has been plaguing them in the waking world. Lucid dreamers are the superheroes of the dream realm. "Do you not see this as a positive, Lori?" the shrink finally asked. "Wouldn't you say this is a good thing?"

Lori thought about it. "No . . . to be quite honest with you, I don't."

The shrink looked as though he had been squirted with cold water. "Can I ask why not?"

Lori thought about it some more, thought long and hard, before finally replying: "Because basically I don't want to get involved in these dreams."

The shrink let out a sigh. "But Lori, they're a part of you. They're who you are. I mean . . ."

"Well, then maybe that's the problem." She gave him a hard look. "I don't want anything to do with them. Maybe I don't want to know who I really am."

This was a half-truth. The real reason Lori Blaine did not want to experiment with such things was the prospect of seeing what was on the other side of that door.

The shrink started to say something else when the morning bell sounded—an electronic drone that summoned students to class like cattle to the meatpacking factory.

The shrink closed his file folder and rose to his feet. "Okay, Lori. I understand. This kind of thing can be . . . difficult." The man thrust out a manicured hand. "Let's keep the dialogue going."

Lori stood. "Sure."

They shook hands.

On her way out, Lori heard the shrink calling after her: "And promise

TWO

According to the Guinness Book of World Records, which Lori verified on the Internet, a British man named Tony Wright set the world record for sleep deprivation by staying up 266 hours (a little more than eleven days). Lori Blaine was only on her third day and was already starting to flake out. She barely made it to the lunch bell.

"And how exactly do you plan to maintain this foolhardy endeavor?" Hugo Stipple asked somewhat rhetorically as he and Lori crossed the crowded, malodorous cafeteria with trays of food-like matter known as "goulash." The room doubled as the gymnasium. The bleachers were now folded up and tucked behind a collapsible wall, the harsh fluorescent light shining down on the cavernous carnival of clatter.

"It's called caffeine, Hugo, you should look into it," Lori replied, giving wide berth to a table full of 'Straps. The 'Straps (short for "jockstraps") were the steroid cases, the football players and wrestlers, who ate together in packs. The stereotype was that the 'Straps were mean, shallow thugs who pushed everybody around. Lori found this to be—like all stereotypes—oversimplified and inaccurate. Lori knew 'Straps who were soft-spoken, shy, and gentle. She knew 'Straps who were Brainiacs, and some who were very cool and friendly . . . and some who were, of course, mean and shallow creeps. It depended upon the person.

But the stereotypes would not go away—especially in that cauldron of tribal warfare known as high school.

Part of the problem was that the kids at Valesburg Central, out of sheer survival instinct, tended to congregate in narrowly defined cliques. The Fundies (short for "trust funders") were the rich kids, who supposedly were nasty, ruthless, amoral snobs. Not true. Lori knew a Fundie named Callie Rossler who spent her summers working at a homeless shelter. The Stoners were supposedly lazy, drug-addled, flaky, clueless idiots—but Lori knew a Stoner named Dave Hardesty who had written three plays and a novel.

"All I'm saying is, if you're not like extraordinarily careful you could like die and stuff," Hugo said as he and Lori took their seats at the Goth table. Spurned by most of the student body, the Goths at Valesburg Central occupied a wholly obsolete corner of the teenage jungle—as useless and anachronistic as vinyl record albums. Being a Goth was so "1990s" it wasn't even rebellious anymore. Technically, Lori Blaine was not even remotely Goth—other than her natural proclivity for brooding—but she gravitated toward the anachronistic styles and melodrama. With her Rasta cool and rebellious nature, she fit right in.

"Not careful about what?" asked Amanda Absinthe (formerly known as Amy Schwartz). She was the smallest of the three Goth girls. She had pink hair on one side and raven black hair on the other, and she wore onyx-dark lace that brought to mind a miniature Anne Rice.

"Nothing you need be concerned about," Lori said with faux cheerfulness, opening her carton of milk. Clad in her leathers and dreads, she affected a certain seniority around the other Goths, like an emissary from some exotic island nation. At the moment she was pretending to be interested in the foul-smelling roadkill casserole on her plastic plate, while she pondered what to say about her little "issue." The chaos of the lunch hour swirled around her. Voices rose in an atonal symphony of hyena laughter and barking rants.

The Goths usually sat in the lower-class district of the lunchroom, and now Lori gazed around their pathetic little "Loser Zone" at all the other disenfranchised cliques: the Brainiacs over by the steam tables, with their ever-present laptops, discussing episodes of *Dr. Who* and chess moves . . . and the Espies, pushed up against the wrestling mats, huddling together in their little gulag of wheelchairs, oxygen tanks, metal braces, and slurred speech. (Espies was short for "extra special persons," a recent politically correct upgrade from the more common phrase, "special needs," which, after all, would be wrong, since the latter suggests they "need" something.)

For a single instant Lori's gaze fell on Davy Kettlekamp, a tall, lanky, pimply kid sitting by himself on a windowsill behind the Espies. Silently eating his meager sack lunch, dressed in tattered denim overalls like some refugee from a Mark Twain story, Davy was burning holes in the rest of the student body with his angry, hostile, eerie stare.

Nicknamed "Ichabod" by the wags at the student paper, probably because of the boy's prominent Adam's apple and jug-handle ears, Davy was another example of what Lori thought of as the fallacy of stereotyping: Not all poor farm kids from the disadvantaged corn belt surrounding Valesburg were the plain, mild-mannered, salt-of-the-earth types from the *Little House on the Prairie* books. Some of them were as mean as snakes, and as scary as Ichabod Kettlekamp.

"Lori's trying to avoid sleep," Hugo blurted, poking a finger at his goulash, wrenching Lori's attention back to the Goth table. Once upon a time, for a few months, Lori and Hugo had pretended to be girlfriend and boyfriend, but neither could stomach the messy rituals that went along with the charade . . . such as dating . . . and sex. Sex seemed like some obscure far-flung objective to be addressed later in life—like a financial annuity or an insurance policy—but God knew she received plenty of portfolio advice from the elders. When Lori turned thirteen, her mother had presented an elaborate presentation on the reproductive system, complete with PowerPoint visuals and a Q and A section—the woman was a born advertising executive—and the whole experience had mortified Lori.

"Oh my God, that is so exquisitely *Lori*," commented Rachael Deathcraft (formerly Rosemary Donowitz) with a flourish of her lace-gloved hand. She was the ersatz leader of the Goths, with the contents of an entire silverware drawer pierced through various parts of her upper anatomy. She wore a black veil over her long, acne-scarred face, her big, intelligent eyes caked with so much eyeliner she looked as though she were wearing a burglar's mask. "We heartily approve!" she enthused.

"Thanks . . . I think," Lori muttered, moving her goulash around her plate. As the unofficial emissary of cool, she sometimes wondered if she served a sort of *token* role for these people, the only sister-girl in the lily-white world of makeshift black masses and Cure reunion concerts. Still, the Goths seemed to look up to Lori, often asking her advice on matters of supreme importance such as how many candles to light at one of their parties or the best body part on which to festoon a pentagram tattoo.

"Is there a reason for this fool's errand?" asked Wyatt Hellstrom from the other side of the table. A heavyset kid in a death-metal T-shirt, Wyatt was the oldest of the group, a senior on the six-year plan who played bass in the garage band known as Bela Lugosi's Gall Bladder.

With a sigh Lori started to say, "All I'm simply trying to is—"

"Nightmare evasion," Hugo broke in, gobbling the barely edible substance in front of him. The others nodded thoughtfully at this information.

"I adore nightmares," Amanda mused. "They give me grist."

"They give you what?" Wyatt inquired with an arched brow.

"Grist for the mill," the young lady elaborated. "For my art projects."

"Well, they give *me* stomach cramps and explosive diarrhea," the

14

heavy kid commented. "And I'm not talking about my nightmares; I'm talking about your art projects." Everybody laughed at that one. Except Lori. "Nightmares can be pretty freaky, though," Wyatt added. "I remember one where my Granny Rose was the lead singer for this band and after this one show she tried to put her tongue down my throat."

Groans issued from every single person at the table but Lori.

Absently playing with her food, her head down, she mumbled something that, at first, no one heard. Hugo looked at her and said, "Sorry—what was that?"

"The old gray mare ain't what she used to be," Lori muttered, her voice barely a whisper now, her gaze fixed on the mystery casserole decomposing on her plate. "Strangely enough, the word comes from a German word *Nachtmahr*, meaning night demon or goblin, but the demon is not really a demon, it's *you*. It's just your body's metabolism. It's just your brain dieseling like a car that won't shut off. Like Dickens said, 'An undigested bit of beef, a blot of mustard, a crumb of cheese, an underdone potato. There's more of gravy than of grave about you.' And that's really all it is—you're digestive juices working while you're asleep, kicking your mind into gear and creating little flicker shows. It doesn't mean anything. There's no . . . like . . . *prophecy*. There's no symbolism, all that Freudian crap . . . Jung . . . there's no psychological significance, no clues to past lives. Nothing. It's just . . . anchovy pizzas, memories of B-movie jump scares . . . fueled by overactive imaginations. They're just annoying, that's all. And I'm so done with dealing with them. But they don't mean shit. Trust me. They're not even worth talking about."

For a moment, the silence that followed this odd, unexpected soliloquy from Lori seemed to stretch for an endless amount of time, the others at the table taken by surprise, their rapt, open-mouthed stares lingering, until Hugo finally broke the spell. "Well, one thing's for sure," he said. "The food in this place is enough to give you nightmares."

Oddly, nobody even offered as much as a chuckle at this little witty retort.

Although nobody said it aloud, everybody was thinking the same thing: Lori didn't sound like she believed a word of what she just said.

After lunch, the Goth gang went their separate ways. Lori had a free hour, so she avoided the crowded corridors by slipping outside and trudging across the school campus. Her battered and outmoded iPhone—its operating system about a half dozen generations old—was out of battery. So instead, she crossed several acres of crumbling brick towers, bordered by parking lots and Victorian streetlamps. It was September, and cold and damp in Illinois, the sky pressing down on the school grounds like a gunmetal gray blanket.

The library wing was the furthest building north, adjacent to the town's main drag of strip malls and office parks. Covered with dead ivy, it looked like a medieval monastery. Lori went in the double doors and blinked at the warm, foul-smelling air, which reeked of musty paper and dried sweat and old floor wax.

On the second floor, just past the librarian's counter, Lori found a vacant computer terminal. She plopped down and tapped into the district-wide database, her platform boots forming puddles beneath the table. She did a search for lucid dreaming and came up with about a million entries. It was difficult keeping her eyelids open and her head from lolling forward, but after staring at a few websites she started narrowing her search.

Lori had a basic layman's understanding of lucid dreaming, but now that the concept was moving from the abstract to the *oh-shit-this-is-really-happening*, she wanted to figure it out, look under the hood, and understand it better. This was how she dealt with things that scared her. One time, when she was only seven years old, she hired the neighbor boy—Jimmy McCauley—to stand outside her window with a Coleman camp lantern and slowly sweep it across the side of the house. The idea was to replicate the spooky shadows moving across the dark interior of her closet, which were plaguing her at night. She paid him in Sweet

Tarts and candy corn—a fee well spent—after realizing that the eerie, animated shadows were from the headlights of passing cars.

Now she got down to the inner workings of lucid dreaming. According to one source, scientists in the 1970s figured out that certain people with high "alpha" activity during sleep—which basically means their brain waves are the same as when they're awake—are able to recognize they're having a dream *during a dream*. This ability, according to test subjects, leads to a kind of superpower.

Anything becomes possible. The dreamer rules the world of the dream.

More interesting to Lori were the different ways in which lucid dreamers become lucid. One category was the accidental discovery—the dreamer basically stumbles onto the fact that she knows she's dreaming—which was basically what had happened to Lori. Another method was to use a memory device called a *mnemonic*. Before going to sleep, the dreamer sketches a picture of a sign that says "This Is a Dream." They stare and meditate on the sketch until the image is burned into their memory. Then, after falling asleep, the dreamer will actually see this "sign" pop up in their dream—in essence a notification that the dream has begun.

There were plenty of other methods—little handy ways of bringing on lucid activity—but Lori was starting to get dizzy with dread. She found case studies of people who were driven insane by the phenomena. One man in India was sent into a vegetative state after being caught in a dream for weeks. Another woman from Des Moines, Iowa, was reduced to a brain-damaged paraplegic after trying to reverse-engineer her dreams of childhood abuse.

One thing was becoming clear: this was not something to be taken lightly. And the more she read about it, the more Lori had a terrible feeling that if she wasn't careful, the dreaming could become the "tail wagging the dog" (instead of the other way around).

The dreams could control *her*.

When Lori finally left the library—after blowing off the rest of her classes that day—it was dark outside. Her tobacco-brown dreadlocks flagging in the wind, she slunk home through the cobblestone streets of Valesburg. Her PVC-black purse slung over one shoulder, she walked as though drunk, the lack of sleep making her legs wobbly and her balance shaky. Her breaths plumed in puffs of vapor in the cold air as she passed under aging gas lamps.

A nineteenth-century river town only half a mile from the banks of the Mississippi, Valesburg was a true throwback to the days of cotton picking, slaves, and steamboat gamblers. Over the years nobody had bothered resurfacing the ancient paving stones, or renovating the old Victorian buildings along Main Street, or even upgrading the plank walkways. Today Valesburg looked like something out of an Emily Brontë novel retrofitted with Taco Bells and 7-Elevens.

Lori's house was on the north side of town, a little shotgun wood-frame job, which her mother had desperately tried to keep as tidy and charming as possible after the divorce. Alas, the front yard was overrun with crabgrass, and the trellises over the front door were clogged with dead roses as sickly and shriveled as little black prunes.

That night, Lori was making her second pot of French Roast Extra Bold in the Mr. Coffee when she heard her mother's voice behind her.

"Honey, please," the woman pleaded, and Lori turned to face her with a jerk.

"What . . . oh, hi."

"You can't stay up forever," Allison Blaine opined. The woman was standing in her robe and high-top sneakers, shaking a plastic pill bottle at Lori. It made an almost musical noise. Allison's dishwater-blonde hair was pulled back from her weary face. She was once beautiful in a freshly scrubbed farm girl sort of way, but life had deepened the lines around her pale blue eyes and tugged on the corners of her mouth.

Lori sighed and turned back to her coffee. "It's a temporary thing, Mom, I assure you."

"You can't function without sleep, kiddo."

Lori fiddled with the coffeepot. "It's just until I get a handle on things."

"What things, Lori?"

She shrugged and gazed at the coffee dripping into the pot. The *plop-plop-plop* of the chocolate-colored liquid could very easily hypnotize Lori if she let it. "Various and sundry items cropping up in my dreams," she murmured.

Lori's mom looked down. A pale strand of hair hung in her eye. "I remember when your father and I split up." She brushed the hair from her eye and looked up. "I went through a period of time when I was having bad dreams every night of my life. I mean, multiple nightmares. Every single night. It went on for months. I thought I was losing my marbles. But you see, here's the thing. It's like the weather. If you don't like it, all you have to do is wait. It'll change. You don't need a therapist to tell you this. It's going to get better. You just have to know, honey, they're going to go away. It's what makes us human. It's what separates us from the animals."

Lori was staring at the coffeepot. "And what is that, Mom? What separates us?"

"Hope, honey. *Hope*. You just have to hang in there." She shook the pills. "Dr. Simonson gave me these. He said they wouldn't interact with the Ritalin."

Lori turned and looked at the pills in her mother's hand. "What are they?"

"Mild sleeping pills."

"Mom—"

"I know what you're thinking," she said and took a step closer. "These are mild tranquilizers; they'll just relax you so you can get some rest."

"But what about—"

"Dr. Simonson claims you won't even dream on these. You'll just sleep."

Lori thought about it. She never realized how desperately a body could crave sleep. She was lost in the desert, and the pill bottle was a mirage—a cool pond in the shade of a lush palm tree—but there were dark objects drifting below the surface of this mirage that scared her, sharks swimming around the depths of her subconscious. She preferred to stay away from the mirage, stay thirsty and dry, but . . .

After a long pause, she rubbed her eyes. "Okay, fine, fine, fine. I'll take them."

Allison Blaine was already at the sink, filling a plastic cup with water.

THREE

Studies have shown there are five stages of sleep. The first two usually last only a few minutes. Stage one, known as "slow-wave sleep," is where the sleeper begins to doze, and brain activity slows down. This is the state Lori Blaine found herself in that night only moments after flopping down, still fully dressed, on her rickety brass bed.

She lay dozing amidst the clutter of pop culture that occupied every last square inch of available space in that inner sanctum she called a bedroom. The walls were plastered with clippings from fashion magazines, old flyers from obscure alternative rock concerts, pictures of Bob Marley, and a wide array of cryptic, spooky photos that she had snapped with her old-school Brownie camera—empty alleys, fogbound streets, close-ups of Rorschach oil spills across weather-beaten pavement, and various and sundry homeless people smiling toothless grins at her lens.

Stage two of the sleep cycle is a transitional phase. Brain waves peak randomly during this stage, with no purpose, like an orchestra tuning. As Lori burrowed into her tangle of blankets that night, she slipped furtively into this phase, her stubborn brain still racing. The last bleary, semiconscious thoughts that registered in her mind were half-formed fragments of her day—like fleeting film clips and bursts of static on her shortwave mind-radio—forming a haphazard collage of sounds and images. She saw the school shrink in his Mr. Rogers cardigan clicking his pen, nodding thoughtfully as he made notes . . . and she heard the dripping of her boots on the ancient parquet floor of the school library . . . and she glimpsed flickering flash-frames of dream researchers attaching electrodes to the heads of hapless subjects.

Then came stage three.

Stage three rolls in like a gentle rain blanketing the mindscape, drowning everything in its white noise. Also known as delta sleep (or deep sleep), this stage causes brain activity to practically shut down like a computer screen cutting to black. That night, Lori lingered in this third stage for nearly two and a half hours, as still as a stone, her chest barely rising with each slow, silent breath. Her body needed to catch up, replenish itself, before moving on to the next stage, which was the most mysterious to scientists.

Sleep researchers think of stage four as another transition—even deeper than the delta stage—a kind of dark, empty, featureless waiting room—preparing the brain for the final and fifth stage of sleep, which is known as REM, or rapid eye movement. This is the place where dreams live. The eyeballs begin to twitch and jitter under the sleeper's eyelids like chicks trying to hatch. In stage five REM sleep, the eyes begin to see things, vivid things, which do not exist in the waking world.

That night Lori Blaine reached this stage at precisely 1:11 A.M., her bedroom still blazing with light. She dreamt she was walking along a frozen lake in the dead of winter. Dressed in the same clingy, sleeveless, red-satin dress that she wore to the junior prom that autumn, she could feel the bitter wind on her bare arms, tossing her hair—she wore her braids in an updo, gathered in back, with snaky bangs stylishly dangling across her eyes, courtesy of Rosemary Donowitz's mom, who was a beautician in town—and somehow it all made sense: the lake, the dress, the wind, the anxious feeling of being late, the way things always have their kind of logic in dreams. She picked up her pace.

Faint cracking noises drew her attention down to her black, open-toed, faux suede high heels—her mom spent an entire afternoon helping her choose those shoes—and now she saw that the ice was thin beneath her feet. Each stride was sending hairline fractures across the milky white ice. She sped up. She was late for an appointment, and she was in trouble. The cracking noises rose around her. Her heart raced. She glanced up and scanned the horizon.

The long, vast, serpentine lake was bordered on either side by thick pine barrens, the forest stretching up a steep slope into the gray winter sky. It was getting late. Night was rolling in. Lori could smell woodsmoke and feel the cold aluminum metal of snow on her face. Jesus, she was so late. She was going to catch hell.

She trundled along as speedily as her high heels would carry her.

Oddly, the vivid setting—the frozen lake and the palisades of thick pine trees hundreds of yards in the distance—seemed very familiar to her. This being a dream, she had no idea why everything seemed so recognizable. But it did, and that was the weirdest part. She almost expected things to go from bad to worse, as they often did on this lake, wherever this lake was.

She scanned the horizon. Her pulse quickened. In the distance, she could see the faint silhouette of something on the ice—like an inkblot in the shape of a human being—and despite the fact that it was over two hundred yards away, Lori could see it was an old woman. Hunched in a rocking chair, clad in black, her face obscured by a black cowl, the crone was working on something in her lap. As Lori approached, the danger became apparent.

The old lady was knitting, her back turned to Lori as she approached—the enormous needles in the woman's hands dripping blood on the white ice—and Lori felt like screaming. This woman was evil. That much was certain. Lori could see the Technicolor scarlet blood running in rivulets across the surface of the lake under the woman's rocker as she knitted and softly hummed a disturbing tune. The rocker creeeeeeaked . . . and the woman hummmmmmmmmmmmed . . . and the ice crrrrrrracked . . .

and the blood trickled and dripped and ran in runnels across the glacial alabaster surface of the lake.

Lori slid to a halt about twenty-five feet away from that terrible old woman in the hooded black cowl. She struggled to turn around and flee, but her high heels were slipping and sliding on the ice and the blood. The old woman stopped knitting. Lori opened her mouth to scream but no sound would come out as the crone stood up on brittle, bony joints, whirling around to face Lori.

The wind blew the hood off the woman's cranium and revealed a horribly burned face, as shriveled as a petrified gourd, with cadaverous eyes that smoldered like embers. Lori scuttled backward and fell on her rear. The crone levitated, hovering a few inches over the ice, slowly and menacingly floating toward Lori.

No matter how hard she tried, Lori could not emit a single sound. The old woman loomed above her like a giant bird of prey, raising the blood-tipped knitting needles, preparing to thrust them down into Lori's heaving midsection . . . when all at once Lori saw something out of the corner of her eye that changed everything.

Twenty feet away, a tiny square of fabric had slipped off the arm of the rocking chair—a tapestry hewn from yarn and thread and beads, presumably the masterpiece on which the old woman had been laboring—and now Lori saw the filigree of letters monogrammed into the cloth, spelling out a simple message:

This is a Dream

Lori stared at the tapestry and thought about it and suddenly smiled. She sprang to her feet. She felt an odd fluttering at the base of her neck, like a plucked string inside her nervous system. The air rumbled with distant thunder and the old woman froze in midair above her as though pickled in aspic. And that's when Lori found her voice and let out a booming cry: "GET THE HELL OUT OF MY DREAM, BITCH!!"

The woman's face puckered suddenly, her flesh beginning to fizz and bubble as though reacting to acid. The knitting needles slipped from her grasp and clattered to the ice, vanishing as if made of smoke. Rising up into the sky like an errant kite, the crone convulsed and arched her back and emitted a strangled cry as though burning up from the inside out. Lori watched.

The old lady vanished then on a puff of air as abruptly as she had appeared.

Lori did a victory dance in her high heels and shimmering red dress that rivaled the craziest end-zone dance ever performed by any game-winning NFL showboat before a national TV audience. In her Michael Kors heels she danced and strutted and spun pirouettes that would have put an Olympic ice skater to shame. She sashayed and did the boogaloo and jigged and reeled until she saw the other figures in her peripheral vision closing in on her like predators.

At least a dozen clones of the old woman—their faces radiating pinched evil beneath their cowls—began closing in on Lori from all directions, sliding demonically on cushions of icy air. Some of them carried elongated knitting needles, dripping with pearls of blood, others gripping scythes and machetes in their skeletal fingers. Lori remained calm. She pivoted toward the closest one. The crone pounced at her, and Lori calmly executed a graceful scissor kick.

The high-heeled pump—its toe as pointy and sharp as a dagger—struck the old lady at the knees and sent the hag sprawling to the ice. More came toward Lori. She spun and kicked and lunged with the aplomb of a samurai—sending crone after crone staggering backward and tripping over their own spindly legs. Weapons hurled through the air. Cries filled the dream—the caws of old arthritic crows—as the monstrous ladies fell, one by one. Some of them broke through the ice and sank into frigid oblivion, while others landed on their rheumatic spines and puffed out of existence on plumes of black smoke.

Lori finished off the last one and let out a yawp of victory—her voice as strong as a clarion now. She stood for a moment in the center of the ice, catching her breath, as the last of hags melted out of existence. Lori giggled and started to turn away from the battlefield when she saw another sight way off in the distance that caught her eye and made her breath stick in her throat.

Barely visible in the icy vapors of the forest, lying in shadows about a hundred and fifty yards away, it was hanging there with no logic other than the logic of dreams. And Lori stood there for an incalculable amount of time, staring at it, clenching and unclenching her fists. In fact, she lost track of time.

In dreams, time makes no sense. It's a mathematical equation with no solution. Lori might have been standing there on that ice for a single moment that seemed to last a lifetime. Or perhaps she had been standing there for a lifetime that seemed to last a single moment.

And don't even *try* to calculate the amount of real time—from the perspective of the outside world—that Lori spent in REM that night.

Lori Blaine was in another dimension now, a dimension she would come to know as REMspace. It had a texture as tactile as the real world. A smell. Burnt orange rinds and axle grease and cinnamon and gunpowder. It had a certain kind of light, too, which reminded Lori of an old black and white movie that had been *colorized*.

She was thinking about all this when she finally realized what she was looking at embedded in a dense netting of foliage more than a hundred yards away.

She froze.

She stared.

* * *

When Lori was twelve, her mom took her to the Art Institute of Chicago. The big, gray, marble fortress had stood on Michigan Avenue for over a hundred years. Twin lions, green with patina and pollution, flanked the great steps like sentries. Inside, the air was thick with dust and mildew and the smell of ancient fabric.

Lori and her mom had made an entire day out of the visit, bringing their sack lunches and eating on the veranda with the pigeons. But it was a special exhibit inside the modern wing that had truly taken Lori aback.

At the time, Lori had just started dreaming about the door and was still trying to figure out what it meant, and whether it was important or not, when she had happened upon the Ivan Albright wing.

Ivan Albright was a famous painter, best known for his extreme detail and dark themes. His most famous work was the *Picture of Dorian Gray*, a decaying zombie in a silk frock coat, which appealed greatly to the Gothy side of Lori. But far more disturbing and haunting to the girl was a single painting lurking in the far corner of the exhibit.

Lori had spent endless moments staring at that tall, narrow canvas with the strange and mysterious title, *That Which I Should Have Done I Did Not Do (The Door)*. She wondered if the painting was an omen, or some kind of supernatural sign. It was a locked door, painted in deep shades of black and indigo, its panels rotted with wormy holes and scars, a shriveled corsage of funeral flowers hanging near the top.

Over the years, since that moment when she first saw the Albright door, Lori's dream door had become more and more like that painting.

Now, in her nightmare, this very instant, she slowly strode across the ice of an imaginary lake toward an object that would turn out to be the closest three-dimensional rendering of the Art Institute painting she had ever seen in a dream. It taunted her from the shadows of the forest, straight ahead, radiating danger, beckoning to her. And the closer she got to it, the more its dimensions revealed themselves.

At least ten feet high, with long, blackened, charred panels like burnt strips of skin, the door had a knob that was old and tarnished. As dull as a rotten tooth. And there was a keyhole, through which a dim strand of light spilled out at her like a finger. If ever there was a door that begged to stay shut—to remain locked, in fact—this was it. Lori did not need to know—did not *want* to know—in fact had spent the past five years *worrying* about and *dreading*—what was on the other side of that door.

She started to turn away.

Then she paused.

At that moment, in the dream, Lori remembered what the shrink had said about lucid dreamers, how they can work out their problems and control the content of their dreams. Maybe Lori could finally conquer this door issue by simply creating something harmless on the other side.

All she had to do was simply *will* herself to go through the door.

Then all she had to do was imagine something harmless on the other side.

She turned back to the door. She was standing closer to it now. Without even moving, she was standing right in front of it. Her breath puffed in blooms of vapor in the freezing air as she regarded the door up close. She could see the peeling paint, the tarnished hinge plates. She could smell the rotting wood, and she could feel an even *colder* draft leaking through the seams of the thing.

She took a deep breath.

The doorknob was cool to the touch. She turned it. The door was not locked, and the bolt clicked as the tumblers opened.

Heart hammering in her chest, Lori swung the door open on squeaking hinges.

FOUR

On the other side of the door stretched a deserted black tunnel, like a root cellar or a forgotten bomb shelter. Lori looked around. The tunnel extended in every direction that she gazed, as far as she could see, before vanishing into the gloom. The air was dank. Clammy and cool and drafty.

For a long while Lori stood in that open doorway, frozen with indecision.

Was she manufacturing this place? It was so detailed and vivid. The tunnel ceiling, which hung only inches above her, featured stalactites like rock formations in an underground spring. The walls, which were the color of moon dust and cigarette ash, dripped with moisture. But these were not the strangest parts.

The strangest parts were the signs of human alteration. The floor had been inlaid with an endless boardwalk. Light bulbs hung in tiny cages every few feet, dangling from exposed power cable. Switch plates were mounted on the walls, connected to snaking power lines. The low hum of a generator somewhere vibrated the floor.

Was Lori imagining all this? Could a dreamer—even a very talented lucid one—purposely construct such a place from scratch?

Something caught her eye in the glistening grain of the tunnel wall a few feet away. She fixed her gaze on it. It looked like a shiny egg or a glass bulb petrified into the stone. She ventured a few steps from the doorway.

She was unaware that the door had slowly drifted shut behind her, clicking softly.

She knelt by the egg-shaped object. It was an eyeball. It was looking at her. The wall was looking at her. She sprang to her feet, gasping, as the wall blinked. More eyes opened like blisters popping open in the stone. The tunnel was checking her out. Hundreds of eyes now seemed to look her up and down with suspicion.

Backing toward the door, she decided to get the hell out of there.

But the door was locked. Lori frantically jiggled the doorknob. It was futile. The bolt was sealed as tight as a weld. Her pulse racing now, Lori was just starting to panic, when she heard a low, menacing, growling noise come from the shadows behind her.

She slammed her back against the door and peered into the distance.

She couldn't exactly see it. Or even hear it. It was more of a feeling. Something enormous was coming—something far more dangerous than a few knitting needle–toting old ladies. And if Lori had been forced to describe the noise it made—mostly in her brain at that point—she would have said it sounded like the lowest note in a pipe organ, the snore of a beast, the rumbling of a leviathan, as old as time itself, and as evil as the farthest reaches of the universe.

Lori ran.

In the opposite direction.

Head lowered, teeth clenched, hands balled into fists, she ran as fast as she could, the soles of her pointy platform boots echoing in the slimy darkness.

She could see a bend in the tunnel ahead of her, and she charged toward it. Whatever was coming toward her, it was beyond horrible . . . beyond Lori's comprehension.

She reached the bend in the tunnel and lurched around the corner.

And ran directly into two figures blocking her path.

"WHOA!" The younger figure—a boy—let out a yelp as he jerked out of Lori's way.

The boy, who looked to be in his late teens or maybe twenty at the most, was dressed in soiled work clothes—like those of a heating and air conditioning installer—his tool belt festooned with strange devices that Lori couldn't identify. He held a long, slender, metallic object, which Lori, at first, thought was a cane.

Lori stumbled sideways, banging into the second figure, an older man dressed in dark overalls, also soiled and workmanlike.

"I knew it!" the man said, shoving Lori off him with a grunt.

"What's going on? What's the—? Who are—?" Lori backed against the moist stone, breathing hard, her gaze shifting from figure to figure.

At that moment, in the dream—or whatever this was—Lori was stricken with a realization that she could not fully understand. These two individuals standing before her were strangers and yet, somehow, they seemed so real, so specific, that Lori was instantly certain that they were indeed *real people*. Or *had* been real. Or were *projections* of real people. Or *something* like that.

"Holy shit, you made it through!" The boy was staring at Lori as though she had just laid an egg. Later, trying to describe the boy to Hugo, the best Lori could do was say he looked like a young Johnny Depp. He had pale blue eyes and long, unruly brown hair that looked as though it had been cut by a weed whacker. He had tattoos and wore a lot of bracelets and beads, and he had a cigarette behind his ear. He tapped his cattle-prod apparatus on the tunnel floor. It made a hollow ringing noise as the boy turned to his friend. "She made it through! I told you it was bound to happen!"

"Be that as it may," the man muttered, gazing past the boy. The man was in his late forties, gray at the temples, and chiseled like a park ranger or a cowboy. A small chain dangled around his neck with keys, a crucifix, a Star of David, and many other unidentifiable objects. "There's a Bogy in the vicinity, so we'll have to sort this out in the office."

They each grabbed a handful of Lori's satin prom dress, then spun her around and started hastily ushering her back into the shadows from which they had appeared. Lori's heels awkwardly clopped on the stone floor as she stumbled along, and she tried to will the whole scene away as she did with the ninja old ladies. But for reasons she would soon learn, the tingling sensation at the top of her cervical vertebra had vanished. She felt as feckless and drained as a dead battery.

"Can we slow down a second?!" She nearly tripped and fell, they were moving so swiftly. She could sense the change in air pressure around them as the presence—or the entity or the monster or whatever it was behind them—closed in. The deep, baritone, snarling noise rose and vibrated the tunnel. The very walls seemed to react to it. The eyeballs embedded in the slimy stone snapped shut, the surface of the wall sprouting goose bumps.

"Just hang in there," the boy advised as he dragged Lori along.

"Can I ask where the hell you're taking me?"

"Somewhere safe," the chiseled man informed her with a weary sigh.

They reached another intersection, turned a corner, and headed down another side tunnel.

"It probably smelled her coming through," the boy ventured, pausing and pulling an object off his tool belt. The thing resembled a flashlight with multiple lenses and wires tangled around it. He pointed it at the interesting tunnels and thumbed a switch.

A flash of brilliant silver light like a camera strobe changed the shape of the tunnel. With a blur the walls instantly shifted.

Lori gasped.

A new tunnel materialized to their left. It looked like an office corridor with wall-to-wall carpeting and recessed lighting. A bank of elevators became visible. The chiseled man dragged Lori toward the doors. "We need this like a hole in the head right now," the man grumbled.

The boy pressed the DOWN button. "You can't stop progress, Pops."

"Progress is it?"

The doors opened and Lori was shoved into the enclosure. They pressed the LL button, which Lori in her daze assumed was the lower level, but the lower level of *what*? The lower level of her dream?

The faint sound of Muzak—Lori would later realize that it was an old song from the 1960s called "The Girl from Ipanema"—droned in the background. The elevator doors closed and the enclosure rattled downward.

"What's done is done," the boy mumbled as the elevator descended.

Lori was biting her fingernails. She looked at the young man. "If it's not too much trouble, would you mind telling me what the hell is going on?"

"Progress," the older man murmured glumly.

The doors opened and the boy yanked Lori out into another bland corporate hallway with inverted lighting and gray carpet. They made their way down the corridor to an open doorway marked DIRECTOR.

"Just let me do the talking," the boy said as they paused outside the doorway. He knocked on the jamb. "Mrs. Waverly! It's Nick and Pops!"

A gravelly female voice from inside: "For heaven's sake, come *in* already."

They entered a cluttered office. Metal shelving units brimming with file boxes crowded every inch of wall space. Giant flexible conduits and mail tubes hung down from the ceiling. A few shriveled houseplants sat on top of huge, old, retro computer terminals, which flickered and crawled with data of some sort, strands of numbers and geothermal maps and contours of landscapes pulsing and changing. It looked like the control center of an absentminded mad scientist. "What is this?" the voice said from the corner.

"Okay let's everybody stay calm—" the boy began to say.

"What is going on?" An old woman in a motorized wheelchair rolled into view. She wore a knit shawl over her camouflage army fatigues. Her deeply lined face was crowned with blue-rinse hair. Her sagging, gray eyes fixed themselves on Lori. "What in the blue blazes is *this*?!"

Lori started to say something when the boy suddenly piped in.

"Okay, remember when I wrote that report on lucies?"

"Lucies?" The old woman did not take her watery eyes off Lori.

"Lucid dreamers," the boy corrected himself. "And the possibility of leakage."

"Leakage?"

"Nick," the man named Pops warned, starting to take over. "You know we can't—"

"Remember when I said it was possible," the boy went on, "that sooner or later one would slip through."

"Don't tell me," the old lady said with a forlorn nod toward Lori.

"Ma'am, with all due respect," Lori started to explain, "I was only—"

"She was spiking, Mrs. Waverly," the boy broke in. "She's been a lucy since she was knee-high."

"What do you want me to do about it?" the woman grunted. "We got Bogies all over the 'scape, I'm down one Exterminator, and I got an archy coming in next week for a blasted committee meeting."

"All I'm saying is, she could be useful as a—"

"No, absolutely, posi-tootin-tively NO!"

"Ma'am, if you just hear me out—"

"Zap her back," the woman in the wheelchair ordered.

"Ma'am—"

"Do it now, Nick, before she fuzzes out on us and I'll have to fill out another form J-X."

"But—"

"Gimme that thing," the man spoke up. He grabbed the cattle prod from the boy. "I'll do it."

Before Lori could say another word the man named Pops lifted the blunt end of the prod, aimed it at Lori, and pressed the tip against her temple.

* * *

"Whoa!"

Lori jerked awake.

Still dressed in her sweat-damp thrift-shop garb, still on her bed in her cluttered room, still on top of her covers, she sat up with a start and tried to focus.

Her room was filled with people, blurry and indistinct at first.

"Well lookie here," a voice said. It was adult, male, and unfamiliar. What in God's name was this strange person doing in Lori's bedroom, hovering over her bed? "Susie, looks like we can put the paddles away," the man said.

"Honey?! You okay?" This voice was familiar. Allison Blaine came into focus kneeling next to Lori's bed. She was dressed in her agency attire—a navy dress and jacket—and her expression was tight with alarm. Her hair was pulled back in a tight ponytail. What was going on? Her hand was cool on Lori's brow.

"What's all the—" Lori could barely speak. Her mouth felt like an ashtray that needed emptying.

"God, you gave us a scare," her mother said with a sigh of relief.

"Freaky," a voice said from over by the door. Hugo Stipple was standing there, watching, fidgeting in his black denim jacket.

Lori was baffled, dizzy, sore. "What the hell is Hugo doing here?"

"Honey—" Allison started to formulate a response and stopped herself.

The paramedic on the other side of Lori's bed rose to his feet, sticking a small penlight back into his shirt pocket. The name badge said EARL. A big, beefy dude with pork-chop sideburns, dressed in a powder-blue uniform, he turned to his partner, a younger woman standing over by the window, snapping her chewing gum. "Get her pulse/ox, Suze, and let's pack it up."

The lady medic, who was also dressed in blue, was stuffing a couple of electric "paddles" back into their carrying case, which was shoved up against the window. Faint sunlight glowed outside. Was it dawn? Lori recognized the "de-fib" paddles, equipment designed to revive a patient whose heart has stopped. This realization made Lori sit up straighter.

"Mom, what exactly is going on?"

"Honey, these nice people are just going to make sure you're okay."

"What time is it?"

"It's almost six thirty," Allison told her as the female paramedic knelt down next to the bed and pressed a cold stethoscope to Lori's sternum. The lady smelled of cigarettes and spearmint gum. She looked up at her partner and nodded.

"Six thirty in the morning?" Lori guessed.

"No, Honey, it's six thirty in the evening."

"Excuse me?" Lori felt her stomach lurch. The paramedics started packing up to leave. "Would you mind running that by me again?"

"Girlfriend," Hugo said gravely by the door. The sound of the word *girlfriend* said it all. In Hugo's limited vocabulary, the word *girlfriend* could hold many meanings: admiration, shame, excitement. The way it sounded now, though, smacked of absolute, unadulterated shock.

"I checked on you this morning," Allison was babbling now, "before I left for work, and you were fine, at least I thought you were fine, so I figured I'd let you sleep, but when you didn't show up at school, Hugo dropped by, and he noticed your breathing was not—"

"*Girlfriend,*" Hugo piped in. "You were like *dead to the world.*"

"Dead is right," the guy with the sideburns said with a smirk, handing Lori's mom a clipboard with a pink sheet of paper for her to sign.

"Thank God you're okay," Allison remarked then, standing and signing the release.

"I've seen babies sleep so soundly you can't even get a pulse," Mr. Pork Chop commented, tearing off a receipt. "It's nothing to worry about." He offered Allison a smile, and then, before making his exit, he uttered one final comment, as though summing it all up with a shrug and a single exasperated word: "*Teenagers.*"

As if that explained everything.

FIVE

The next day they arrived at the DeKalb Medical Center at 5:30 P.M. on the nose. They had driven most of the afternoon—up the snaking blacktop that wound north along the Mississippi, past the ancient locks and dams, then across the vast brown farm fields of central Illinois—and now both mother and daughter were officially exhausted.

Allison let Lori off at the main entrance and then went to park the car. Lori hauled her overnight bag—which was packed with pajamas, toiletries, her diary, an iPad mini, makeup, smartphone, ear buds, clove cigarettes, and her leather pouch of good luck charms—through the glass doors and across the tiled lobby to the reception desk.

Lori told the receptionist why she was there, and the silver-haired woman gave her a look and then tapped on a keyboard. She found Lori's name, took her insurance card, tapped the keyboard some more, and then directed her to the lower level.

A few minutes later Lori was following an obese nurse down a tiled corridor.

"The sleep clinic's fairly new," the woman explained as she waddled toward the last door on the right. "Just started up last spring."

"Good to know," Lori said, mustering as much enthusiasm as possible.

As she trudged down the hall behind the nurse, Lori made a faint, metallic clanking noise—the collective jangling of her chains, bracelets, overnight satchel, and the studs on her shopworn black leather jacket. She sounded like a gunslinger entering a saloon.

"It's completely painless," the nurse said, pausing in front of the door, sliding a magnetic card through a lock. The door clicked open with a beep. "Very relaxing, in fact."

That morning, when Lori's mom had told her she would be spending the night in a sleep clinic, Lori had envisioned a scene out of a 1950s science fiction movie. She had imagined a mad scientist who called himself the Sandman, and a series of iron-lung contraptions and wires and bubbling flasks everywhere, and high-voltage electrodes wired to pillows, and a female assistant who looked like Vampira in a white latex mini and nurse's hat, and a gigantic soul-sucking glass chamber hanging down from the ceiling known as the Dream-a-Tron 6000.

"Don't worry, honey, it's no big deal," Allison had assured her at breakfast. Staring down into her corn flakes, Mrs. Blaine's face had been drawn and pale and deeply lined as though she had slept on the wrong side of the bed.

"Mom?"

"Yeah, honey?"

"I don't mean to pry, but are you all right?"

Allison Blaine had taken a deep breath then, forcing herself to swallow a spoonful of soggy cereal. "I'm fine, honey. I'm just . . . a little blue is all."

"Mom, please. I may be tired but I'm not brain dead. A little blue?" Lori gave her mother a look. "A chemical imbalance is not just 'a little blue.'"

"Who told you I had a chemical imbalance?"

"Mom, I'm not a six-year-old."

She smiled. "You're telling me. Listen. I'm fine. Okay? Everything's fine."

"Really," Lori had commented skeptically. She knew that her mother's heart was broken. It was broken in multiple places by Lori's dad, and also by the guy whom Allison had been dating last year, and also by her boss at the agency who had passed her up for a promotion. But what Lori didn't know was how far into a deep, black hole Allison Blaine had fallen.

"More importantly, how are *you* feeling?" the woman had finally said.

Lori gave her shrug. "I'm . . . quite well, actually." She wondered how much she should tell her mom about the dream door, about finally going through it, about the bizarre people on the other side. Lori wondered how much she should talk about the strange sense of . . . *relief.*

She could think of no better word for it. She felt an odd sense of relief that she had finally worked up the nerve to go through the door and had not died or lost her sanity. Of course, the jury was still out on the latter assertion. But she definitely felt—secretly, deep down, in her private thoughts—that the world on the other side of the door was more than a mere dream.

She would never be able to explain this to anyone, nor would she try, but the sheer *mystery* of what was on the other side—even the creepiness of it—made her feel something that she hadn't felt in years. Maybe ever. It was a sense of . . . wonder? Excitement? Power?

Now, less than twelve hours later, Lori found herself about to enter the lair of the mad scientists and the Dream-a-Trons.

She followed the nurse through the door and was greeted by a very bland room with a couple of ordinary beds and a few physicians in unassuming white coats. In almost every way, the space looked like a hotel room. The beds were made. There were a couple of dressers, a bureau table, a few coffee tables with magazines, and even crappy hotel art on the walls. Seahorses and wheat fields. Nothing menacing or even the slightest bit medicinal.

Upon closer inspection, though, Lori recognized a few telltale giveaways. In one corner was a video camera. A rack of medical monitors was positioned next to one of the beds, and along the far wall stretched a long mirror, much bigger than that in your standard Holiday Inn. Lori guessed it was the kind of two-way mirror you might find at a police station. She was sure there were doctors behind it, even now, watching the proceedings and making notes.

"Have a seat, Lori," one of the doctors said after Allison had returned from the parking lot. The older woman kept her coat on and stood behind her daughter, nervously wringing her hands. "Just need to get a little information," the doctor said, flipping open a chart.

Lori sat down on the edge of the bed, feeling a little ridiculous. They asked her all the standard questions. Was there anything she was allergic to? Had she ever had a seizure? Did she have any metal inside her body? Finally the nurse rolled a metal cart over to the bed and asked Lori to use the bathroom and then slip out of her clothes and put on her pajamas. Lori did as she was told. Her pajamas consisted of torn black leggings and a ratty old thermal underwear top that looked like it once belonged to a hobo but was eventually discarded in disgust.

A minute later they were putting electrodes under her small breasts, on her slender wrists, and around her ankles with Velcro. The plastic leads were cold and made Lori shiver as she lay down on the bed, her head propped up on a pile of pillows, her Medusa tangle of dreadlocks now splayed across the bedding like a nimbus of tentacles. The doctor explained that they would be monitoring Lori's heart and respiration during sleep. "What we're looking for is any kind of apnea," the doctor said then. "Sleep apnea is basically a condition where sleep brings on respiratory problems."

Allison stared at the doctor. "Problems meaning . . . ?"

"Meaning there's a breathing issue." The doctor put his pen back in his breast pocket. "Or sometimes there's even a pause in breathing during sleep." He looked at Lori. "We understand you had some issues with breathing the other night."

"She certainly did," Allison answered with an edge in her voice.

Lori found herself wanting to go to sleep. For the first time in as long as she could remember, she wanted to dream again. She wanted to go back through that door, regardless of who was standing around this place, watching her, monitoring her, writing stuff on clipboards.

"Well, we're going to get to the bottom of it tonight," the doctor said with a practiced smile. He had silver hair and looked like an airline pilot. "All we ask is that you relax and try to get a good night's sleep."

"I can handle that," Lori said with a nod.

"Listen to Sleeping Beauty here," Allison commented under her breath.

They turned the lights down. The doctors and the nurses exited through a side door. Allison lingered. "You forgot your teddy bear," she said with a smirk.

"Mom, please."

"Honey, don't worry, it'll be over before you know it and we'll go stuff our faces with pancakes."

Lori looked at her mom. "I'm not the least bit concerned about this thing, Mom." She reached up and brushed a tendril of a dreadlock from her eye. "And you shouldn't be, either."

"You're right." Allison leaned down and softly kissed Lori's forehead. The look in the older woman's eyes—a mixture of love, sadness, regret, and fear—was heart breaking. "I love you, sweetie."

"I love you, too, Mom."

Allison turned and headed for the side door that led into the observation room.

"Mom?" Lori called to her.

Allison paused in the doorway. Computers ticked and whirred in the background. "Yes, honey?"

"Stop worrying."

Allison smiled and nodded and then vanished inside the shadows behind the mirror.

For nearly an hour Allison Blaine sat on a metal folding chair in the corner of the observation room, gazing through the glass at her daughter settling in for the night in that artificial hotel room. Lori wrote in her diary for a while, yawning a couple of times. At one point an electrode slipped off her rib cage under her tunic, and a nurse had to go back into the room to resecure it.

The observation room was more of a closet than a room, the walls paneled and the ceiling made of acoustical tile. The air smelled of coffee. Two technicians in powder-blue lab coats sat at a control console, playing cards, eating ham and cheese sandwiches, and absently glancing at the pulse/oxygen monitors, as though keeping track of baseball scores. They made Allison nervous.

"Looks like we got a sleeper," one of the technicians announced.

Allison nearly jumped out of her skin. "Is she okay?" she asked.

"Looking good," the other technician, a younger guy with a ponytail, announced with a mouthful of sandwich. "Heart rate's normal."

Allison gazed through the mirror. Lori was out cold, her diary tented over her tummy, the wires poking out from under her threadbare thermal top. "She looks like a homeless person in those PJs," Allison mused to herself.

"I had some with little frogs on them when I was that age," the older technician said without looking at her. "Little froggies and flies."

"Froggies and flies," the younger technician commented wryly.

"Looks like she's entering stage three," the other guy said, glancing down at his monitor.

Allison sat forward. "What's that mean?"

The technician spun around on his chair and explained the five stages of sleep. He patiently explained the final stage—REM—as the Holy Grail for sleep disorders. He explained how REM was the dream state, and afforded the sleeper the deepest rest. "So we'll be looking at changes in respiration," he said finally, "which might keep her up in the shallow waters."

Allison let out a pained sigh, and she started to say something else, when the older tech spoke up.

"Houston, we got REM!"

They all looked through the two-way mirror at the slumbering young woman, whose eyeballs jittered busily under her lids.

* * *

Lori could not find the door at first. She dreamt she was in a deserted movie theater. It was a familiar place called the Orpheum Twin. A narrow, cavernous chamber of plaster walls and tattered velvet seats. The place was the only theater left open in Valesburg after the ravages of the recession, and it had the customary sticky floors and faint stench of old popcorn butter in the seat cushions.

Lori had seen one of the *Twilight* movies there—the third or fourth sequel, she couldn't remember which—just last week with Hugo and Rachael. But now the place was eerily empty, cluttered with trash and unidentifiable plastic body parts from discarded mannequins, as though the apocalypse had come.

For some reason, in the dream, Lori was pacing the stage area, a small thrust of hardwood that protruded out in front of the torn projection screen. Once in a while the theater put on live shows there, children's theater on Saturday mornings, puppet shows or charity events. Lori was waiting for someone or something to happen. She saw no door. No sign of life anywhere.

Then it hit her: You can go anywhere . . . do anything . . . make anything happen. She imagined herself a performer . . . a comedienne . . . a ventriloquist. She felt the hairs on the back of her neck bristle and that strumming sensation in the marrow of her spine.

All at once, in the dream, she was dressed in a sequined bustier and feather boa like some retro dancehall queen, and she was standing at the mic with a ventriloquist's dummy cradled in her arms, a doll with a hinged mouth, which looked suspiciously like Hugo Stipple.

"How many Goths does it take to change a light bulb?" she said into the microphone. Whoops and hollers rang out from the darkness of the audience, but before anybody could shout an answer, the Hugo doll squawked, "None! They'd rather sit in the dark and cry."

Out in the shadows, the packed house roared with laughter and cheers, and simultaneously lit their cigarette lighters—which looked like a constellation of twinkling stars—at which point Lori launched into another light bulb joke, purring into the mic, "Okay, how many Goths does it *really* take to change a light bulb?"

Right on cue the Hugo dummy wisecracked, "Three! One to change the bulb and two to discuss Lord Byron's Grand Tour and the creative use of opium in a metaphysical environment."

In the dream, out in the audience, her friends applauded and nodded their heads appreciatively, and even the 'Straps and Fundies whooped and hollered.

On stage, Lori sprouted sequined bat wings like some garish character in a bad road tour production of *A Midsummer Night's Dream*, and she flapped her wings, and she gracefully levitated above the crowd with the Hugo dummy still in her arms . . . floating, floating . . . across the audience . . . out through the front foyer of the theater . . . and into the glittering night.

The cool, clean wind caressed her face. The tops of buildings passed down below in a blur. In the distance the river glistened in the moonlight

When she finally landed—maybe a mile away—she was buzzing with excitement. She had touched down on the edge of the rolling farmland, and it had never looked so beautiful to Lori. The Hugo dummy had vanished, its absence as sudden as a jump cut in a film. The indigo silhouettes of trees in the distance, the inky black ocean of soybeans—all shimmering with moonlight—made Lori's heart swell with happiness.

And that's when she saw the door.

She saw it out of the corner of her eye at first—as she always did—floating in the moonbeams. But when she turned and focused on it, she realized it was embedded in the side of an ancient, gnarled oak tree.

"There you are," she said, walking over to it. As she approached, she saw the strange inconsistency of the gray door installed in the massive, petrified trunk of the two-hundred-year-old oak. It looked as though hobbits or elves had made their home there.

"Let's see if anybody's home," Lori muttered under her breath as she grasped the knob, opened the door, and went through it to the other side.

SIX

"Whoa! Whoa! Whoa!" The younger technician—the one with the ponytail—sprang to his feet. He noticed something alarming on the monitors.

"What is it? What's wrong?" Allison stood up. Her heart raced. The airless little cubicle seemed to close in around her. She had been cooped up in that coffee-smelling observation cell, staring through the glass, watching her daughter sleep for nearly three hours now. She had almost drifted off to sleep herself. But now her senses crackled like overloading terminals. "What's the matter with her?"

"Take it easy, folks," said the older tech, spinning his swivel chair, taking a closer look at a long paper printout curling out of the EKG monitor. "Nothing to worry about."

"Look at her temp, Jerry," the younger tech said, indicating a small digital number blinking on the monitor screen.

"Her pulse/ox is spiking, sure," the older guy muttered, reading his screens. "But, hey, the girl's in deep REM . . . having a nightmare most likely."

"I think we should get the resident on the blower," the younger tech said. "A temp spiking that fast? Even in deep REM?"

"What's going on?!" Allison demanded. She could see her daughter writhing in sleep-agony in the other room, the girl's expression contorting.

"She's burning up," the younger tech warned.

"Just having a bad dream," the older tech murmured, clicking a pen and making a mark on the printout sheet as it spat from the EKG.

"I think she's going into A-fib," the younger tech cautioned, glancing at the heart monitor.

"Goddamn it, wake her up!" Allison pushed her way past the younger tech and threw open the door. She rushed around the corner, burst through the side door, and lurched into the fake hotel room.

Within seconds, she was hovering over her daughter, shaking her awake.

What Allison Blaine didn't know—in fact, had no way of knowing—was that she was already too late.

* * *

The moment Lori emerged on the other side of the door—entering that high-definition world behind her dream—she felt heat. Sweat broke out under her clothes—at some point, her sleepwear had metamorphosed back into her leather jacket, ripped jeans, and boots—and she could see flames flickering in the depths of the deserted tunnels. Superheated air blew through the passageway, the blast furnace bathing her. It pressed in from both ends of the tunnel. But worse than that, far worse, was the baritone growling noise and sense of horrible doom coming toward her from her immediate right.

She reacted instinctively. Whirling away from the menacing sound, she took off in a dead run for the opposite end of the tunnel.

As she fled the terrible noise and smell, she felt her flesh crawling, the back of her neck prickling with terror, the coppery taste of fear in the back of her throat. She was learning something new about her dreams:

The horror was palpable. Physical. As sticky and redolent with dread as any waking trauma.

She could see orange flames straight ahead, licking up both sides of the intersecting tunnels. Everything was a blur. But somehow, in her chaotic thoughts—as she raced toward that intersection—Lori realized that this place had somehow fallen under the spell of something dark and powerful.

She reached the flaming intersection and instinctively turned right.

Now she hurried down a side tunnel. The walls were oozing. The darkness flashed and flickered. And the odor was incredible. It was a black, ashy smell like burning tar . . . but worse. It choked her. It got inside her brain as she ran. It threatened to knock her over. She couldn't think straight. Where the hell were those people she had encountered last time? She reached another intersection and decided to take the tunnel on the left.

Bad choice.

She ran directly into a fog bank. The thick smoke—the smoke of burning rubber—engulfed her. Blinded her. She nearly tripped and fell. Coming to a full stop, she coughed and tried to wave it away. She began to back out of the smoke, retreating toward the intersection. But when she heard the deep, low, threatening snarl coming from behind her, she paused and turned around.

She froze.

She stared.

The terror crashed down on her, drowning her, carrying her off in its current like a riptide.

The thing stood—if that's the word—perhaps ten feet away from Lori. At first glance, it looked like a column of smoke rising up and brushing the tunnel ceiling, silhouetted against the glow of heat behind it. But the more Lori stared at it—mesmerized by the otherworldly horror of it—the more her eyes absorbed its contours and alerted her brain that *this was no column of smoke.*

For one horrible instant, the fear held her rapt. Petrified. She could not move a muscle as she gaped at the vaporous thing before her. She couldn't breathe as she registered the smudgy black entity's true nature. This realization took only seconds—maybe less, maybe only microseconds—it was hard to tell in this world. Time was stretching like putty again. But when the thing began to move, Lori turned and plunged back into the smoke.

Another bad decision.

The problem was, Lori had caught a glimpse of the thing's face right before she managed to spin and flee into the haze. Just a fleeting glimpse that could not have lasted more than a nanosecond. But it was more than enough to see the deep-set lupine eyes and the hairless skull rising up with its cloven nose sniffing the air.

Now the thing chased Lori through the black miasma of smoke.

Lori ran willy-nilly with no direction or purpose other than *away*. Away from the slithering black humanoid thing on her heels.

She ran as fast as she could, considering she was completely blind. She covered quite a bit of distance, too, judging by her strides. But of course she had no way of knowing. Distances were as elastic over here as the passage of time. And before long, Lori felt the hot, noxious breath on her neck. She could hear the galloping skitter of claws in the fog behind her . . . gaining on her. She tried to change the course of events with her lucid powers but was unable to get even the slightest tremor of a vibration in her spine. Once again, for some reason, she was a dead battery.

When she burst out of the smoke, she found himself in another world.

A vast canyon of shimmering black matter rose up in all directions, as far as the eye could see, honeycombed with dark pockets and shadowy cavities, and more tunnels, tunnels everywhere, tunnels leading to God-knows-where. Alien light shone down from overhead, and an endless phosphorescent river ran through the heart of the gorge. It looked like an uncharted planet bathed in purple light. It took Lori's breath away, so much so that she didn't see the ledge right in front of her. She tripped and fell over the edge.

The slope was treacherous and steep, and Lori slid on her belly down the spongy black surface. Her teeth rattled as she plummeted over bumps and stalks of unearthly flora. Her mind swam with terror.

She landed in a ravine. Bones aching from the fall, head spinning, she tried to muster enough strength to rise back to her feet and find a hiding place. All at once, her fear sharpened and intensified. Her terror rose like a symphony changing keys, moving into a higher register. It was as though she were reduced to her infantile, primal self. Tiny. Insignificant. She could hear the ghastly noises of the winged creature up there on the ledge somewhere. It was coming for her. The great leathery wings made a drumbeat that vibrated the air and echoed across the dark, alien gully.

The chasm rose on all sides. The honeycomb of caves went on forever and ever and ever. Innumerable. Imponderable. Impossible. It looked like an infinite beehive stretching for millions of miles under a low, roiling, stormy, toxic sky. It looked like a race of giant wasps or moles lived here. But Lori did not have enough time to study the chambers closely—or even get her bearings—because the thump of giant bat wings had multiplied.

Lori looked over her shoulder.

She could not even muster a gasp or a scream—or make any sound whatsoever—because what rose up behind her in the sky was beyond her comprehension. Like a squadron of prehistoric winged creatures, a dozen or more Bogies now started launching off the edge of the cliff. It looked like bouquets of poisonous black flowers blossoming. They fanned out across the midnight sky with great wings thundering rhythmically.

And then they dove.

Straight toward Lori Blaine.

The flash came out of nowhere—at the precise moment the Bogies were about to tear Lori apart like a piñata—and it filled the valley with a brilliant blast of magnesium-hot sunlight. It made an audible sound—a *WHHOOOMP!*—like a depth charge exploding underwater.

Lori flinched and stumbled backward, falling to the ground. She landed on her rear end, and blinked, and tried to see through the blinding glare.

Above her, the Bogies were scattering, soaring back up into the air, shrieking in unison. Their screams were indescribable. Lori covered her ears and clenched her teeth at the amazing noise—a trillion fingernails on a blackboard—so enormously loud it practically rattled the canyon.

"You happy now?!" a voice rang out behind the glare.

"Wh-what?" Lori was still trying to gather herself, trying to focus on the owner of this new voice. She struggled to get air into her lungs.

"C'mon," said the voice. "Before they regroup."

Lori felt a hand on her blouse sleeve, and she jumped. She realized a figure was standing next to her.

Dressed in khaki brown overalls and clanking tool belt, he flipped off his lantern. The light died, plunging his angry, handsome face into shadows. "This way," he said, and yanked Lori across the ravine toward a winding trail that snaked up one side of the gorge.

They moved quickly. The air was vibrating with wings. The Bogies were circling, regrouping in larger numbers. Lori could feel the cold draft of hunger on the back of her neck as they scaled a narrow path toward the closest cave. Finally Lori managed to speak.

"I don't mean to be . . . *rude* . . . or ungrateful," she uttered between breaths. "But what the hell is going on?"

"You really messed things up last time, coming through with no warning," the young man said, breathing hard, dragging Lori up a winding path strewn with sparkling cinders. Lori's brain was spinning. They reached a plateau and the young man said, "The place is infested with Bogies now, all smelling new blood. This way, come on!"

They hustled along a row of caves embedded in the moist, spongy cliff. The air smelled of coal dust and ash—like the pit of an archaeological dig—a very, very, very old smell. Like the floor of a fossilized ocean. The young man paused and peered into the mouth of a cave. He shook his head. "Too old! Come on!"

Stumbling along behind him, Lori bit down on her terror and said, "May I ask what you're looking for?"

"A shortcut!"

"Okay . . . alright . . . again . . . at the risk of being tedious, I need to clarify something." Lori fought the dizziness and cold currents of dread coursing through her to formulate her thoughts. "This is all a dream, right? It's my dream. I'm the one dreaming this, correct?"

"Not exactly," the young man said, pausing to grab something off his tool belt. "It's complicated. You got to this point through your own dream, but now you're beyond the threshold. Let's put it that way." He had a small brass cylinder in his hand. It looked like a shotgun shell with a cross engraved in it. "We don't have time to get into this now," he added sourly, snapping off the cylinder's cap. The thing sparked like a road flare. "Or should I say, *you* don't have time."

In her confusion and alarm, she decided to try and just go with it. Partly out of instinct, and partly out of fascination with this scruffy young dude in the orphan rags and workman's uniform, she began to realize there was something going on here that transcended the surreal details of an ordinary nightmare. From the deep set of Nick's sad eyes, his irises as pale blue as the ocean at dawn, to the jut of his strong chin, whiskered with a five-day growth of beard, to the profusion of beads and leather bracelets and strange bling and tats adorning his body, this handsome young man was simply too specific for a run-of-the-mill dream. Not to mention the fact that, despite her terror, she found herself mesmerized by his face. At last, she swallowed her panic and said, "And . . . so . . . what exactly are we doing now?"

"It's a mixture of holy water and gunpowder," he said unceremoniously and tossed the object across the plateau. It bounced off the cliff, then landed on the ground and popped open like a firecracker. Technicolor pink smoke poured out of it. "Keeps the Bogies away long enough to get outta here! C'mon!"

He yanked her toward a smaller opening in the cliff about ten yards away.

They reached the mouth of the smaller cave—an aperture no bigger than the width of a manhole cover—and the young man waved an instrument in front of it. "Good, good . . . this one's a young one. Come on, you first," he said.

"What?"

"C'mon, get in there!"

"All right, I'm going!" Lori climbed through the cave's opening.

Plunged into darkness, she crawled on her hands and knees for several feet, the air as cool and musky as that of a root cellar. The texture of the cave was like most: glittering gray sandpaper.

The young man was right behind her. "There it is!" his voice echoed through the channel a moment later. Lori stopped when she saw the membrane.

It was as though they had traversed a giant ear canal, and now they crouched in front of an enormous eardrum. In the darkness the membrane was just barely visible, embedded in the side of the cave.

Upon closer inspection, Lori saw that it was a fleshy, flexible film of skin the color of elephant hide. She knelt inches away from it, wondering what the hell she was supposed to do now.

"On my count," the young man said, squeezing next to her, fiddling with another device in his hand. "Push your way through it. Ready?"

"No!"

"Three, two, one—"

"Wait!"

"GO!"

The young man named Nick shoved Lori through the membrane.

If asked to describe it, Lori might have thought of the sensation of pushing through a giant casing of Silly Putty—that shiny, flesh-tone substance that is both resilient and tacky. Her face stretched the tissue like a vacuum mold and then snapped the membrane open.

There was an audible breath of air as Lori tumbled through the membrane and fell to the floor of a brightly lit room. Lori lay there, stunned for a moment, taking in the bizarre change in atmosphere, blinking fitfully, as though she had just awakened.

It was a child's room. But not your ordinary child's room. It looked like a nursery designed by Salvador Dali or Lewis Carroll. The pink papered walls rose at odd angles. The hobbyhorse in the corner was chewing on the curtains. The crib was as high as the ceiling, and the mobile of butterflies spun and fluttered with reanimated insects.

The sound of a child crying drew Lori's attention over to the far wall.

A little girl, no more than three years old, stood ankle deep in marshmallowy muck. Dressed in a pink pinafore and saddle shoes, she was trying to get to a small rubber ball about ten feet away—and she kept trying and trying—but her legs were caught in the sticky white mire.

It was hard to look at.

It was also apparent to Lori—all at once, like a splash of water in her face—that she had entered someone else's dream.

SEVEN

Much of what Lori encountered in those next few seconds made no sense whatsoever—the spangled light coming down from some high source, glittering in the air like the shaken contents of a snow globe; the odor of cinnamon and rust; the soft churning of some offstage engine, the faint vibrations coming up from beneath the child's spongy bedroom floor as though the entire scene were steam-driven by invisible turbines. But at the same time, Lori—being a quick study—was starting to formulate an understanding of the mechanics of this world.

Her comprehension ran on two equally complex, parallel tracks. On one track, she was beginning to accept the fact that this elaborate dreamscape that she was in, regardless of its source, seemed to have a geography to it . . . as well as physical laws and a weightiness and severe consequences for those who took it too lightly. She could no longer simply dismiss these troubling events as "just a dream." *These* nightmares had teeth and could bite . . . and quite often her lucid skills were useless. On another track, however, she was starting to process the possibility that this little funhouse nursery—as well as everything else she was experiencing in this topsy-turvy world—had some inchoate connection to the *real* world. The waking world. The place where people breathe actual oxygen and get sent to school therapists and bleed when they're injured and die when their time is up.

Reeling from all the contrary emotions flowing through her, both fearful and galvanizing, Lori was about to say something to the little child in the dream room when Nick, the mysterious hunky dude in work clothes, burst through the portal, climbing into the child's nightmare with the casual ease of a stock clerk searching for a part.

"Come on, come on, gotta keep moving," Nick said to Lori as he brushed himself off and headed for the other side of the nursery.

"Fine . . . fine . . . I'm right behind you," Lori mumbled, climbing to her feet.

The nursery was in a higher definition than the tunnels and the canyon, the colors more vivid, the sound of a music box tinkling in the background. It was like being in a virtual reality exhibit.

The little girl looked up as the intruders walked passed her, the teardrops on her cheeks as real as diamonds. Lori nodded to her. "Afternoon, sweetheart."

Nick was already on the other side of the room, waving a device across the pink wallpaper. "Come on, Lori, your time's running out," he warned.

Lori paused and smiled at the child. Then she looked across the room at Nick. "How did you know my name was Lori?"

"Long story," he said, thumbing a switch on the device. Another membrane appeared in the wall like a photograph developing.

Lori looked back at the little girl. The child had stopped crying, but still . . . she looked so crestfallen, so discouraged. "She can't get to her ball," Lori murmured almost to herself.

"Don't fraternize with the dreamers, Lori."

Lori looked at Nick. "She just needs a little help."

Nick let out a sigh. He turned and looked at Lori. "We're not even supposed to be here."

"But she looks so tragic."

Nick rolled his eyes. "Okay, okay . . . go ahead. Fix it. But be quick about it."

Lori walked over to the rubber ball, picked it up, and brought it back to the child. The little girl stared, dumbstruck, as this unexpected savior loomed over her. The marshmallow quicksand vanished.

"Next time," Lori said softly to the child, patting her little downy head, "you'll realize you're dreaming, and all the bad dreams will go away after that."

Nick watched this with mounting interest. He smiled to himself, walked over to Lori, and offered her a hand. "Nicely done," he said with a grin.

Lori patted the girl one last time, took Nick's hand, and walked with him through the next membrane.

In order to get back to headquarters, they had to cut across half a dozen more dreams—mostly those of children, which, according to Nick, were easier to navigate. They encountered weird landscapes made of Lego bricks. They crossed rivers of cough medicine. They circled around mountains of stuffed animals. They snuck through a nightmare that some kid was having about the Wizard of Oz, the sky dark with flying monkeys and smoke writing that said WAIT TILL YOUR FATHER GETS HOME! And they even passed through the dream of a boy whom Lori recognized from Central.

Ichabod Kettlekamp, the lanky farm kid with the burning stare, was dreaming he was out in the blazing sun of his family's cornfield, fighting a plague of man-eating Venus flytraps with his hedge clipper. From a distance it was almost comical to watch. The gangly, pimply-faced teen was out in the high grass, his overalls drenched in sweat, his huge Adam's apple bobbing busily as he slashed like a mad ninja with his yard tool. Lori and Nick hurried unseen a hundred yards away along a split-rail fence.

"I *know* that person," Lori remarked, indicating the mad slashing farm kid in the distance. "He goes to my school, skulks around the cafeteria, giving people the willies all the time."

"Dreamers from the same general vicinity usually cluster together in here, but not always," the young man explained as he took Lori's hand and gently ushered her toward the far property line. The sun was hot on the backs of their necks. "I've seen a dreamer from Pakistan next to one from Peoria."

A twinge of adrenaline stitched through Lori's midsection. It occurred to her that if all these dreamers she was encountering here actually existed in the real world—and the connection between nightmare and reality was keen and robust—then this Nick dude must exist somewhere in the waking world. This stirred up all sorts of interesting emotions in Lori that buffered her fear—excitement, self-consciousness, yearning, and even a little insecurity. "You never explained how you knew my name," Lori said to him after a moment.

"They got all kinds of files on all kinds of dreamers," Nick explained as they reached the edge of Ichabod Kettlekamp's dream and then pushed their way through another rubbery membrane embedded in a chicken coop.

They emerged into a long, deserted, dimly lit passageway, and the sudden contrast between the two environments—the sun-washed air of the farm boy's dream and this grimy, airless, rotting tunnel—was spectacular. Lori noticed the channel walls here were originally stone, or perhaps ancient plaster, and then reinforced with massive, riveted iron girders the color of gangrene, and then retrofitted over *that* with some other rusty steel alloy, and then retrofitted over *that* with miles and miles of steel mesh, and on and on, like a layer cake of brutish industrial endoskeleton. But the strangest part was the unstable nature of the tunnel, the way it seemed to swim with microdots, pixilated in Lori vision, as though its very fabric were a faulty signal from a faulty satellite.

"We knew you were a lucy," Nick was elaborating, hustling down the passage. "We knew your name, we knew everything about you, but nobody thought you'd make it through."

"'Lucy' meaning lucid?" Lori asked, trotting alongside the young man.

"Precisely."

"So what we're doing now—all this dream hopping—if it's not exactly me dreaming, then what *is* it exactly?"

The young man pulled a digital device from his belt and checked the elapsed time. "Long story . . . and you don't have that kind of time. C'mon. This way. One more shortcut."

He led her through another membrane and into the dream of a twelve-year-old boy having a lot of anxiety about his Little League baseball team.

The dreamer—a freckled kid with big ears—was in left field, gazing up at a pop fly that would not fall. The baseball hovered way up in the blue sky like a stubborn helium balloon, while the voices of angry parents shouted nasty threats from the bleachers. The dream was extremely detailed: the smell of manure and sweaty leather and freshly cut grass, the trilling of birds.

"You keep saying I don't have much time," Lori said, jogging across the grassy outfield, heading toward another membrane, which was embedded in the center field fence just beneath the scoreboard. One of the other kids in the dream—the center fielder—was watching the intruders with a vexed expression. "What happens when my time runs out?" Lori continued pressing the issue. "I turn into a pumpkin?"

Nick glanced at her without breaking stride. "That's actually not too far from the truth."

"You're going to have to elaborate on that."

"You end up a vegetable. It happened to me." He swallowed hard as he said this. "I don't recommend it."

Lori thought about this for a moment. "So you're not just a figment of my imagination."

"Ha-ha, very funny."

"No, I'm serious. I had a feeling you were real—or an *artifact* of the real world—or however you say it."

"*WAKEspace.*"

61

"Pardon?"

"We call it WAKEspace. And yes. I'm a real person . . . a lucy like you." He glanced over his shoulder, his expression darkening. "Did you hear that?"

"Hear what?"

"Nothing, never mind. Come on, follow me, keep moving, chop chop!"

They reached the fence and Nick gently shoved Lori through the portal.

She broke through the rubber skin and tumbled into the clammy darkness of another corridor. This one looked like a catacomb that had been rotting for centuries under some ancient ruin or seventeenth-century madhouse. The walls were hewn from scarred, moldering, gray marble, then reinforced with endless rows of crisscrossing iron rebar, puffing red rust with each footstep. The only illumination came from flashing yellow signals blinking at every intersection.

Nick entered this gloomy passageway and then urged Lori onward, quickly, toward the distant shadows.

Breathlessly, hustling along to keep up with him, Lori started to ask, "So what was it that turned you into—"

"I overstayed my visitor's pass," he said. "Had to stay on full time." He checked the digital counter again. "But that's not going to happen to you."

"So your name's Nick?"

"That's right. Nick Ballas. It's Greek. Family's from Missouri. They call it the Show-Me State. Isn't that lame? I'm not sure why they call it that."

"How much farther do we have to go, Nick?"

"Not far. Distance is weird in here. A mile is like a few inches. An inch can be a thousand miles."

"Excuse me?"

"I told you it was hard to explain."

They turned another corner and hurried down an increasingly narrow passageway, lined with steel girders and work lamps. It was obviously under construction—or had been many eons ago—and was now abandoned.

Nick stopped and glanced over his shoulder once again with those knitted brows. "You must have heard *that*," he muttered.

"Heard what?"

"You better pray we didn't—" He stopped himself.

"What?"

"Never mind, come on," he said and continued hustling along.

"What is this place exactly?" Lori asked him. "If we're not in a dream right now, where are we?"

"It's got a lot of names."

"Like for instance . . . ?"

"I don't know . . . the In-Between . . . the BACKworld. You don't understand . . . I could get in deep trouble for talking about this stuff."

"Why?"

"Never mind why."

"Who's the woman in the wheelchair, Nick? Is she your boss?"

"She's the supervisor, works for the Company."

"What company?"

Nick let out an exasperated sigh. "We call it the Company. It's not really a company." He pointed at a large industrial elevator about fifty feet away, barely visible in the gloom. "C'mon, I'll explain it on the way down."

They reached the freight elevator—a pair of vertical doors that connected in the middle like massive jaws—and Nick thumbed the DOWN button. A moment later the floor vibrated and Nick yanked the doors apart with a leather strap. The hinges squeaked.

Lori followed him into a moldy enclosure lined with old packing blankets.

But just as Nick was reaching for the lever to yank the doors shut, he called out, "GET BACK!"

It happened so quickly, all that Lori saw, initially, was a dark blur out in the tunnel.

"DON'T LOOK IN ITS EYES!" Nick shoved Lori deeper into the enclosure, while simultaneously pulling a tool from his belt.

The Bogy was already halfway into the freight elevator, its long, oily, sinewy arm thrusting like a sword. The smell was like the bowels of a goat. The sound was a broken diesel engine revving.

Lori turned and dropped into a crouch. Nick threw himself on her, as though shielding her from a blast, as thorny black claws protruded and reached for them . . . scraping Nick's back . . . Lori crouching down, blinking, gasping, trying to utter a response. The claws made a whispering sound in the air. The arm was made of smoke. Or maybe it was a ghost.

"STAY DOWN!"

All at once, Nick turned and thumbed a switch on his nightstick, and a blade popped out of the nose.

Lori would realize later—she was too freaked out right then by the sudden attack to notice anything but the Bogy—that Nick's blade was actually a crucifix whose base had been sharpened on a whetstone. Nick executed a perfect spin with the razor-sharp crucifix-sword, then sliced through the offending arm.

When the shriek rang out, Lori slid into a sitting position on the floor and covered her ears. In this enclosed space the noise was unbearable, unfathomable, as palpable as acid. It felt as though Lori had her head lodged inside an air horn on an eighteen-wheeler.

The Bogy screeched and folded its massive wings against its spine and recoiled back into the corridor like black vapor being drawn up through an air vent, as Nick madly punched the DOWN button.

Something had tumbled across the floor—a piece of debris or skin— which Lori caught out of the corner of her eye. The doors rumbled shut. Nick fumbled for another tool on his hip. It was a glass vial, wrapped in ornamental gold leaf. He raised the vial to his mouth and bit into the cork, pulling it out with his teeth.

What he did next he did very quickly, with the casual precision of a mechanic sealing a joint. Flinging holy water on the severed hand, which lay smoking on the floor, he recited a prayer or incantation or litany—maybe in Latin, Lori wasn't sure; she had flunked that class last year—the words hissing out of the young man by rote: "*Sacerdos ab ordinario delegatus rite confessus aut saltem corde!*"

The magical fluid sputtered and hissed on the black humanoid hand on the elevator floor, the fingers curling inward like a withering flower. Within seconds the hand was a smoking puddle of goo.

Lori realized the elevator was moving. Built to convey great loads, the rattling carriage descended slowly. The stench that filled the enclosure was like tar baking in a furnace. On the floor, Lori coughed and tried to speak. "What . . . ? How do they . . . ? What the hell *are* those things?"

Nick sealed the vial of holy water and was clipping it back on his belt. "Parasites," he mumbled.

Lori realized her heart was pounding harder than she had ever felt it pound. Nick gently helped Lori to her feet. She took deep breaths.

For a single instant she had gotten an up-close and all-too-personal glimpse of the Bogy, and it was not pretty. Unlike a dangerous wild animal or even a crazy person, the physical nature of which you could at least grasp—the foaming mouth, the whites of the eyes, the fangs, the drool—a Bogy was a hazy apparition. It left in its wake a disturbing jumble of impressions.

Lori thought of burn victims, the skin charred to a blackened crisp. She thought of her dream the other night of the old woman with the burned face. But she also had the impression of a shadow, a projection on a wall, like those distorted, ghostly silhouettes you see in old silent vampire movies. But worse than that, far worse, was the feeling that trailed after these things like an odor. It was the feeling of utter desolation. Black, empty, cold desolation. Like a cemetery in the middle of the night.

"Look, I'm sorry," Lori finally said to the mysterious young man. "But you're going to have to give me a little more to go on here than just 'parasites.'"

Nick sighed and leaned against the freight elevator's side wall as it rattled downward.

"Okay, fine. I'll tell you everything. But in case anybody asks . . . you didn't hear it from me."

EIGHT

The elevator vibrated on its slow-moving, rickety course toward the lower level as Lori listened intently to the young man's spiel. She swallowed hard and stared at the black stain on the floor of the enclosure. "Okay, slow down," she finally interrupted him. "You're talking about *demons*? Old-school Catholic evil spirits—that sort of thing?"

He looked at her. "I know, I know . . . intelligent girl like yourself, IQ off the charts—you'd never believe in such horse crap, right?"

"Well . . . actually," she said with a shrug, and thought about it for a moment.

Lori Blaine had always considered herself an agnostic. She believed in some kind of higher power but also believed that the physical universe was so vast and complex it was incomprehensible to something as puny and clunky as the human mind. Science had proven that the universe was finite, and was expanding, and had a beginning, middle, and end. And there was something *before* the universe—cosmologists called it the "singularity"—which begged the question: How did it all get started? But demonic entities? To Lori, the whole concept of fallen angels was something out of musty old hymnals and B movies. It was a way for the faithful to ameliorate human cruelty and greed and brutality—blame it on the boogeyman. The devil made us do it.

At last, she shrugged and said, "Anything's possible, I guess."

Nick smirked. "That's probably the closest I'm going to come to getting anything like an open mind out of you." His grin faded. "They're real, Lori. Trust me. But here's something most people don't know about them. Where do they go between gigs? Where do they hang out when they're not busy possessing people and stuff?"

She looked up at him and didn't say anything. She had never really given it much thought.

"Nobody ever talks about that, do they?" Nick looked almost irritated. "Where do the demons go when they're not busy making people's head spin around? Hell? Schenectady? Where do the demons live, Lori?"

Lori stared at him, a cold ice pick of realization running through her midsection. "*Here*," she said almost under her breath.

"Bingo."

Lori was just beginning to process this when the young man spoke up again. "Now. For twenty bonus points and a chance to win the lawn furniture . . . do you know exactly how a demon gets inside a person?"

He didn't have to explain. Lori was almost in a trance now, her traumatized brain calculating all this. "They enter through dreams." She uttered this in barely a whisper. "They get into a person through their nightmares."

"You're good, Lori. I told Mrs. Waverly. I told her you were very smart and now look at you."

The elevator was slowing down, rattling toward its final resting place, the gears shrieking beneath them.

"We call it LIMBOspace, or LIMBOworld," the young man went on. "But it's not what you think. It's neither REMspace nor WAKEworld. It's *in between*."

Lori thought about this. "You're talking about . . . what? *Purgatory*?"

"Not exactly. Nobody's dead here. Not yet." The young man measured his words. The elevator was grinding to a stop. "The word *limbo* means border. That's what we do here, Lori. We guard the border."

"You mean . . . ?"

"We keep the demons out of people's dreams. It's a full-time job, Lori."

Lori processed this as she noticed little things about the young man that she had not noticed before. The tattoos, for instance, peeking out of his sleeve and adorning his neck: a Sacred Heart, a scarab, a Celtic cross, sun spirals, nautilus shells, yin and yang symbols, eyes, pentangles, and triple moons. Letters were inked on the backs of his hands, one below each knuckle, forming the Latin words *Pater Magna*.

The elevator thudded to a stop, and Nick grabbed the strap. But before he yanked it open, he glanced over his shoulder at Lori. "I probably don't have to say this again, but let me do the talking."

Nick gave the strap a yank, and the doors suddenly yawned open.

A sandpapery voice greeted them: "Isn't this cozy!"

The voice was accompanied by a blinding, celestial beam of light, which shone in Lori's face.

"I can explain," Nick said, shielding his eyes from the harsh light.

Lori could barely make out the figure sitting in a wheelchair in front of the freight elevator. The old woman held a lantern and quivered with fury. She wore her customary camo fatigues. Behind her stood a tall, graying, chiseled man in work dungarees, gripping the handles of the wheelchair. Lori remembered Nick calling the man Pops.

"Do you have any idea what you've done?" the old woman wheezed. She was out of patience and out of breath.

"Mrs. W . . . if you could please go easy with that light and let me explain."

"Get your butts out here!"

The light dimmed, and Lori saw that the elevator had come to rest on the edge of a cavernous warehouse the size of a concert hall. She followed Nick off the elevator and onto the painted cement floor, standing sheepishly behind him as he faced his inquisitors. "I didn't have a choice in the matter," Nick told them, his voice echoing. "She drew a whole flock of them in through the back door."

Lori noticed the warehouse was a regular arsenal of exotic weaponry and arcane equipment. Metal cases marked with Latin words rose up to the high ceiling on all sides, illuminated by massive scoop lights. Aisles were lined with racks and shelves brimming with modified crucifixes in all shapes and sizes. Some of them were sabers, some were bludgeons, and some were hybrid rifles with air tanks filled with God-knew-what.

"They have no inkling about what they've done," Pops marveled to the woman in the wheelchair.

The old lady glared at the young man. "Damn it, you brought one into the 'scape!"

"I know, I know, I'm aware of that," Nick said. "But we managed to fend it off with a—"

"I'm not talking about the Bogy in the back hall!" the old woman barked. She palmed her toggle switch, and the wheelchair jerked forward until it bumped Nick's shins. Nick flinched as the old lady snarled at him, "I'm talking about a Shadow! Got into somebody's 'scape."

Lori's head was spinning again. She thought she heard footsteps, echoing, somewhere off in the shadows of the warehouse, coming this way.

"What do you mean?" Nick's face went pale. "We sealed every flap behind us!"

"Oh really?!" Without taking her fiery gaze off Nick, the old woman jerked a thumb toward the older, chiseled man. "Tell him, Pops!"

The gray-haired man pulled a scroll of printer paper from his back pocket. "Seems you dragged one into the 'scape of a young farm kid."

This got Lori's attention. She glanced over at the chiseled man, who was unfurling the scroll. The printer paper unrolled, falling to the floor as though it were Santa's naughty list. The man searched the names. "Name of . . . Kettlekamp? David Raymond Kettlekamp?"

"*Ichabod*," Lori murmured, and was about to tell the man and woman that she *knew* this boy, that he was a student at Valesburg Central, but the sound of footsteps tugged at Lori's attention. Someone was approaching from one of the adjacent aisles.

"Okay, we'll fix it, we'll fix it," Nick was saying, his voice taut with nervous tension. He had obviously made a major blunder that Lori would soon comprehend in ways she could never imagine. But before she could jump in and say anything, the footsteps drew near.

A voice rang out from the shadows of a neighboring aisle. "I hate to be the bearer of more bad news," the voice said with calm authority. It was a male voice, sturdy and confident, as clear as a bell.

The old lady snapped her gaze toward the mouth of the aisle. All heads turned toward the voice. Lori felt a loosening in her gut as the newcomer stepped out of the aisle and into the light.

"It seems our new friend here is fast approaching zero hour," said the newcomer.

A man of indeterminate age, perhaps somewhere in his thirties, he stood in a cone of overhead light, his lion's mane of hair catching a halo of golden radiance. He wore a long, dark, floor-length coat, a duster, like a gunslinger, and his chest was clad in battered silver armor. A long, gleaming broadsword hung from a scabbard at his waist.

Lori would find out later that this man also happened to possess a very impressive pair of wings, which were currently tucked and folded beneath the fabric of his long coat. The man reminded Lori—and this association popped into Lori's mind unbidden, instantaneously, despite the chaos whirling about her—of Roger Daltrey, the lead singer for the Who. Lori would eventually learn that this was the Archangel Michael—the head honcho of this little guerrilla unit—but right now, right this instant, things were happening too quickly for niceties or introductions.

Before Lori could utter another word, the man with the golden hair approached, his sword clanking against his hip. He came to within a couple feet of Lori and looked into her eyes. Lori could have sworn she heard the man say something else, but his lips did not move. It was as though he simply *thought* the words at Lori—"*You're a wild one, aren't you?*"—but almost instantaneously the mysterious man turned to the others and said, "Better get moving."

The archangel's words triggered a series of responses from his three colleagues. Mrs. Waverly spun on her wheelchair with a sudden whirring noise toward Nick, who was fumbling with the digital timer on his belt, all the while muttering, "Oh my God, oh my God, oh my God, I forgot, I forgot, I forgot—"

"What's wrong—" Lori started to say, but froze when she saw the digital display in Nick's sweaty palm. The elapsed time, which was running backwards, was showing 00:00:06 . . . then :05 . . . then :04 . . .

. . . and due to the slippery nature of time in LIMBOworld—or perhaps due to the sudden shock of adrenaline coursing through Lori at that moment—the next four seconds seemed to slow to a crawl.

She could very clearly hear her own voice saying, "What happens if—"

Nick was reaching for his little electronic cattle prod on his belt in urgent, dreamy, surreal slow motion. His voice had softened to a breathy whisper. "I was told the boss wanted to meet you. I should have gotten you here faster. I'm sorry. My bad. I wish you could stay." His eyes met hers, and the moment stretched like taffy. "Full disclosure?" He smiled nervously, lifting the prod. "I'm starting to miss you when you're not around."

Behind him, Mrs. Waverly's voice called out: "*NICK, FOR GOD'S SAKE STOP WITH THE PUPPY LOVE AND ZAP THE POOR GIRL ALREADY!!*"

Lori felt that strange, electric flutter in her spine as she willed time to slow down. The passing seconds crawled, broke down into components, dripped like a leaky faucet. She was doing this—manipulating time as she had never done before—prolonging this moment of gazing into the eyes of this gorgeous, rough-hewn, mysterious young man. "I know," she murmured in extreme slow motion, her voice like a rattle of heat lightning, "I miss you, too."

The prod swung up—00:00:03—and Lori flinched at a spark in her face.

"Until we meet up again," Nick whispered, and Lori was certain that she was the only one who had heard him. Nick's voice was drowned by the booming sound of the digital timer.

TICK! Lori jerked backward.

TICK!

A voice cried out, "NOW!"

—00:00:01—

The cold tip of the prod touched Lori's forehead.

NINE

Lori awoke with a start. She was somewhere else all of a sudden, somewhere unfamiliar that smelled of disinfectant. She heard dripping noises, a rushing of air through a narrow tube, the soft beeping of monitors. She blinked and tried to focus. She could feel the pressure of restraints around her midsection, her wrists, her collarbone, and ankles. A thin mist cooled her face. She desperately needed to pee.

Eyes shifting, gazing around the room, she saw blurry shapes coming into focus one at a time. An armchair, a tile floor, venetian blinds, a bank of machines, diodes, lights, displays flickering.

She realized, all at once, that she was strapped to a padded bed in an unfamiliar hospital room. It was not the sleep clinic room in which she had drifted off last night. Outside the door, footsteps were approaching, echoing in the corridor. They were running. The urgency of these footsteps only added to Lori's disorientation.

In that horrible instant before the door swung open, Lori made note of several disturbing details. A tiny atomizer, like a small dental instrument, was aimed at her lips, periodically moistening them. Her lower body, covered with a sheet and bound with leather straps, felt numb. Feeding tubes snaked off entry ports on the back of her hands, and the cold sting of a catheter poked like a splinter through her lower regions. The gagging sensation in the back of her throat was from a ventilator tube running down her nasal passage.

She had drool on her cheek.

The door burst open.

"Oh my . . . oh. Oh." The middle-aged nurse froze in the doorway like a deer staring down the barrel of a shotgun, her half-glasses perched on the end of her nose. "Look at her, look at her."

Lori tried to speak but could only manage a garbled, breathless moan, the tubes clogging her throat. She wanted to say, WHAT THE HELL?!

The nurse came over, licking her lips nervously, looking as though she were searching for the right words. A mixture of emotions crossed her face as she checked the monitors: shock, excitement, nervousness, professionalism, and something resembling a student about to be quizzed. Finally all these emotions resolved themselves into a fake, upbeat cheerfulness, every statement ending in a question mark: "I'm just going to check something here? Nothing to worry about? Everything's looking good and—"

Lori moaned. Tried to speak. But all that came out was a strangled cough.

"Gonna take a little practice to speak again? Can you hang in there for me? Take this one step at a time?" She glanced nervously at a chart clipped to the foot of the high-tech bed. "We're going to get the doctor in here now? Get you checked out?"

"Mmmm."

"I know, I know . . . it's a little strange right now, huh? Just hang in there for me, okay? Okay?"

The nurse hurried out of the room. Lori's mind reeled. Why couldn't she feel her legs or talk?

A commotion out in the hall drew Lori's attention over to the door.

A young doctor came in with a weird smile on his face, like he was about to present Lori with an award. "Well, well, well," he said, warming up the stethoscope with the palm of his hand. He had a mop of chestnut hair combed back into a fashionable pompadour. He gently pulled the cuff off Lori's rib cage. "This is quite a pleasant surprise."

As the doctor listened to Lori's heart and checked her blood pressure and looked at her pupils with a penlight, Lori continued to notice troubling details: She was dressed in a hospital smock. Her arms looked strange, riddled with bruises, and sinewy, roped with veins, like someone had sucked the air out of them. And perhaps the most disturbing detail of all, the doctor—whom Lori had never met—seemed taken aback, his astonishment thinly veiled with small talk.

"Good strong sinus rhythm, blood pressure looks good," he said, glancing from a monitor to Lori and back to another monitor. "I know it's a little tough to speak right now, so why don't we just blink once for yes, twice for no. That okay?"

Lori blinked once for yes.

"Can you follow what I'm saying pretty well?"

One blink . . . yes.

"Can you see okay?"

One blink.

"Swallowing's not a problem?"

One blink.

"Can you touch your nose with your right hand? With your index finger?"

Lori touched her nose.

"Can you try and move your head for me, like a nodding motion, can you do that?"

With great effort Lori nodded, and then tried to speak again in a breathless whisper: "Hhh-hh-howw—"

"It's okay, it'll come," the doctor encouraged her. Then the man waved his finger slowly in front of Lori and asked her to follow it with her eyes, which she had no problem doing.

The doctor pulled a stainless-steel instrument from his pocket and moved to the foot of the bed. "I'm going to ask you if you feel any sensation down here when I do this," he said, uncovering Lori's bare feet. "How about now?"

Lori felt something cold and metallic graze the sole of her foot.

Lori blinked once . . . and then blinked again . . . and then again . . . and again. She wanted to scream. What the hell had happened to her in the sleep clinic? Why couldn't she speak?

"Jennifer, could you help me with these linens?" the doctor asked the nurse.

Right then, as the nurse came around the foot of the bed, Lori heard shuffling footsteps outside the door. Then she heard the sound of a familiar voice.

"Oh my GOD!"

In the doorway, two slender figures, dressed all in black, stood gaping in at the room. The tall, gangly Rachael Deathcraft (aka Rosemary Donowitz)—her raccoon eyeliner framing her bulging eyes—stood with her hand to her mouth in amazement. Hugo Stipple stood next to her in his leather jacket and hoodie, transfixed by the medical miracle.

"Looks like you've got visitors already," the nurse said as she peeled back the blankets.

Lori stared at her own legs. She stared and stared. Aghast. Thunderstruck.

She knew now. By the condition of her legs, she knew now why they were treating her this way, why she couldn't talk, why her body felt as though it were encased in concrete. Her legs had faded from their customary tobacco brown to a pallid khaki color. They looked like the legs of a prisoner of war—pocked with sores, atrophied and shriveled— the legs of a very small, very skinny, very emaciated seventy-year-old woman.

She looked at the doctor and forced the words out on a whispered gasp: "How long?"

The doctor didn't answer at first. He was measuring his words.

Meanwhile, Hugo and Rachael cautiously came in the room and stood at Lori's bedside. They too seemed to be searching for the proper words.

"*How long!?*"

This time Lori found her voice, and it came out of her on a hoarse, rusty gasp of pain and confusion. It was directed at all of them and none of them. It was directed at the world, at the universe: *How long have I been asleep? How long have I been in this bed?*

"Lori, I understand you're dealing with a major type of situation here," the doctor said, rubbing his dry palms together. "This is a difficult transition and we need to—"

"How! Long!"

"Lori, you have to remember—" the doctor began to explain when another voice piped in.

"Girlfriend . . ." Hugo leaned over Lori's bed rail and put a sympathetic hand on her shoulder. "You were in like a coma."

Lori looked at her friend. "A coma?"

"Yeah. Sort of." Hugo looked at the others, then back at Lori. "For like a long time."

"How long, Hugo? How long was I out?"

The doctor stepped back, letting the young people do the dirty work. Hugo glanced at Rachael. "How long has it been? Like . . . we're seniors now . . . so . . ."

Rachael looked at Hugo, chewing her lip, then she gazed down at Lori. "I dunno. It's been like . . . a little over a year?"

The word seemed to hang in the air. A *year*.

TEN

Lori wanted to see her mom. But for some reason everyone seemed to be avoiding the subject. They needed to do more tests first, they needed to draw some more blood samples, they needed to talk to Lori about physical therapy and insurance and all kinds of trivial matters that didn't even remotely approach the importance of seeing her mom.

At last, just before dinner, the doctor with the chestnut hair—his name was Pyne—materialized in the doorway of Lori's room with his hands in the pockets of his immaculate white lab coat. "Hey, I wanted to mention something about your mom," he said softly, speaking with the gravity of someone carefully parsing words.

Lori looked up at him from her bed. She was propped up against a stack of pillows, a spiral notebook on her lap, her cell phone close by. She had been making notes, trying to remember the events she had undergone in the dreams that were already wavering in her memory like tendrils of smoke vanishing in front of her face. She frowned. Why was everybody tiptoeing around the subject of her mom? She looked at the doctor and said, "Is there a problem with my mom? Why isn't she here? I tried to call her but the voice mail keeps answering."

"First of all, Lori, let me assure you that your mom is fine." The doctor pulled a chair next to the bed, sat down, and thoughtfully picked at a piece of lint on his perfectly creased slacks.

"When can I see her?"

"How about right now?" The doctor smiled. "She's in the waiting room downstairs."

"Fantastic. Send her up." She sat up straighter, stretching her sore neck, gathering up her overgrown braids and cinching a rubber band around them. Her dreadlocks had gone to seed during her spell in dreamland, sprouting mossy whiskers and split ends that curled off the tips like kudzu vines. Now she did her best to contain them within a ponytail.

The doctor pursed his lips. "One thing, though—"

"What the hell is the problem?" Lori felt a twinge of fear stitch coldly through her midriff. Her lower extremities were tingling as though they had not yet fully awakened. In fact, that was *indeed* the case. Lori was improving rapidly. Notwithstanding the atrophy—in the mirror Lori thought she looked like a living skeleton—her limbs, according the doctor, had not been permanently damaged. At this rate she would be up and about soon—albeit with the aid of a walker. "Can my mom see me or not?"

"She can, yes, absolutely, but before you talk to her, I need to prepare you for something."

"Prepare me?"

The doctor sighed, cleared his throat, and measured his words. "There's a thing called the Health Insurance Portability and Accountability Act—HIPAA for short—which prevents me from discussing certain aspects of your mom's treatments."

"Treatments for what?"

The doctor looked at her. "Lori, dealing with your condition hit your mom hard. As I'm sure you know, she's been struggling with clinical depression most of her adult life . . . and unfortunately she's never quite found the proper cocktail of antidepressants."

Lori stared at him. "What are you trying to tell me? Did my mom go off the deep end?"

Another sigh from Pyne. "No . . . not at all. She's fine. Again, I'm not at liberty to discuss specifics, but you should be aware that your mom has been through a lot. At a certain point . . . with your condition stalled . . . she upped her dosage of Paxil, and when that was ineffective, she went through a series of ECT treatments, which can be . . . tough."

"ECT treatments?" Lori searched her bleary memory. "You're talking about shock treatments?"

The doctor was shrugging. "It's not as medieval as it sounds."

"Jesus, why would she—"

"Electroconvulsive therapy can be a lifesaving treatment. Really. Trouble is, your mom responded poorly. We had her here as an in-patient for a while. Just as a precaution. She's doing a lot better now."

"Shit," Lori muttered softly. She chewed her fingernail and stared at the threadbare linens bunched around her skinny ankles.

"She just might be a little . . . *tentative*." The doctor looked at Lori. "It affects your short-term memory." He smiled. "I just thought you should know."

She nodded. "Can I see her?"

His grin widened. "I'll go get her."

The first thing Lori heard was the loping footsteps of someone running down the corridor. These were unmistakable—her mom's Fendi boot heels—clopping down the parquet flooring of the hallway. Lori had heard this sound many times in her life. Once, when she was in the first grade, there was a tornado warning and the students were evacuated to the school's lower-level boiler room. Sitting in the darkness of the cellar with the other kids, petrified, little Lori heard those same high-fashion soles clamoring down the steps, and all at once everything seemed as though it were going to be okay. Years later, when she was in junior high and going through the first of many rebellious phases, Lori got busted for shoplifting. She would never forget hearing those Fendi heels rounding the corner of the entrance outside the police precinct house, coming to both liberate and scold. The clamor of those heels trumped any natural disaster, penetrated any authority, and now they approached Lori's door with percussive purpose . . . accompanied by the trademark squeal of Allison's pet name for her daughter. "PEEWEEE!" The woman appeared in the doorway. "PEEEWEEE! You're back! Oh God, you're back!"

"Mom!" Lori's voice cracked with emotion. She sat on the edge of her gurney bed, arms reaching for her mother, who stood in the doorway in her customary work clothes—smart navy blue Donna Karan dress, simple elegant pearls, and those ever-popular Fendi dress boots—grinning with eyes brimming with tears. Lori found her own eyes welling up. "Oh my God, it's so good to see you."

"My sweet Peewee," Allison Blaine uttered as she lurched across the room and practically tackled her daughter. To Lori it felt as though she were being hugged by a perfumed grizzly, her mother's grip so tight it cut off her air. "I thought I lost you . . . thought I lost you . . . thought I lost you," the woman murmured into the damp nape of Lori's neck, her breath hot with sorrow and smoke.

"I'm fine, Mom."

Allison stepped back, hands still cradling Lori's face, brushing dreadlocks aside. "I ought to smack you a good one for scaring me so much."

"I'm okay."

"What did the doctor say?"

"He said I'm a medical miracle and my cholesterol even looks good."

Allison hugged Lori some more, and softly said, "I thought you'd never come back to me. I can't believe it. You're back, you're as good as new."

"Yep."

Allison wiped the tears and snot from her face, dug in her purse for a Kleenex. "They kept saying 'inconclusive' and I sat by your bed and read to you and sang you Bette Midler songs and one day I brought brownies and ate them all myself . . . oh my God it's so good to see those brown eyes."

Lori watched her mother weep. She reached up and daubed a tear off Allison's cheek. "They told me you had a rough go of it."

Allison swallowed and furrowed her brow. "What do you mean?"

"Pyne said something about shock treatments?"

Allison stared at her daughter for a moment, then sighed and waved it off. "A total waste of time."

"Mom, did you really—"

Allison chuckled ruefully. "I've decided I was just born depressed." Her smile curdled a little. "The truth is, the only thing that seems to work is Napa Valley cabernet sauvignon and double chocolate chip Häagen-Dazs." Her smile faded. "And you."

Lori smiled, reached out, and pulled her mom into another desperate hug.

This time, it was Lori who did the embracing with the vigor of a large woodland mammal.

Over the course of that next day, Allison explained in layman's terms—using medical phrases she had overheard here and there—what exactly happened one year ago in the sleep clinic on that fateful night.

In a nutshell, Lori had not responded to the technicians' attempts to wake her from a troubling REM state. Lori's heart had fallen into arrhythmia, and her pulse was off the scale, and her temperature had spiked to 108. But no matter what they tried—pin pricks, lights, noise, shaking her, cold packs to the face—she would not awaken. It was as though she were trapped in the REM stage.

Later, the two specialists running the lab that night had confessed to the hospital's internal investigative board that they had never seen anything like it.

The next day, exhibiting signs of being "AC" (atypically comatose), Lori was moved to the long-term care ward. That's when Dr. Pyne came into the picture. After a whole battery of tests, the neurologist realized that Lori's condition was not only rare, but also unprecedented.

Lori was trapped in what the neurologist called a "locked-inside" state. This is a condition where the brain acts as though it's awake, but at the same time, the body is physically exhibiting signs of being unconscious. It's not sleep. It's not a coma exactly. It's a strange trance state that Pyne first encountered in medical school texts. Allison remembered Pyne rhapsodizing about it in the hospital lounge one evening, and she had written most of it down in her diary.

Supposedly, according to the doctor, only a few cases of the phenomenon existed in recorded medical history. One was an Indian Yogi who had slipped into the condition during a long session of transcendental meditation. Another case involved a Native American man in a nursing home who had left a rambling note about being on a vision quest. These cases had become infamous as urban folk tales among neuroscientists . . . but now Dr. Edward Pyne was a believer.

"You should have heard him ranting and raving about it," Allison said in the cafeteria that night. Lori's crutches leaned against the table, and a chessboard lay between the two women amid the empty cottage cheese containers and Diet Coke cans. They had been picking at the food for an hour, pretending to be interested in the chess game, but as the cafeteria cleared of people, the conversation kept circling back to Lori's marathon dream.

"What do you want to know about it?" Lori asked finally, sensing that Allison was dying to get into it. "Ask me anything and I'll tell you the truth."

Allison shrugged, a little nervous tic tugging at her lip. "I don't know. What was it like? Were you dreaming? Was the door involved?"

For a brief instant Lori considered telling her mom everything. The truth of the matter was, Lori didn't have the energy. Not right now. She wanted to tell. Maybe she would in due course. But right now, she simply said, "To be honest with you, I don't remember much of it."

"Do you remember that night?"

Lori looked at her. "In the sleep clinic?" She gave a shrug. "Not very well." She rubbed her eyes. "I remember having a nightmare and then . . . it's all kind of nebulous."

"'Nebulous'?"

She sighed. "It was like . . . I lost track of time." She shrugged. "It's a little difficult to articulate." Lori thought about it for a moment. "Okay, I know this sounds certifiably insane, but I think there might be something to these dreams."

"Okay."

"What I mean is, there may very well be something going on here that's far more complicated than your basic recurring nightmares."

"Alright." Allison had a strange look on her haggard, weary face. Lori had a hard time figuring it out. The woman looked curious, and also suspicious. "And . . . ? So . . . ?"

Lori looked into her eyes. "Mom, I promise you I will tell you everything . . . just as soon as I get a little more information."

"Information about what?"

Lori took a deep breath. "Information about . . . a person in the dreams." Lori swallowed hard, licked her lips, and then added, "I think there's some major connections between the dreams and reality."

There was a pause. And finally Allison grinned at her daughter. "Of course there's a connection, honey," Allison said then. "Dreams are where we work out our problems. Even nightmares. Especially nightmares."

"Yeah, I've heard that before. But what if they're more than that?"

"They *are* more than that."

Lori looked at her. "Okay . . ."

"They're full of symbols, honey. I read up on it. While you were in the coma. I read a lot of Carl Jung. For instance, when you dream about other people, you're actually dreaming about parts of yourself. Did you know that?" She looked down and seemed to ponder it for a moment. The lines on her face were prominent, her breathing labored. "Come to think of it, there's a lot of material about doors." She looked at Lori. "Does your dream door open inward or outward?"

Lori thought about it. "Inward. I think. No . . . outward. It opens outward. Actually I'm not certain one way or the other."

"If it opens inward? It might represent something like . . . your desire for inner exploration . . . or like . . . self-discovery."

"Hmm."

"If it opens outward, it might mean, like, you want to connect with others. Or be more accessible. Or maybe develop relationships or whatever."

"That's . . . interesting."

"And there are mystical meanings, too. Like oracles. Signs and portents. Allegedly. I mean, you wouldn't believe how much literature there is on doors. Is there a doorknob or a handle?"

Lori thought about it for a moment. "A knob."

"A knob means unexpected luck. Are there hinges?"

"Sure . . . I guess . . . yes, absolutely. I mean, it's a door. Hence it has hinges."

"Hinges bring family into it, hinges are family issues. God knows you have plenty of those." Another weary smile and then a big sigh. "I'm ranting now. I better be careful or Pyne's gonna have me back on lithium." The silence pressed down on them. "Bad joke. I'm sorry." She narrowed her eyes and looked closer at Lori. "You okay, honey?"

Lori yawned. "Yeah. I'm just—" She fell silent and yawned again.

"You look exhausted, sweetheart."

Lori nodded. "Yeah. I guess I'm just procrastinating."

"Procrastinating over what?"

Lori took a deep breath and looked at her mom. "Over going back to sleep."

ELEVEN

Lori's dream felt different that night. It felt *engineered* somehow—artificial, virtual, fake—as though someone or some *thing* had implanted it in her brain. Maybe it was the texture of the sunlight shining down on her street as she found herself outside her house on Monterey Court, sitting on her Schwinn ten-speed bike.

She hadn't ridden the bike since eighth grade. Lately she had been getting around on foot, or would borrow her mom's rust-bucket Toyota. She wouldn't *dream* of riding her old Schwinn. Literally. She wouldn't dream it . . . unless somebody had inserted it into her subconscious.

Overhead, the sky was robin's egg blue and the little bungalow at 5720 was freshly painted, the roses crowning the trellis over the front door in full bloom, their blossoms like daubs of beautiful Technicolor red in a lovely oil painting. Birds sang overhead.

It was the perfect summer day. Picture postcard perfect. In other words, *too* perfect. In other words, the exact *opposite* kind of day Lori Blaine—brooding hipster—would normally dream.

Lori noticed there was a map Scotch-taped to her handlebars.

She pulled it off the bars and looked at it. Hand-drawn with little diagrams and arrows, the map pointed the way to a house at the end of

Monterey Court. The address was 6800—an address that did not exist in the real world—and a single phrase was scrawled above the hastily sketched house: GO HERE NOW!

Lori obliged.

Pedaling down the street, passing the manicured lawns and kaleido-scopic flowerbeds, she wondered if she should control this dream. She knew she was dreaming now, and she had the power now to change the course of events, but for reasons she would soon learn, it was probably better to follow the directions that the dream was giving her.

She arrived at the nonexistent house at the end of her block.

In the real world this parcel of land was an overgrown grove of elm trees and wild undergrowth, the mouth of the state forest preserve, which had become a makeshift dump in recent years—the repository of old tires, broken refrigerators, cinder blocks, and mangled lawn jockeys. But in this dream, the property featured a lawn as groomed as a putting green, and a two-story white Cape Cod that looked like a home John F. Kennedy might have lived in back in the 1950s.

Lori parked the bike at the curb, leaning it against the storybook mailbox. She put the map in the hip pocket of her shredded black jeans and strode up the charming little daffodil-bordered walk to the front porch. For some reason, Lori was not surprised to see that the front door was *the* door—the gray, mysterious door about which she had been dreaming since she was twelve—with its mystic knob.

She didn't knock. She didn't ring the doorbell. She didn't even hesitate. She expected it to be open, and when she turned the knob it was, indeed, *open*.

What she found inside was like something out of a brochure. *Beautiful Homes and Gardens of Northern Illinois*. The entryway smelled of pine and floor wax, and a lovely copper chandelier illuminated the threshold with rose-colored light. The living room was spacious and filled with the kind of overstuffed sectionals and easy chairs that make you want to cuddle under a blanket and watch an old movie on a lazy Sunday afternoon. The entertainment center featured CDs of all her faves: Evanescence, Ziggy Marley, Reel Big Fish, All-American Rejects, Akon, Sublime, and Gnarls Barkley. DVDs of her favorite movies—and only her favorites—were stacked neatly beside the Blu-ray player: *Little Miss Sunshine*, *Beetlejuice*, *Donnie Darko*, *Pan's Labyrinth*, Coppola's *Dracula*, *Edward Scissorhands*, and on and on. There was an iPad mini loaded with her favorite books and magazines and artists. Lori didn't notice it at first, but there was something odd about the selection—despite the fact that these were all her favorites, the assortment seemed stuck in the year she had turned eleven. She wasn't absolutely certain about it, but it seemed as though all the titles were the best of 2006.

Just beyond the living room, an enormous bathroom clad in gleaming subway tile featured a black oval hot tub, candles softly flickering, and all her favorite makeup and fashion products neatly arrayed on the marble counters: black eyeliner sticks from Urban Decay, temp tattoos from Manic Panic still in their little paper vials lined up on the sill, and primitive steel jewelry in every conceivable make and design hanging on ram horns and steampunk-style sculptures—again, styles that were all the rage in 2006. Nobody but Lori would notice such a subtle distinction . . . but somehow, in the recesses of her mind, it seemed significant.

Across the hall and around a corner, Lori found a showroom-elegant kitchen with a gigantic, gleaming Sub-Zero refrigerator, fully stocked with her favorite foods: individual servings of double-chocolate fudge pudding in silver chalices, and fresh raspberries still beaded with dewy droplets of perspiration, and stainless-steel canisters of homemade whipped cream, and bowls of hand-spun sugar skulls, and ice cold bottles of Yoo-hoo, and imported pints of ginger beer from Martinique.

Five minutes later, Lori was savoring her second helping of raspberries and cream when she noticed a single piece of plain white paper propped on a coffee cup on the dining table across the kitchen.

She went over and picked up the notepaper and saw that someone had written her a message:

Lori—

I don't have time to explain but something terrible is happening. I made this dream for you so you could just chill out while you recover. Enjoy the stuff and don't go anywhere. Stay inside. And keep track of your time. The timer's on top of the TV in the living room. Don't get cute with any of your lucid tricks. And wake yourself up before the timer runs out. And above all, do NOT—I repeat—do NOT answer the door. No matter what. Do NOT answer it. We'll get back in touch when things calm down—hopefully.

—Nick

Lori read the note a second time just to be sure she was seeing what she thought she was seeing. Then she folded it in two and put it back on the table. All of sudden she didn't feel so terrific about being in this dream home—despite the luxurious accommodations. The vague sense of dread that was turning in her gut changed to a sort of longing. If forced to admit it, she would have to confess that she missed Nick. She really wished he were here. She couldn't remember ever missing somebody like this. What the hell was happening to her? She pushed the feelings back down inside her and went out into the living room.

On top of the plasma TV sat a rectangular digital counter. It currently read 01:53:11. A little less than two hours of dreamtime left before she turned into another pumpkin. She sat down on the cushions of the massive sofa and thought about it. What if she missed the deadline again? What if she went beyond the point of no return? Would she end up like Nick?

She wondered how he had made this dream. How did he know that Lori liked chocolate pudding and Nine Inch Nails and Coppola's *Dracula*? And more importantly, who in the world would be knocking on this door?

She found a remote on the coffee table and fired up the TV. She stared at the blank pixel dots. Evidently the dream world had ended its broadcasting day. She powered up the iPad mini—her favorite books, of course, all available on Kindle—and she stared and stared, trying to forget her troubles, trying to engineer the dream.

But she couldn't concentrate. She kept waiting for the time to run down.

And she kept listening for someone or some *thing* to knock on the door.

TWELVE

As it turned out, no one came to call. In fact, for the duration of that week, Lori Blaine dreamed each night of that luxurious Cape Cod with its deep pile carpet, high-definition TV, and gourmet kitchen. In the dream she spent her time *indoors*, staying put, staying out of trouble—just as Nick had recommended—watching movies and experimenting with different kinds of makeup and listening to music and just generally keeping to herself.

She received no further correspondence from Nick, and she heard no knock at the door.

And in each dream, when the timer would approach zero, Lori would stand up and slap her face until she awoke in her hospital room, the sun streaming in through the blinds. It was a technique Lori had developed spontaneously, without putting much thought into it. Lucid dreamers can do that. They can exit their dreams fairly easily. Unfortunately, Lori found herself agonizing over the extent of her abilities to engineer her dreams. Her power to change things seemed intermittent, at best inconsistent, and that was bothering her. She wondered if the old wives' tale about dying in your dreams was true: if you die in the dreamscape, you die in reality.

The days were long and difficult that week. Once she was out of her wheelchair for good and allowed to rely solely on the crutches, Lori struggled through a series of painful exercises to strengthen her legs. She went through an endless gauntlet of tests and scans. The doctor claimed that he was pleased with Lori's progress. And Lori was told that she would be able to go home in a few days.

She slept soundly and well that week. The fact was, she was growing fond of the little hideaway in her dreams. It provided her with all the empty calories and downtime her heart desired.

She almost wished the dream house would always be there, waiting for her.

But she knew better. She knew her dreams would be changing very soon . . . probably for the worse.

That Friday, Allison Blaine dropped by the hospital with homework for Lori. The truth was, even handicapped with the loss of an entire school year, Lori could have passed her senior exams with her eyes closed. But what Allison did *not* know—nor did the doctors have any clue about—was the fact that her daughter was working on a special homework project that was not authorized by any school. She was now taking secret side trips during her long, painful, therapeutic walks around the mazelike corridors of the medical center, silently slipping into the empty nurse's lounge when nobody was looking. There was a desktop computer in there, and Lori needed the added memory, as well as a printer, in order to pull some key artifacts off the Internet. Her iPhone was an ancient generation and was getting spotty service in the hospital. She need to be sure about something . . . and it had to do with the St. Louis area.

The following Monday, just before breakfast, the chestnut-haired doctor came into Lori's room with a clipboard and the smile of a used car dealer. "Good news, young lady," he said. "You're going home."

Lori was leaning against the sink, pulling her long, shiny, fuzzy dreadlocks into a massive ponytail. Her hair was way too long—its year of growth making her look like a Rastafarian priestess—but she had no energy to give herself a trim. Her legs were still weak but functioning better every day, her skin had returned to its normal healthy butter-scotch tone, and her mind was clearer every day. "That's terrific," she said, looking up at him through her big, clear, intelligent brown eyes, wiping her hands in a towel.

"Just need to fill out a few forms, and we'll get you out of this place."

Lori limped over to the bed, buttoning up her floppy fisherman-knit sweater. She sat down and signed her signature on a series of dotted lines, not really bothering to read any of the insurance forms or legal waivers. Dr. Edward Pyne watched with that big corporate grin. "You're a real success story, Lori."

"Thanks . . . I think?"

"I understand we got a request from the University of Chicago to do a paper on you." Pyne informed her of this as if handing out a merit badge.

"A what?"

"A scholarly paper, Lori. You're the Miracle Girl. Never seen anything like it."

"Yeah . . . um . . . that's cool and flattering and everything . . . but I'm not sure that's a good idea."

The doctor looked crestfallen. "Why is that?"

"I'm going to have plenty of my own papers to write if I want to ever be a senior."

"Look . . . I never really got into this with you," the doctor said then, lowering his voice, sounding a bit melodramatic. "Medicine is sometimes . . . well it's not an exact science. But this was . . . this was a complete anomaly."

Lori was gathering her personal items, her leather satchel and her purse and her coat, then pulling her tattered leggings up over her sore legs. "Yeah, well, let's hope it's also an *isolated* anomalous event."

"Just be careful, Lori," Pyne said. His expression had changed. All at once he looked almost grave. "You have a unique structure to your brain."

Lori stopped packing. She smiled. "I'm sure my mom would agree with you . . . not that she would mean it as a compliment." Her smile faded. "If you don't mind, though, I'm going to ask you to elaborate on that."

The doctor took a breath, as if considering a boundary he was about to cross. "Without getting too technical, Lori, there's a part of everybody's brain that's like an on-off switch. It's called an RAS, or reticular activating system." He paused, a very dramatic pause here. "You have two of these."

"I'm sorry . . . what was that?"

"Think of it this way, Lori. You have a switch in your brain that's like an override. I've heard about this kind of thing—read about it—but I've never seen it up close. Not one of my colleagues has seen anything like it. It's basically like a delta wave generator, as though you can mass-produce dreams."

Lori stared at him. "I'm not really following. What are delta waves again?"

The doctor smiled. "They're the brain's electromagnetic activity that is most closely associated with REM sleep. Sleepwalkers have a similar makeup during sleepwalking, but it's all delta wave activity. The sleepwalker is like a puppet. Daydreaming is gamma activity, the mind wandering. You on the other hand have the ability to achieve REM in a fully conscious state, Lori. It's like having X-ray vision."

Lori gave it some thought and let out a sigh. "Can it help me get into Harvard Law School?"

Dr. Pyne chuckled uneasily. "Just be careful, Lori. That's all I'm saying. Your scans are all clean; you're doing great." He closed his file, then clipped the forms together. "We'll have you come back in a few weeks for a follow-up." He walked over to the door. "But Lori . . . just be careful out there. That's all I'm saying."

"I will, Dr. Pyne. Don't worry. I have an aversion to trouble." She gave him a smile. "I'm highly allergic to it."

Another awkward chuckle from the doctor. "Any-hoo . . . let me get the nurse to call your mom."

"Um, you know what?" Lori spoke up then, reaching for her crutches. "You don't have to do that."

"Excuse me?"

"I'd like to surprise her."

"That's kind of against hospital—"

"I know it's probably against the rules, but could we perhaps bend them a little for the Miracle Girl? Just this one time?" She practically batted her eyelashes at him. "Pretty please?"

The doctor nodded knowingly. "Of course, of course. So you have a ride home?"

"Absolutely. I got a friend I can call."

"Okay then . . ." Pyne looked as though he should say something else but could think of nothing and simply nodded and walked out.

Hugo Stipple showed up at the medical center a few minutes before noon in his stepfather's Chevy Geo. Lori had to laugh as she shuffled through the exit doors on her crutches and saw the miniscule vehicle waiting for her at the curb with its rust pocks like measles speckling the cat-vomit yellow exterior. She threw her crutches in the back seat and climbed into the passenger side. The car smelled like sour milk. Death metal music roared out of the speakers.

Behind the wheel, Hugo grinned at Lori and said something that was drowned by the music.

"Dial it down, Hugo—please!" Lori hollered.

Hugo complied. "Sorry. Whassup?"

"Feel like taking a road trip?" Lori pulled a folded piece of paper from her purse. It was a MapQuest printout that Lori had snuck out of the nurses' lounge.

"Always!" Hugo grinned. "Where to?"

Lori glanced at the printout. "Carlinville, Illinois, just north of St. Louis. Probably . . . like . . . what? Maybe five hours or so?"

Hugo looked at her. "What's in Carlinville, Illinois? Other than cows and rednecks."

"I'll let you know when we get there."

"Let's do it," Hugo said, slamming the shift lever into drive and then goosing the gas pedal.

They tore out of the parking lot in a cloud of carbon monoxide.

Within minutes, they were tooling down the main drag, past strip malls and office parks, heading toward the interstate. Hugo cranked the music back up.

Lori yelled over the thunderous drumbeat. "The way you drive, we'll make it in four!"

They took US 39 down to Interstate 55, and then cut through the central part of the state—zigzagging across the cornfield counties of Tazewell, Logan, and Menard—the endless acres of cardboard-brown crops rushing past them, as desolate and vast as the Sahara Desert.

It was early September. The sky was low and dark, but the weather held for most of the trip. They stopped for gas twice—the Geo was burning oil and in bad need of a tune-up. At a truck stop south of Springfield, Lori called her mom on Hugo's cell. She assured Allison that everything was fine and that she was getting homework from Hugo and that she would be home later that night.

Back on the road, the two of them talked about everything *but* their destination. Lori just kept avoiding the subject, explaining it had to do with a "missing person." She figured it would take too much energy to explain the whole situation with the dreams . . . and the mysterious young man named Nick . . . and the fact that Lori was going to Carlinville to find out once and for all if the people in her dreams were real.

The strangest part was, neither of them noticed that they were being followed.

The mysterious black vehicle behind them had been tailing them ever since they left DeKalb. Keeping its distance, lurking three or four car lengths back, the stalker went unseen for nearly three hundred miles.

That was the strangest part.

And also ironic.

Ironic because all that Lori had to do was turn around and peer into the distance behind them—and see who was driving that mystery vehicle—to confirm the fact that her nightmares were about to spill over into reality.

THIRTEEN

The official name of the place—such a tongue twister it barely fit on the knotty pine sign planted in the ground at the end of its gravel drive—was the St. Vincent de Paul Long Term Acute Care Hospice and Nursing Facility.

Lori and Hugo arrived at the place just as the sun was setting over the high dormers and turrets. The waning light gave the ancient building a spooky Addams Family flavor. Once upon a time, the place was probably a single-family home—probably the residence of some coal baron or steamboat tycoon—but now the massive Victorian edifice housed a respected nursing home.

On her way to the front entrance, scuffling along on her crutches— her tall, lanky form wrapped in a many-buckled leather waistcoat over her ratty sweater, leggings, and beat-up Doc Martens—Lori surprised herself. She paused on the sidewalk, leaning on one crutch, gazing down at a little shriveled bed of daffodils along the edge of the walk. It had been a dry summer, and the little purple- and peach-colored blooms were brown around the edges.

"What are you doing?" Hugo asked.

"Nothing." Lori picked a small bunch of daffodils and carefully nestled them in her coat pocket.

They went inside and found themselves in a reception area that looked more like a grandmother's sewing room than a lobby of a high-tech nursing facility. The air reeked of menthol and old hard candy petrifying in crystal bowls. Catholic icons were everywhere: on the walls, behind glass cabinets, engraved into paperweights on coffee tables, even woven into the doilies on the arms of the colonial sofas and easy chairs. It looked like a crucifix store.

A gray-haired nun greeted them at the front desk. She looked up at them over the tops of little square eyeglasses as thick as ice cubes. "Now, how may I help you two fine young people?"

Lori swallowed her nerves, leaning on a crutch. "I'm here to see a patient, Ballas is the name." She spelled it. "First name Nick."

The nun pecked at a keyboard. "And you are . . . ?"

"Lori Blaine." She spelled her last name. Then, indicating Hugo, she added, "My friend's gonna wait out here for me."

Hugo nodded.

The nun thoughtfully chewed the inside of her cheek, scrutinizing Lori and her wild dreads tied up on the back of her skull like slumbering boa constrictors. "And you're a . . . relative?"

"Actually I'm a cousin . . . distant but . . . yeah, a cousin . . . a distant cousin . . . twice removed.""

The nun arched an eyebrow. "You do realize that visiting hours are almost over for the day."

"I understand that, yes," Lori said with as much deference and politeness as she could whip up. "I just wanted to stop in and . . . say a few prayers for him."

The nun exhaled a thoughtful breath. Then she opened a leather binder on the countertop in front of her, spun it toward Lori, and said, "Please sign in with your name and address and relationship to the resident and time of day." She glanced at the clock on the wall, the one with the Sacred Heart and crucifix emblazoned on its face. "It's 6:47 P.M." The nun wrote a number on a Post-it note. "He's in one eighteen. Take a left at the fountain."

Lori did as she was told, writing her information in the registry. She turned, gave a nod to Hugo, and then trundled off toward the central hallway.

It took Lori quite a while to find the room. Slowed down by the crutches, and still groggy from her experiences in the DeKalb sleep clinic, she passed room after room of whispering ventilators and beeping life-support equipment. She tried not to stare. But she could not help stealing glances inside each of the open doorways, the inert, skeletal figures lying inside each room, alone, forgotten, and frozen in their mechanical wombs, tubes coming out of every orifice, blank faces as stony and pale as chalk.

Lori had almost forgotten Nick's last name—despite the fact that she hadn't been able to stop thinking about him since their last encounter. Like a melody that would not leave her mind, she kept thinking about his face, his scraggly whiskers, his soulful eyes. But the last name still eluded her. The enigmatic young man from the dreamscape had only mentioned it once in that second dream.

As soon as Lori had come out of her twelve-month stupor, she got her hands on a pen and some scratch paper, and she wrote down as many details from the dream as she could remember. She wrote down *Ballast* first. And then *Bollas*. After doing the Google search in the nurse's lounge, though, the search engine actually spit back a correction in the form of a question:

Did you mean: Ballas 208 results shown

At first, none of the entries caught her eye. There was a Major Dunleavy Ballas Military School. There was a Facebook page for somebody named Nancy Ballas, and another one for somebody named Mark Ballas. There were Twitter sites, and Ballas dry cleaners, and the Ballas family reunion scrapbook site. Finally Lori's cursor froze above the following entry:

The Nick Ballas Critical Care Benefit—S.L. Post Dispatch

Lori clicked the entry and the screen filled with an archival page from the St. Louis newspaper. The article was dated May 12, 2006—a little over eight years ago—and featured a high school picture of a boy of fourteen or fifteen, with pale blue eyes and sandy blond hair sweeping across one side of his face. Lori had stared at that little thumbnail for a long time.

At fifteen years of age—with that same bed-head hairstyle—Nick Ballas looked like the kind of boy whom Lori's late grandmother Helen would call a "real pistol." His lips were curled into a droll little smile that seemed to say, *No worries . . . I got this.*

The bulk of the article was about a charity concert organized by Nick's school to defray the massive costs of Nick's healthcare (after his sudden and tragic descent into brain death). It didn't say much about Nick himself, or his family background. But it did mention his current residence at the St. Vincent de Paul Long Term Acute Care Hospice and Nursing Facility, in the sprawling metropolis of Carlinville, Illinois. There had never been any doubt in Lori's mind that the dreamscape was inextricably linked to the waking world—that there was a complex, reciprocal, and terrifying interconnection between the dreams and reality. Nor had she ever really doubted that Nick was a real person. But despite all this certainty, she desperately needed to see the real Nick with her waking eyes. She needed so badly to connect with the flesh and blood Nick Ballas.

She reached the end of the nursing home's main corridor and paused.

The intersection was dominated by a huge marble fountain of the Blessed Mother pouring holy water into a sacred pool, illuminated by yellow floodlights. Lori recognized the landmark, turned left, and followed the room numbers until she found 118.

Her heart was beating as she pushed open the door and entered the warm, dimly lit room. The bed was facing the window, so Lori approached the occupant from behind, her pulse racing in her ears. Ventilators hissed and clucked. Monitors softly beeped. She could see the top of his head. She came around the side of the bed.

"*Nick?*"

Looking down at him, Lori did not even hear her own voice in her own ears. The whisper of shocked recognition came out of her on a breathy, choked utterance as she stared at the sad little bundle of flesh and bones nestled in the folds of that motorized bed.

The young man was practically unrecognizable. His body had shriveled over the years into a spindly stick figure. His skin was the color of tapioca pudding that had dried and congealed. His face—that was the worst part for Lori—had lolled to one side and stared emptily at the acoustic tiles of the ceiling. Drained of color, drained of life, drained of everything that was once Nick Ballas, his face had sunken into itself, as gaunt as a skull. His staring eyes reminded Lori of buttons.

"*Um . . .*"

Lori stood there for an eternity. She didn't even notice the tears burning in her eyes. She never imagined this moment would be so sad. She had envisioned it being an incredible victory—like Newton's apple hitting the ground—proving once and for all that she wasn't insane. Her dreams were real. But this—

She pulled the little wilted daffodils from her pocket and gently laid them on the bedside table. Should she put them in water? Would he ever see them? She just stood there for endless minutes, staring down at him, trying to connect the feisty, courageous young Turk of LIMBOworld with this ragged doll of a human being, when she realized she was hearing a strange sound underneath the drone of life-support machines: a faint scratching noise, like the claws of a rat struggling to escape a cage.

She looked around the room. Where the hell was that noise coming from?

Lori noticed a few personal items scattered here and there, collecting dust. Family photos of Nick and his parents, standing in front of their Greek restaurant in St. Louis—it was called Cross Rhodes Café—smiled down at Lori from a shelf over the ventilator. A few high school pennants hung on the wall, a few wilted flowers drooped out of dusty vases on the windowsill. The scratching noises rose, as though the rat or the mouse or the cockroach—or whatever it was—was in the throes of a feeding frenzy.

That's when Lori saw out of the corner of her eye the bloodstains.

She looked down at Nick's bed and saw the source of the scratching noise. His corpse-like hand, curled into a claw, was busily scraping at the edge of the mattress. Either through some damaged nervous system tic, or perhaps some stray electrical impulse from his brain stem, it had been at it so long and hard now, the jagged, untrimmed fingernails were bloody.

At first Lori didn't notice the letters. She only saw the deep scarlet stains smudged across the mattress like blurry tadpoles. And those cadaverous fingers, like talons, kept scratching and scratching, until Lori realized they were actually forming the lines and whirls and curlicues of crudely drawn letters.

She stared.

And stared.

All at once a jolt of fear constricted her throat, the cold current coursing through her veins, raising gooseflesh down her back and across the backs of her legs. She felt dizzy. She could make out a childish word peaking out from under Nick Ballas's left hand. The letters were runny and poorly formed, and partially hidden by Nick's trembling hand. But Lori could plainly see two words forming in blood scrawl on the fabric of the mattress. "Automatic writing," Lori would later learn, is what psychologists call it:

YOU

This was the first word Lori was able to decipher. And in the moments before she fled that sad, dusty chamber of beeps and deathly stillness, she saw another word on the mattress beneath those horrible clawing fingers. This second word, which Lori was barely able to decipher in the streaks and smudges on the fabric, was just below the first:

ARE

Right then, as Lori's brain registered this second word, she happened to glance across Nick's paralyzed midsection. On a wave of nausea and terror, Lori realized—all of this occurring within mere seconds—that Nick's other hand on the other side of the mattress was jerkily composing two additional words. These two additional words formed a complete sentence. It was a simple, declarative, four-word sentence.

But Lori hardly had time to even compute the meaning of it when a noise yanked her attention to the doorway across the room.

"Excuse me?" A middle-aged priest in a black frock coat was standing in the doorway with the nun from the lobby. They looked worried, suspicious, nervous. "Miss?"

"I'm sorry. I need to—" Lori struggled to get her bearings and swallow back her fear. "I need to—"

"Young lady, if we might just have a word with you for a moment?"

"I need to go," Lori said, and grabbed her crutches, and hobbled toward the door. She pushed her way past the puzzled priest and nun.

"Miss!"

It was too late.

Lori was already halfway down the hallway.

She was shuffling toward the exit as though the building were on fire.

"You want to tell me what's going on?" Hugo said as he turned the ignition key and fired up the rattletrap Geo, which coughed up a belch of exhaust across the nursing home parking lot. Darkness had fallen, and the streetlights illuminated the gravel lot in their eerie glow. "What did you see in there?"

Lori sat on the passenger side, her crutches between her legs, her fingernails digging into the edge of her seat as hard as Nick's fingers had clawed at the edges of his mattress. "Just go," she said. "Get us out of here."

Hugo shook his head and slammed it into gear. He screeched out of the parking lot, throwing a wide wake of rocks and debris. The Geo squealed around a corner, then boomed back down the main road.

"Dude," Hugo blurted, his hands glued to the steering wheel, the green glow of the dashboard shining off his mousey features. They were already halfway back to the interstate. "I am seriously considering, like, dumping you at the next bus depot if you don't tell me what's going on."

Lori gazed out at the rushing darkness, the passing strip malls blazing with sodium vapor light. She didn't say anything at first. She was exhausted and hungry and dizzy with nervous tension. She wondered if it actually might be best for both of them—at least best for Hugo—if Lori were dumped at the nearest bus station. Lori knew she had to tell Hugo *something*, but how was she going to explain the importance—even the existence—of those four words smeared on the edges of a brain-dead young man's mattress:

YOU

ARE

And then. On the other side of the mattress. The final two words of the message. Under the claws of Nick's right hand:

IN

DANGER

Finally Lori said, "Hugo . . . dude . . . I don't . . . I don't even know where to start."

"Just for the hell of it, why don't you try, like, maybe, the beginning? That's always a good place."

Lori let out a tense breath and nodded. "You're right. You're right. Okay. You remember the door I was telling you about?"

In the darkness Hugo scrunched up his nose. "Don't tell me we're back to *that* again? What's that have to do with missing persons and Carlinville, Illinois? Who *was* that in there?"

"You have no idea," Lori said. "Hugo . . . here's the situation. Essentially, I think I've gotten you mixed up in something that's not exactly . . . safe."

There was the briefest pause then. They were climbing the entrance ramp to the interstate. At this time of night, in this remote rural area, the river of pavement was deserted, snaking off into the dark void. Hugo pulled the Geo into the fast lane and gunned it.

The little bucket of bolts shivered as it accelerated past forty-five . . . past fifty . . . past fifty-five . . . then finally topped out at sixty and change. At this speed, the engine sounded like an opera singer with a sore throat getting tortured.

The Geo's top speed was probably somewhere south of seventy miles per hour. Built for maximum economy, with a body about as sturdy as a balsa wood model, the Chevy Geo was never going to win any drag races. But it had served the Stipple family well over the years, especially since Hugo's stepfather was a part-time pipe fitter and full-time loser, living off of unemployment checks.

"I hope you're planning to elaborate on that 'not exactly safe' part," Hugo finally said, his knuckles on the steering wheel showing white in the darkness. Lori was getting the feeling that her friend was a lot more nervous than he was letting on.

"Look, I know it sounds like I'm a couple of instruments short of an entire orchestra," Lori said then. "But it all started when I went through that—"

She never finished the sentence.

What had begun as a vague, uneasy feeling that they were being followed now washed over Lori like a tsunami. She felt a presence looming behind them in the darkness—even before the headlights made themselves known—like a cold finger touching the back of her neck.

She twisted around in her seat.

She saw the headlights.

They were a quarter of a mile behind the Geo—

—but they were closing that distance so quickly they looked like the eyes of a hungry predator.

PART TWO

EXTREME SHOCK

"Hell is empty and all the devils are here."
— William Shakespeare

FOURTEEN

In the seconds before the crash, the passage of time seemed to slow down, almost as though Lori were caught in another dream, but this wasn't a dream—this was real. This was Interstate 55, and this was Hugo Stipple behind the wheel of his stepfather's ailing Chevy Geo with the sour milk smells and the shrieking six-valve engine that was hardly bigger than that of a go-cart. This was the cold darkness of night and the desolate black sea of cornfields rushing alongside the tiny car on either side, with no sign of civilization for miles and miles.

And this was a pair of hungry headlamps like the glowing pupils of a dragon bearing down on the Geo with startling speed, impossible speed, almost supernatural speed.

In the midst of those endless moments before the collision, Lori felt that horrible, lethargic quicksand of fear gluing her to her seat, choking off her words, keeping her mute and frozen. She wanted to warn Hugo, wanted to say something, but her brain had seized up, shutting down like a computer crashing. Information overload. And in the jumble of thoughts jamming her fractured mind at that moment, Lori felt something stirring in her that was beyond her vocabulary, beyond her ability to articulate. She had felt this feeling only a few times in her life.

The feeling usually came during moments of great emotional trauma, moments of change, moments of transformation—as though Lori were crossing over a threshold. They were times when Lori felt—deep down—that everything would be measured, from that moment on, as either *before* or *after* what was about to happen.

Lori felt this feeling on the day her dad left. Her father, Michelangelo "Mikey" Blaine, a thin, dark-complexioned, handsome Jamaican, who was employed as an English literature professor at Knox College, had been a private man. Quiet, moody, even mysterious to the eleven-year-old Lori. And that terrible morning—a little over six years ago—when Mike Blaine had announced that he was moving out, proved to be one of the worst moments of Lori's young life. "Everything comes to an end, Lori, even the best things," Mike had said of his marriage that morning as he strolled with his only daughter along a deserted river walk as barren, windswept, and lonely as a family crypt. "But you're going to have to grow up quickly, Lori, and take care of your mother."

Lori remembered crying that morning, sobbing like a newborn infant freshly slapped on the ass. And maybe that's what she was. A baby being yanked into the harsh light and cold air of reality. But she also remembered feeling something else that morning—something far more powerful than sorrow—something buried deep in the core of her being—something that she felt right now.

It was shame—a deep, humiliating, festering *shame*—as potent and dangerous as uranium in a nuclear reactor.

Lori blamed herself for her parents' split. Simple as that. It didn't matter what the relatives had said, or the school counselor, or all the well-wishing family friends: Lori knew her parents were happy before she came along. Then Lori popped into the world and ruined everything.

"Is that a cop?" Hugo craned his neck to better see the vehicle gaining on them in the rearview mirror. Hugo's voice sounded thin and shaky with uncertainty. "He's like coming at warp speed."

"Give him room," Lori heard herself say, sounding as nervous and edgy as Hugo.

"I *am* giving him room—I'm practically driving on the shoulder."

"Are you speeding?"

"That's a good one—in *this* piece of crap?"

"He's probably chasing somebody else, somebody ahead of us. He'll go around us."

It took another ten seconds or so for the mystery vehicle to reach the Geo. Lori envisioned whoever it was—state trooper, undercover cop—swinging out into the fast lane at the last possible instant and then zooming past the Geo in a slipstream of swirling leaves. But what if he didn't? What if he didn't?

As the seconds ticked down, Lori could feel that same cancerous, inarticulate, invisible shame building in her—the same sort of shame that had turned her inward after her parents' divorce. It was the itch she couldn't scratch, the wound she couldn't dress. It turned her into a brooder. It changed her from an all-American Girl Scout type into a silent, sullen mope. It was why she started painting her nails black and listening to ska and keeping her mouth shut and piercing her eyebrows and growing her dreads and dreaming of the door. Shame. And now it was too late, it was too late, because she had gone through that door, *she had gone through it,* and she had caused another disaster, a disaster far worse than divorce. She had brought this on herself, and on her friend, and maybe even on the whole waking world—

—YOU ARE IN DANGER!

"What the hell?!"

Hugo's voice was as taut as a guitar string that was about to snap.

"Looks like he's speeding up." Lori twisted around in her seat to get a better view of the oncoming headlights. They looked like two full moons, reflecting their radiance on the pavement below, like moonlight rippling on the surface of rushing, roaring rapids. They also looked close together, and high powered, which told Lori they probably belonged to a sport utility vehicle or a small truck or a jeep.

"The guy's really moving!"

"Just keep it steady in this lane, Hugo. Just stay calm and keep it steady."

"Jesus Christ, he's gonna—"

"No he's not; he's going to pull around us, I assure you. It has to be a cop."

"He's gonna hit us, Lori!"

"No he's not!"

"The hell he isn't—sweet Jesus, look at that! Lori, he's gonna ram us!"

The last conscious thought that washed over Lori Blaine before the impact was a fragment of a dream, a memory from her long, strange trip into LIMBOspace. It was curious that she would think of this now—in the frenzied countdown to the crash—but she did. She thought of the man with the golden hair, the rock star figure with those Roger Daltrey curls and that gleaming broadsword, who had appeared in that bizarre warehouse in the bowels of the tunnels. Now, in this last millisecond before the sick crunch of metal, Lori thought of that mysterious winged figure. She hadn't realized it at the time, but when that strange man—who would turn out to be the Archangel Michael—had sent that silent thought (*You're a wild one, aren't you?*) into Lori's brain, like a depth charge between her ears, the eruption sent a wave of emotions crashing through her. It included sorrow and guilt, but also a deeper sense of something being revealed, a secret being told. It had to do with the word *wild* and the puzzle that was Lori Blaine, but it was all too fleeting and vague to figure out all at once. And it was certainly not something she was going to figure out right now, not in the last nanosecond before the collision, as the two menacing headlights flared behind them like twin supernovas—

—right before the nauseating metallic crunch.

Before her parents split, when Lori was still a model student at Calvin Coolidge Elementary School, the county fair was a favorite summer activity for the Blaine family. Lori would count the days until the local truck lots would sprout vast networks of big-top tents for the 4-H exhibits and pie eating contests. Down the middle of the fairgrounds ran the midway, a wide gravel walk that offered a feast of forbidden sights and sounds for a ten-year-old. From the two-headed cows and bearded ladies of the Oddities Emporium to the endless rows of rip-off games like the Dish Toss and the Ping-Pong Throw, the midway was catnip for an impressionable young girl like Lori. But her favorite part of the carnival lay at the south end. In a cloud of carbon monoxide and blaring rock music churned the corridor of thrill rides. This was the home of the Zipper and the Alpine Bobs and the Gravitron and the Mega Drop and the Himalaya. But Lori's favorite—especially at night, when the carnival was bathed in its Technicolor neon glow—was the Spider.

The Spider held you in its thrall by strapping you into a rusty metal car at the end of a huge gantry. When the engine fired, the Spider would lurch into motion. The gantries would rise and fall as the center spun, and the effect was a jerky, vomit-inducing ride up and down an invisible slalom. Gravity would yank you in all directions, and you either lost your lunch or shrieked with joy.

That was a long time ago.

Tonight, at the point of impact, Lori found very little to be joyous about as the Geo lurched across the centerline in a drunken facsimile of the Spider ride.

"HOLY SSSSSHHHHH—" Hugo Stipple yelped a garbled cry as he wrestled the steering wheel. The Geo swerved wildly. Tires squealed. The engine screamed, and for one terrible instant it felt to Lori as though the little subcompact was about to tip over.

Then Hugo yanked the wheel in the opposite direction and the car swerved back the other way. More squealing tires, and a battering ram of gravity pushing Lori and Hugo into their seat cushions.

"LOOK OUT!"

Lori's frantic wail dissolved into teeth-rattling vibrations.

The Geo had drifted across the opposite lane and onto the shoulder, its tires drumming across the corrugated warning track. Sparks jumped in the darkness. Hugo cried out and struggled with the wheel. A ghastly scraping noise rose up as the front right quarter panel sideswiped a guardrail.

Then the Geo swerved back onto the road, careening across the fast lane.

The serpentine motion jostled the interior, making Lori dizzy with adrenaline. She could barely see the wash of the Geo's headlights zigzagging across the brown burlap wall of cornstalks lining the interstate. It looked to Lori like a tattered curtain running the length of some vast, sinister, medieval amphitheater.

Lori tried to wrench herself around to get a better glimpse of their attacker.

The nameless assailant drove a pickup truck. That much Lori could see in the flashing darkness behind them. Flames spurting from vertical exhaust stacks, the thing was roaring toward them for another taste of bumper.

The truck's windows must have been tinted—or maybe it was just a combination of panic and confusion, exacerbated by the dark of night—because Lori could only make out a ghostly silhouette behind the wheel.

"FLOOR IT, HUGO!" Lori shrieked, trying to ignore the fact that the thing behind them looked familiar.

"I GOT IT PINNED!" Hugo cried with his hands welded to the steering wheel. The Geo was swerving like an out-of-control go-cart, but by this point Lori realized it was probably Hugo's terror that was making the car swerve.

Lori gazed through the front windshield, into the distance ahead of them, and saw something looming that put a squeeze on her heart.

Looking back on this moment with the benefit of hindsight, Lori would realize that this was probably the first hint of her transformation.

All at once, over the space of a split second, Lori realized what she had to do. The feeling came surging up from deep within her. She was no Amazon warrior . . . no hard-ass gang girl . . . far from it . . . but something inside her told her it was time to protrude the claws and fight back.

Later she would realize that the voice she heard in her head at that moment was the Archangel Michael.

"*Wild*," the voice whispered somewhere deep in the folds of Lori's brain.

The timing could not have been better. The Geo was on a downgrade. The speedometer was edging toward seventy, and they had put some distance—not much, but at least a couple of additional car lengths— between them and the killer truck. Lori swung her sore leg over the center hump. In her weakened state, with her atrophied leg, she could barely manage to press the sole of her Doc Martens boot down on top of Hugo's foot, but it was enough pressure to nudge the pedal.

The engine sang out suddenly, an off-key aria crooned by a rusty fat lady.

"THE HELL ARE YOU DOING?!!!" Hugo bellowed.

"HOLD ON, HUGO!" Lori yanked the steering wheel at the precise moment the Geo zoomed past a long, unbroken, overgrown stretch of cornfield. A piercing screech filled the air as the vehicle went into a skid.

The sudden g-forces slammed both of them against each other. Hugo clutched at the steering wheel, and Lori clenched her teeth hard enough to crack a molar. Thunderous tremors ripped through the Geo's chassis as the tiny car plunged into the cornfield.

A wave of debris crashed against the windshield. The Geo shivered and quaked over the bumpy earth, fishtailing wildly, Lori's foot still pressed down hard on the accelerator. The noise drowned Hugo's scream.

A wall of corn blinded them, and the Geo managed to mow down at least a hundred more yards of cropland before the wheels lost their traction and started spinning wildly in the soft earth.

Lori twisted around in her seat, ignoring Hugo's hysterical cries, as the engine sputtered and died, and the interior fell silent, the air filling with dust and drifting corn silk and Hugo's raving: "ARE YOU NUTS?! ARE YOU TRYING TO GET US KILLED?! ARE YOU INSANE?!!"

There was no time to answer. Lori was transfixed. Through the cracked rear window, above the surface of the ruined corn, she could see the highway in the darkness behind them. The truck had turned sharply only seconds after the Geo's plunge into the field—

—but evidently the truck's center of gravity had proven too high. It was a modified Chevy El Camino with whiskey bumps all around the rust-pocked midnight-black finish, and tires the size of windmills—and now the great, massive, hulking utility pickup went into a roll.

"HOLY CHRIST!"

Hugo's startled cry hardly registered in Lori's ears as she watched the black metal marauder roll at least a dozen times. Doors flapped open. Glass shattered and swirled into the air, the noise approximating a dying dinosaur, as the roof collapsed and the truck slammed down to a halt against a tangled, ancient barbed wire fence.

The impact threw the driver—Lori realized who it was now, and it made sense, it made horrifying sense—at least twenty-five yards across the corn. From this distance, it looked like a giant rag doll being tossed away by an angry child. The driver landed in a clearing, tumbling across a bare patch of ground, bones shattered and arms and legs flopping limply.

The figure came to a rest in a contorted heap, tangled in a giant knot of rusty fencing.

The terrible silence that followed held Lori and Hugo rapt with shock, speechless for quite a while. The only sounds audible now were the ticking of the dead truck's engine fifty yards away in the darkness, and the dripping of some fluid beneath the damaged Geo.

"What . . . just . . . happened?" Hugo finally managed to utter breathlessly to Lori in the silence. Shaking uncontrollably, trying to catch his breath, Hugo still had his hands on the steering wheel. It would take a crowbar to pry them off.

"Hugo, do you know who that was?" Lori gaped at the darkness, breathing hard.

Hugo shivered, gazing over his shoulder at the dead driver fifty yards away. "Emphasis on the word '*was*,'" Hugo muttered in a shaky voice.

At last the spell was broken, and the two of them managed to unbuckle themselves and climb out of the Geo. They stood beside the car for a moment, Lori leaning on the door, catching her breath, her spindly legs throbbing as she gazed at the wreckage in the dark middle distance. It was hard to make out much in the gloomy light—not to mention the forest of stalks standing between the Geo and the wreck—but there was clearly a single casualty lying in a contorted heap in a small clearing visible through the broken corn.

Lori nodded. "Believe it or not, that was—" Lori was about to say "*Ichabod.*"

But something stopped her.

The black El Camino, which Lori had finally recognized a few seconds after the plunge into the cornfield, used to sit on blocks out in front of the Kettlekamp's run-down soybean farm north of Valesburg. It once belonged to Ichabod's older brother, Jimmy, but was handed down after Jimmy went off and got himself killed in Afghanistan. That tragedy left the skinny, eighteen-year-old Ichabod in charge of the family farm, his only companion his angry, senile grandmother, who was drunk most of the time. The El Camino became a home away from home for Ichabod Kettlekamp. Lori had seen the thing countless times parked outside highway strip clubs, hauling pig feed from the farm store, and parked up on Haven's Leap with the flickering glow of a pot pipe behind its tinted windows. It seemed to radiate a kind of hillbilly menace to the other kids at Central High, and whenever anybody crossed paths with the thing they gave it a wide berth. Ichabod Kettlekamp was the class boogeyman, and his truck fit him like a greasy black leather glove.

Lori was about to explain all this to Hugo, but was suddenly stricken mute by what she saw in the hazy distance of shadows and musty dust still rising off the ruined swath cut by the careening truck. What Lori saw in the moonlight fifty yards away held her spellbound for one, long, exquisitely horrible moment.

Ichabod Kettlekamp was moving. Sitting up. Brushing the dust off his greasy overalls. Stretching the kinks out of his broken neck.

He was smiling.

FIFTEEN

"Get in the car." Lori's voice was steady all of a sudden, authoritative, strangely clear in her own ears. Behind her, Hugo was slowly backing away.

"But what about—" Hugo was shaking again, unable to tear his gaze from the apparition fifty yards away.

In the moonlight, across a mangled patchwork of shredded, broken cornstalks, the gangly, greasy, eighteen-year-old was rising on creaking bones, casually bushing himself off as though awakening from a pleasant little nap. His smile, visible even from this distance, looked like the rictus of a skull, all teeth and blackened gums, completely humorless.

"Get in the car, Hugo." Lori heard her own voice, flat and alien in her ears, as though she were reciting lines from a play. Lori had no plan other than to protect her friend, whom she had dragged into this . . . whatever *this* was. But on a deeper level, she suddenly felt as though she were responsible for this terrible turn of events. She had never even remotely considered herself brave. She was no hero. But she was starting to feel as though she had a strange kind of mastery here. She knew all too well that this wasn't dream. This was real. This was flesh and blood and earth and sky. But still, she felt as though she had some kind of edge over this mess. She was a tamer of wild animals, and her animals had gotten loose, and now it was up to her to round them up before they hurt someone. And she used every last shred of pride and confidence and righteous rage to make her legs work right then.

"Good idea, good idea," Hugo babbled and spun toward the Geo.

Lori did not take her gaze off the injured farm kid in the moonlit distance, but she heard the Geo's driver's side door squeak open, and then the shuffling fabric of Hugo's jeans sliding behind the wheel. Lori stood her ground, legs trembling without the crutches. Her fists clenched at her sides.

Ichabod Kettlekamp now began strolling through the corn toward Lori Blaine.

As the farm boy approached, the moonlight shone down and reflected off his baleful smile, making those rotten teeth gleam like brass bullets. Cornhusks brushed across his horrible face as the boy calmly, relentlessly, emotionlessly forced his way through the corn, snapping twigs and bending stalks. A tassel stuck out of his greasy hair like the tuft of a cowlick.

All at once Lori felt that strange mixture of emotions burning in her gut again. She felt shame and anger and that eerie sense of destiny—all captured in the whispered message bubbling up from her reptile brain: *wild*.

"I know what you are!" Lori called out. "I know where you came from. GET OUT OF HIM!!"

The gangly farm kid kept coming, his monstrous work boots crackling over soft, muddy earth, making smooching noises, bending and snapping stalks, his big head swimming above the tassels, smiling its cadaverous smile. His body, all sinew and muscle, hardened by the farm and the sun, moved as though attached to invisible strings. He was maybe thirty yards away now.

Hugo's feeble cry from somewhere behind Lori barely reached her ears—"Come on you piece o' crap!"—the whining groan of the Geo's pitiful power plant like a sick animal. The car would not start; it just kept whining and whining.

Lori closed her eyes.

All at once she remembered a dream from long ago, and she realized something important was hidden in that dream. In the dream she was cornered on the playground by a group of girl jocks who always hated her, and she had no weapon, no way out, nobody around to help her. But she had her voice. She had her dream voice.

She opened her eyes and saw Ichabod Kettlekamp drawing closer. Less than twenty yards away now, clearly visible through a gap in the cornstalks, the farm kid was smiling from ear to ear—a wicked, diseased, perverted smile—and Lori clenched her fists so tightly that her nails began to draw blood.

Hugo's voice was a million miles away now—"Stupid cheap-ass bucket of bolts!"—as he kept grinding the ignition, the Geo refusing to start.

Lori sucked in a huge breath as if preparing to summon a tidal wave of air: "GET! OUT OF HIM!"

On the word *out* a pulse of energy burst from Lori Blaine like a solar flare, punching through the darkness with the force of an invisible wrecking ball, slamming into Ichabod Kettlekamp. It looked as though the farm kid had been decked by an all-star tight end from some pro football team, smashed in the solar plexus so hard he was practically lifted out of his boots. He landed a half acre away, vanishing behind a curtain of corn.

Lori blinked.

There was no time to think about what had just happened. There was no time to wonder if this was what the Archangel Michael had meant when he said Lori was a "wild" one. Lori whirled toward the Geo.

Hugo was still grinding the ignition, cursing the vehicle with a colorful conglomeration of swear words, when all at once the engine fired. A plume of exhaust burped out of the tailpipe. Hugo let out a victorious yawp and revved the accelerator.

Lori climbed in the passenger side, and Hugo slammed down the gas pedal.

For a single frenzied instant the wheels spun in the mud, sending up a spray of earth across the tops of the corn. Then the tires bit.

The Geo lurched into motion. Lori held onto the dash as the car tail-wagged across a couple rows of corn. Stalks flew every which way like bowling pins falling under the churning wheels. Mud sprayed in the air. Hugo cried out, "Come on—come on! COME ON! YOU HEAP OF WORTHLESS CHEAP DETROIT JUNK!!"

A clearing materialized in the moonlight fifty feet ahead of them—a gravel path, a hill, a split-rail fence, and finally—sweet Jesus in Heaven, thank you—the edge of the highway!

Hugo steered toward the fence. Lori tensed her butt cheeks against the seat, preparing for impact. Hugo put the pedal down and the engine screamed as the little car bounded across the gravel access road and then fishtailed up the steep, narrow hill.

The Geo smashed through the railing as though it were kindling, sending shards of sun-bleached wood in all directions. The tires hit the highway, squealing on solid pavement, as Hugo yanked the wheel.

The little car skidded across both lanes. Had there been traffic that night, the two of them would have been creamed. But the interstate stretched in both directions, deserted and desolate. Hugo wrestled the car back in line, and then he stepped on it.

They roared away in a thunderhead of exhaust and shrieking tires.

Lori let out a pained sigh of relief.

Maybe ten seconds later, fifteen at the most, they heard the sound.

At first Lori thought they had blown a tire. The telltale thump sounded like the bang of a broken tread hitting the under carriage, and the car shuddered for a moment.

Considering the fact that they had just put the Geo through the torture chamber of the cornfield—with its rusty fence wires and sharp rocks—a lost tire would not come as a surprise. "I think we just—" Lori started to say, when she abruptly stopped.

The noise had not come from under the car. Lori realized this at the precise same moment the sound of muffled scraping noises traveled across the roof.

"What's going --?!" Hugo had the Geo back up to sixty miles an hour, and now he hunched over the steering wheel with every muscle in his body tensing as he threw furtive glances over his shoulder. His trembling had worsened. He could barely hold onto the wheel.

"I think we got a—"

Before Lori could get the words out something dropped into view outside the front windshield.

"WHOA! WHOA! WHOA! WHOA!" Hugo jerked with terror, the wheel jittering, the Geo swerving. The upside-down face looked in at them with alien calm. Its eyes twinkled with demented delight.

"Jesus," Lori uttered, instinctively flinching, shielding her face.

Despite the wind, and the vibrations of scarred pavement rushing under the wheels, and Hugo's jerky driving, Ichabod Kettlekamp clung to the roof of the Geo like a massive barnacle. He hung inverted in front of the windshield and did something that Lori would puzzle over for days.

"WHAT'S HE DOING?! WHAT THE HELL IS HE—" Hugo struggled to see around the huge face blocking his view, struggled to keep the car on the road. Ichabod Kettlekamp was saying something.

"Of course . . . of course . . . of course," Lori murmured, trying to read the upside-down lips.

It was far too noisy and windy to hear much more than a faint, gravelly drone outside the window, almost like a fly buzzing in Lori's ears. But she could hear enough to know it was Latin, and it was being delivered with sick, contemptuous amusement.

All at once Lori felt a tremendous need to memorize every word this monstrous thing that was once a farm boy was saying to them.

In the jet-engine roar of wind Lori clearly heard the word *substisio*—or maybe it was *substiso*—as well as the word *tardus*. She was absolutely sure about that one. *Tardus*. And something else she couldn't quite decipher.

Over the course of the next few seconds—as Hugo suddenly realized the only way out of this bizarre situation—Lori concentrated as best she could. The last words she heard were *est* and *legio*.

"HOLD ON, LORI!" Hugo hollered and slammed both feet down on the brake pedal.

The disc brakes locked instantly and the car went into a screaming skid. Lori was thrown against the dash—she had forgotten to buckle up—and smacked her chin on the glove compartment.

The intruder was launched into the air in a cloud of vapor and burning rubber.

It was like watching a skydiver plummet without a parachute.

Arms and legs flailing wildly, the farm boy arced out through the air and plunged to the ground. He crashed hard on the pavement and rolled several yards like a sack of dirty laundry.

Ichabod Kettlekamp came to a rest near mile marker number 157 and lay still.

The Geo shuddered to a halt in a fog of smoke. Hugo sat as rigid as a statue, his feet still pressing down on the brake pedal, breathing thickly, white-knuckling the wheel as the smell of hot rubber rose in the darkness. Lori sat back and let out an agonized sigh.

They sat like that for several moments, too stunned to talk, staring at the body fifty feet away, illuminated by the dim beams of the headlights.

"Get out of here, Hugo," Lori said almost under her breath.

Hugo goosed the foot pedal, and the Geo shot forward with a lurch.

They swerved around the body, which lay in a heap near the shoulder—giving it a wide berth—and then roared off into the night.

They never saw the body behind them casually sit up, rise to its feet, and walk away.

"I promise I'll tell you everything," Lori was saying, searching through the glove box, as the damaged Geo chugged down a hill. "Just gimme a minute."

The road ahead of them wound through a small mining community south of Quincy, Illinois, skirting the river, running past dark bait shops and fishing piers. It was almost midnight, and they had put enough miles between them and the accident scene to almost breathe normally again. Hugo wanted to go to the police but Lori convinced him to wait. She needed to figure something out first.

"What the hell are you looking for?" Hugo wanted to know, still spooked and shaking.

"Something to write on." Lori found a Midas muffler shop receipt and pulled the crinkly paper out into the light of the dome lamp. "This is important. I'll explain everything, I promise; I just have to write something down here before I forget it."

Lori clicked a Bic pen she found in the map case and wrote the following words in the margins of the Midas invoice for a tailpipe extender:

Vos mos non subsisto nos.

Is est quoque tardus.

Nos es legio.

It was a rough approximation of what Ichabod Kettlekamp had spoken in the wind and noise of the highway, dangling from the Geo's roof—or at least it was as close as Lori was going to come with her rudimentary yet serviceable fluency in Latin. And the only way to remember it was to write it down. Her cell phone had petered out again when she had tried to ask Siri to translate. Now she would have to wait until she got home to her laptop in order to get the meaning of these sinister-sounding words. "Okay," she spoke up finally, folding the receipt and stuffing it in her waistcoat pocket. "What I'm about to tell you is not to go any further than this car. You understand?"

Hugo shook his head. "Who the hell would believe it if I told them?"

Lori had to agree. She proceeded to recount all the strange events leading up to this night. She described the night she first went through the dream door. She told Hugo about Nick Ballas and the old lady in the wheelchair and the guy named Pops and all the experiences in LIMBOworld. She described the Bogies and the mysterious man with the golden hair who looked like Roger Daltrey. Lori also explained the time limit under which she had been operating in LIMBOworld, and what it felt like to wake up after a year in a coma.

Hugo remained silent for most of this, listening intently, as they drove through nameless little river towns. But when Lori finally described how a Bogy—which is actually a demon—gets inside a person, Hugo spoke up. "You're not telling me what I *think* you're telling me . . . are you?"

Lori looked at him. "What do you think I'm telling you?"

"That Ichabod Kettlekamp is—"

"Yes."

"That he has a—"

"Yep."

Hugo looked as if he was either going to laugh or scream, but he did neither. He simply drove without saying another word for quite a while. Lori could tell that her friend was mulling everything over in his mind.

At last Hugo said, "To be perfectly honest with you . . ."

"Yeah?"

"If anybody else told me this . . . I would have said they were tripping."

"But you believe me?"

Hugo thought about it. "I came to that hospital room at least three times a week, sometimes twice on Saturdays and Sundays. I sat next to that bed and talked to you like a dork because they told me to. I even prayed one time with your mom, and I'm like a total atheist." Hugo looked at her. "Lori, you're, like, my best friend." He thought about it some more. "And I know what I saw tonight."

"Then you believe me."

Hugo licked his lips and looked at Lori. The green light of the dashboard made his expression look owlish, almost gargoyle-like. "Whatever you've gotten yourself into, whatever is going on . . . I know you wouldn't make it up. Who could make this shit up?"

"Good." Lori gave him a nod. "Because I'm going to need your help."

After she got home that night, Lori had a lot of explaining to do.

Allison Blaine had become so worried that she could barely function. She had called all of Lori's friends, and nobody had any idea where Lori and Hugo might be "studying" that night—emphasis on the quotation marks—and finally Allison had called the police.

The cops told her that she should come down to the station in the morning and file a missing person report if she wanted to, but until then, Lori was not officially a missing person—she was simply a teenager who was out too late. Lori apologized over and over, and hugged her mom repeatedly, and told her that she had lost track of time when she saw all the schoolwork she had to catch up on.

She could tell that Allison knew it was all a lie. But for some reason—maybe she was simply grateful that her daughter was home—she decided to cook for Lori. She made her a late-night snack of chicken potpie and banana pudding and oatmeal cookies and milk. "Lots of tryptophan," Allison said as she stood at the stove in her robe, stirring the pudding. "To help you get a more restful sleep, and hopefully avoid those nightmares."

The truth was, Lori could not wait to go to sleep that night. Not only was she exhausted, drained by the confrontation downstate, but she needed to get back to LIMBOworld and figure things out.

Around two that morning, after Allison had said good-night and gone to bed, and Lori was in her pajamas, yawning every three seconds, ready to hit the rack, she sat down at her desk before turning in.

On her laptop she found a translation site online that converted Latin into English—just to be sure. She stared at the flickering screen as the program processed the mutterings of Ichabod Kettlekamp.

When the three lines of Latin were converted, Lori stared for an eternity at the three sentences:

Vos mos non subsisto nos. (You will not stop us.)

Is est quoque tardus. (It is too late.)

Nos es legio. (We are legion.)

SIXTEEN

That night Lori dreamt she was riding her trusty Schwinn ten-speed bike down her street toward the cul-de-sac at the end of the block.

But something was wrong. The sky was no longer a robin's egg blue, as it had been in previous dreams. Instead the heavens now roiled and churned with storm clouds. A cold, clammy wind blew litter across the neglected, overgrown lawns.

As she rounded the turn at the end of the block, and the Cape Cod gradually came into view, Lori got the distinct impression that she was late for something. Maybe she had missed dinner. Maybe she had missed a test. Perhaps her library books were overdue, or a pot had been left on the stove to boil over, or some kind of deadline had come and gone.

She was late and she was in deep trouble.

Then she saw the house and nearly fell off the bike. She slammed on the brakes, and the rear wheel scudded to a stop in front of the monstrosity.

6800 Monterey Court had transformed. The yard no longer looked as lush as a putting green; the front porch no longer radiated the warmth of the Kennedy compound. The house had fallen under the influence of ghosts.

Bordered by a trash-strewn patch of untended weeds, it rose up against the darkening sky like a sore on the beleaguered neighborhood. The years of hard winters and neglect had ravaged the exterior. The weather-beaten roof sagged. The clapboard siding, peeled and gray and pocked with age, looked like the scaly flesh of dead fish.

"Okay . . . whatever," Lori muttered under her breath, climbing off the bike and leaning it against the rusty, broken mailbox. She recognized this new version of the safe house. She knew it well. She knew every boarded-up window, every broken pane of glass.

It was the Marsden house.

As she strode bravely up the walk toward the front door—the door to LIMBOworld—Lori saw the cobwebbed corners and drawn shades of the same "haunted house" that had stalked her nightmares as a little kid.

In the waking world, the old Marsden house had sat vacant and rotting at the top of Pearson Road—the original street on which the Blaine family had lived in their early days—tormenting the nightmares of neighborhood kids. Nobody on the block could even remember who the Marsdens were. Old-timers in the neighborhood whispered about a suicide that had soured the property for nearly two decades. Once in a while, teenagers would work up the nerve to spend the night in the place, but nobody ever made it to sunrise without fleeing the decrepit shadows in terror.

"You're having a dream," Lori reminded herself under her breath as she climbed the rotten, worm-eaten risers of the front porch. "Nothing more than a few delta waves bouncing around your thick skull." Beneath her feet, each tread creaked sickly, like the arthritic vertebra of an old person's spine. Lori crossed the warped porch and stood in front of the door.

She knew it was just a dream.

She knew she was lucid.

She knew she had the power to change events.

And yet . . .

The front door, which was *the* door—the door to the In-Between, the door to the BACKworld, with its familiar flat, featureless, gray-painted metal surface and smooth, stainless-steel doorknob—had never felt as menacing to Lori. She hesitated there on that crumbling porch, paralyzed with indecision, staring at that silent door and the promise of a deeper silence behind it.

Don't go through this door, she heard a voice warn from somewhere deep in her midbrain—an unfamiliar voice, not the voice of the golden-haired man. *Go back. Now. Before it's too late. Do not go inside.*

"Mind your own business," Lori told the voice. Then she grasped the cold metal of the doorknob, turned it, and opened the door on squeaking hinges.

* * *

When Lori was just a first-grader—and an active member of a scrappy little gang of neighborhood ragamuffins back on Pearson Road—she would slam her eyes shut whenever she rode her Big Wheel past the Marsden house, or she would slap her hands over her eyes whenever her mother or father would drive the family car past the place. "It's just an old pile of wood, sweetie," Mike Blaine would tell Lori at bedtime. "It can't hurt you, it can't hurt anybody." But Lori knew better. She knew the place was evil. She had heard stories of teenagers finding human bones in the basement and hearing voices begging for mercy in the attic and smelling the rancid perfume of Mrs. Marsden—the lady who killed herself in the master bedroom. But what haunted Lori most of all was the talk among neighborhood kids of the pale dead faces materializing behind the windows late at night.

Although Lori had never seen such things, and had never set foot in the house, she felt as though she knew every room. She could describe the grand staircase, the narrow hallway on the second floor, and almost every nook and cranny from the many stories told during sleepovers and around campfires. It didn't matter that most of this mythology was lodged in Lori's overactive imagination and did not exist in the real world. What mattered was that the house loomed large in Lori's nightmares—

—and now it loomed even larger as she entered the vestibule inside the door.

She paused for a moment to swallow back her primal fear and keep her wits about her. In the dream she wore torn black leggings, Doc Martens, and a lacy black top that she now nervously brushed off and smoothed down with shaking hands as she looked around the foyer. Despite a few dim light bulbs, which hung from frayed cords throughout the first floor—buzzing and sputtering with failing electrical current—the bulk of the house was bathed in shadow. Lori could see the grand living room just around the corner, with its dusty chandelier of broken bulbs and its sweeping staircase.

Her heart hammered in her chest as she crept deeper into the house.

In the living room, she found the entertainment center, which Nick had left for her in earlier dreams, now demolished and laying in scraps of broken glass and shards of plastic. Each fragment was furry with dust, as though a tornado had passed through the room long ago, and the wreckage had lay strewn across the moldering rug for centuries. The cabbage rose wallpaper, fading and peeling off the walls, was so old it looked like the skin of a corpse.

"Just an old pile of wood," Lori softly reminded herself, her voice sounding weak and tinny, like a voice coming out of a pull-string doll.

In the kitchen Lori found no note. No sign of life. The stained, yellowed tile floor, greasy walls, and filthy countertops were illuminated by flickering, failing fluorescent ceiling fixtures. In the ancient refrigerator Lori found all the goodies that Nick had laid in for her petrifying with rot: meat fuzzy with mold, cheese crawling with maggots, chocolate pudding hardened into shriveled tar, and raspberries dried into little black stones. The smell jumped out at her and made her dizzy.

She was turning toward the sink when the power suddenly went out.

It happened so abruptly that it nearly took Lori's breath away, and she froze in the pitch darkness for a moment. She could not see her hand in front of her face. It almost felt, just for a moment, like being under water. Like being *deep* under water. Like being at the very bottom of the Mariana Trench at the deepest part of the ocean. She couldn't breathe, couldn't move, couldn't think. The darkness made the house suddenly feel enormous, gargantuan, monstrous—

—until she realized once again that she was a lucy, a wild one— whatever *that* meant—and she could make things happen, damn it. She could control things.

She thought of a flashlight, and like magic she suddenly felt the reassuring smooth steel cylinder nestled in the palm of her right hand. The milky-white beam shot out across the kitchen and landed on the opposite wall.

A face stared back at her.

She jumped back with a start, her heart hiccupping with terror.

For a single instant, on a wave of gooseflesh, Lori saw the pale, ghastly face on the opposite wall staring back at her with a horrified scowl. Backing against the fridge, making bottles rattle, Lori flashed back to the stories of ghost faces flickering behind the windows of the Marsden house, and she was about to let out a scream—

—when she realized she was looking at *herself*. She had caught a glimpse of her reflection in a slice of broken window glass.

She exhaled a long, pained breath, pointing the light beam down at the warped linoleum. She let out another sigh and told herself to relax. *Relax and get your act together! Get your feces assembled!*

She let out another breath. It wasn't exactly relief that she was feeling right then. It was much more than that. It was something she was now just beginning to understand. It had to do with courage, yes, but it also had something to do with being lucid—and that feeling that had washed over her when she looked into those blue eyes of the man with the golden hair.

She took another deep breath and raised the flashlight.

And that was when she heard the knocking.

It took a few moments for Lori to comprehend what she was hearing. Somebody was knocking on the door. But what door? She tried to concentrate on erasing the sound, willing it to stop . . . all to no avail. Someone or something else was in control of the dream now, and it seemed as though it was letting her manufacture a flashlight but that was about it. She cocked her head to hear better. The knocking continued in a strange rhythmic pattern of seven repeating knocks—one . . . *two-three*, four-five . . . *six-seven*—but it didn't seem to be coming from the front door. It was the hollow, telltale rap of knuckles on wood. One . . . *two-three*, four-five . . . *six-seven*. Where the hell was it coming from?

Lori aimed the flashlight across the kitchen, and the beam fell on an open doorway. Barely visible in the dust motes floating in the shaft of light was the top step of a staircase. The paint-flaked steps led down to the basement—Lori just intrinsically knew this from the folklore of the Marsden house—and she knew what she had to do.

She started toward the steps.

ONE . . . *TWO-THREE, FOUR-FIVE . . . SIX-SEVEN!!*

The knocking intensified. It boomed and echoed and reverberated through the darkness, rattling windows like thunder. Whoever was knocking was getting impatient. Angry. Insane. Lori approached the door to the basement and paused. All at once she remembered where she had heard the pattern, the weird rhythm of the knocking.

Shave and a haircut . . . . two bits.

Lori's great-grandfather on her mother's side had been a prisoner of war in World War II. His name was Edward Kowalski, but everybody called him Shave. He'd been a pilot during the war. His Spitfire got shot down over the German countryside, and he spent two and half years in a prison camp outside Wiesbaden. Old Shave used to describe how American POWs would authenticate a new prisoner's American identity. They would tap the first five beats of the code against the wall of their cells.

If the new prisoner responded by tapping "two bits," they knew he was a fellow countryman.

Now Lori started down the creaking cellar steps. BAM! BAM-BAM! BAM, BAM! BAM! BAMMMMM! The knocking rose in volume as she descended into the shadows, her flashlight beam falling on dust motes so thick they looked like snow. The knocking thundered. Lori could smell the horrible stench of root cellars and grave dirt, the black odors of decay, and found herself flashing back to Nick's note:

Above all, do NOT—I repeat—do NOT answer the door. No matter what. Do NOT answer it.

In the beam of the flashlight Lori saw the bottom step and a patch of scarred cement beyond it, the rest of the basement shrouded in darkness.

She took the last few steps. She reached the bottom of the staircase and paused on the cold concrete floor. The knocking was off the scale now—ear-splittingly loud, coming from all directions, sonic booms shaking the walls—maybe three or four separate visitors, clamoring to be greeted, demanding to be let in.

Lori swung the flashlight out across the length of the cellar.

It looked like a sewer under a dying city, stretching at least a mile or more into the darkness, far longer than the house or the physical laws of the waking world could accommodate.

BOOM! BOOM-BOOM! BOOM, BOOM! BOOM! BOOMM!

Black fluid oozed from the stone floor. Smoke seeped from cracks in the walls. The stench engulfed Lori, the thunderous noise pounding in her skull.

BOOM! BOOM-BOOM! BOOM, BOOM! BOOM! BOOOOMMM!

The flashlight beam brushed across human skeletons piled in drifts against the crumbling stone pillars. Way in the distant shadows, so far away they looked almost like the stick figures of a mirage, human silhouettes writhed in pain in flickering orange flames. Giant turbines turned. Nameless creatures slithered.

Lori felt dizzy, faint, nauseous. She wanted to wake up, slap herself out of this hellish place, as the beam of light moved across the wall, passing a massive, arched door made of iron, puffing plumes of dust with each impact. BOOM! BOOM-BOOM! BOOM, BOOM! BOOM! BOOOOOOOOMMMMM!

They were all demanding to be let into the dream. The Bogies. The demons. Lori *was* too late. She *would* never stop them.

They *were* legion.

Lori dropped the light, and fell to her knees, and covered her ears.

"Lori! Pssssst!"

At first she didn't hear the familiar voice behind her, barely audible under the noise and her covered ears. Then, when she heard it a second time, she thought she might be imagining it. She thought the Bogies might be getting into her head. An audio hallucination maybe . . . if there *was* such a thing in a dream. Everything was a hallucination in a dream. At least that's what Lori used to think.

"Lori, for God's sake, *behind* you! Turn around! Up here! Lori, look!"

Now Lori was certain she was hearing an actual human voice behind her, and she whirled around in time to see an ancient metal hatch in a giant furnace conduit on the ceiling flip down with a rusty squeak.

A familiar face peered out from the manhole-sized opening in the massive steel duct.

Lori's heart leapt.

"Nick!"

SEVENTEEN

He pulled her the rest of the way out of the basement and up into the enormous ancient duct. Without saying a word, the two of them crawled on hands and knees down a dark channel of corroded metal. Nick wore a miner's lamp on his hard hat. His tool belt clanked. Lori hurried to keep up with him.

They reached a junction.

"This way," Nick said, indicating a manhole cover with an iron wheel mounted in its center. Nick turned the wheel with a grunt. The hatch opened with a rusty squeak, revealing a narrow ladder.

They descended the ladder.

Lori was out of breath, her brain swimming, as they reached the bottom of the ladder and found themselves in yet a *lower* level of the Marsden house, a subbasement, maybe a bomb shelter or root cellar.

They paused to catch their breath. The odor of sulfur hung in the air—a million match tips smoking—and a sense of the very foundation of the dream—maybe even the dream universe itself—shifting under their feet.

Lori saw an enormous Day-Glo pink and green centipede the size of a baseball bat crawling across the cracked cement floor. The walls, barely visible in the dim light of Nick's helmet, bubbled and oozed as though made of volcanic lava. Brilliant orange cinders floated in the air like miniature falling stars, but it was not even remotely pretty. On the contrary, everything had an ugly, garish, disturbing cast to it, like a high-definition snuff film.

"Sorry about the dream house getting hijacked," Nick said, removing the hard hat and shaking the soot from his straw-like brown hair. In the dim light of the lamp, he looked fearless . . . fearless and strangely handsome. He gave Lori a sidelong glance. "You okay?"

"Yeah . . . I . . . actually I was . . ." She groped for the right words. There was something weird going on—weirder than usual. In fact, everything around the edges of Lori's field of vision—the dust motes, the alien bugs, the broken fixtures hanging down, the crumbling cinder block pillars, the maze-like grid of rusty steel ducts stretching off into the distance—undulated and blurred as though all of it were passing under a distorted lens.

"Come on," Nick said, putting his helmet back on, nodding toward the wall of shadows in the distant reaches of the subbasement. "Gotta hook back up with the others."

They found a back way out—a corroded circular staircase behind one of the pillars—and they started up it. Their collective weight made the wrought iron squeak and complain as they climbed.

And climbed.

And climbed.

The steps seemed to go on forever. Clogged with spiderwebs, peeling with ancient rust flakes, the spiral rose up through a narrow shaft of crumbling brickwork, like a chimney, teeming with bugs and vermin and nameless creatures, most of which scattered into cracks every time the headlamp beam fell on them.

They finally reached a landing.

"Stay close," he said, opening a scarred wooden door and ushering Lori through it.

Lori paused. Taken aback by the immense space in front of them, she blinked. "I have a feeling this isn't the Marsden house anymore," she murmured under her breath, not really believing what she was seeing.

If it were possible to build an attic (yes, an *attic*) as big as the state of Texas—or perhaps Antarctica—and then infest it with ghosts for thousands of years, you might *begin* to approximate what Lori was seeing at the moment. Miles and miles of warped, stained floorboards reached into the distance, as barren and wasted as Death Valley, as dark as the Dead Sea at midnight. Mountain ranges of sheet-draped furniture, spider-webbed hat racks, old moldering trunks, and paint-spattered wardrobes lay in the shadowy territories to the east, and to the west, sheer cliffs of ancient fiberglass insulation.

The sky—or what *served* as a sky, hanging dark and brooding over this weird attic-country—consisted of vast stalactites of broken joists and timbers, as immeasurably long as storm fronts, behind which dirty rays of moonlight shone down through a miasma of dust.

"It never *was* the Marsden house," Nick said, tugging on Lori's blouse, urging her onward.

They started across the eerie landscape of gargantuan moldy cardboard boxes and disembodied pieces of mannequins and forgotten doll parts strewn across the landscape like the carnage of ancient wars. Sinister things lay behind the shadows—giant panels the size of warehouse doors, scrawled with Satanic graffiti, decorated with pentagrams and inverted crosses, defaced with the black and sticky residue of blood writing.

"You're going to have to explain that last statement," Lori said, following him. "Can we start by identifying who's dreaming this dream?"

"Another long story," Nick said. "They're tapping into you."

"They're what?"

"Tapping into your fears."

"What do you mean?"

He paused. "We're in a Bogy's dream right now." She stared at him.

He gave her a nod. "It's a parasitic dream and to be perfectly blunt, it's not the kind of place you want to linger in so—"

"Wait!" Lori yanked him to a stop. She burned her gaze into his soulful blue eyes. "Wait a second. I think I understand how it works now."

He looked at her. "How what works?"

"My ability to change things . . . the lucid thing." She felt gooseflesh trickling down her back. "As long as I'm the one doing the dreaming, I can alter the dream. I can change things. I'm God. But if I'm in somebody else's—"

He raised his hand. "Slow down, Sherlock. You're close. But it's a little more complicated than that."

She cocked her head at him. "How so?"

He sighed. "Let's just say I'm supposed to let you discover it on your own." He gently nudged her along. "C'mon, we're late."

They continued across the attic world while Nick explained what was going on. He explained that the demon's dream was infectious. Like a virus. Or cancer. It could absorb and take over the dreams of the innocent. This was one of the ways in which the Bogies had been moving from dream space to wake space over the millennia.

And they had gotten into Lori's hideaway by using her childhood fears as a spider would use a web.

Nick then went on to explain that the balance of power in LIMBOspace was tipping. The In-Between was infested now. A plague had broken out. Bogies were getting into peoples' dreams. Just last night a man in Mumbai, India, had gotten possessed in a dream and was now holding thirteen people hostage at a nuclear power plant. A woman in Seattle had suffered a breached nightmare two days ago and was now on a killing spree. The powers that be had responded by sending reinforcements to the dreamscape.

The Company was in full battle mode now, but it was an uphill fight.

"Wait, Nick, one second," Lori said finally. They had reached a trapdoor embedded in the floor.

"Come on, Sherlock, we're still on the clock," he said, grasping the iron handle and pulling open the trap. "You don't want to end up in an iron lung at St. Vincent de Paul."

They descended a narrow stepladder.

Down they went, down rickety wooden steps, scores of them, Lori lost count, down, down, down into some kind of featureless burrow of hallways.

The area seethed with a mist thicker than a smoke bomb, and it stunk of death and decay and rot. Lori could barely see the thin beam of Nick's headlamp cutting through the fog as they descended.

Lori was burning with questions, things she wanted to tell him, important things. She wanted to tell him about waking up after a yearlong coma, she wanted to tell him about Ichabod, but most of all, she wanted to tell him about the feelings that had been stirring in her ever since she had laid eyes on him in that nursing home in Carlinville.

They reached another landing. She grabbed his sleeve and gently pulled him to a stop. "Listen to me," she said. "Take a breath for a second."

Nick paused in a nimbus of fog. It was as though they were standing in a storm cloud. "I'm sorry . . . go ahead," he said at last.

"This is all my fault, isn't it?" She drilled her gaze into him. "The leakage . . . the plague."

"Not at all, Lori. It happens every once in a while. It happened back in the Middle Ages, the Inquisition."

"You know I saw you," she told him in a softening voice. "The real you, I mean. The flesh and blood you. In Carlinville."

"Yeah, the flowers were a nice touch."

"How did you—"

"We monitor the waking world, Lori."

"How?"

"Through dreams, of course. Even though I'm stuck in this place . . . I'm still . . . *connected.*"

"But the house, all my favorite things. How did you—"

"How did I know about your favorite things? I didn't. You did." He must have seen the puzzled look on her face because he added, "We just provide the soil, Lori, you plant the seeds."

She had no idea what he was talking about. "Okay, but, the thing is . . . those CDs . . . the movies? It was strange—and I might be imagining this—but they seemed stuck like maybe in 2005 or 2006?"

He gave her a forlorn smile. "That's because I went inside back then; that's my incept year."

"You're what?"

"That's the year I started at this job."

She stared at him as this sunk in. She suddenly felt an incredibly strong urge to brush the flyaway locks of brown hair away from his chiseled face. "Can you ever go back?" she asked.

He managed a sad smile. In the mist he looked like a ghost, or one of those sad heroin-addicted models in a Guess jeans ad you see in *Vanity Fair* or *Vogue*. The lines on his face looked a little deeper, his pale blue eyes a little sadder. Lori felt a jolt of longing deep inside her. She wanted so badly to touch his hair. He looked as though he might tear up for a moment. "Not likely," he muttered.

"You know about Ichabod Kettlekamp, though."

"Yeah, he's a problem . . . one of many. But the thing inside him? Lori, it knows you're a condie. Word has spread across the BACKworld, too."

"I'm a what?"

"A conduit, Lori. Between the two worlds." His expression hardened then. "Be very careful. This thing inside the farm kid? It's a Shadow. A higher order of demon, very nasty."

"What do they want? Ultimately, I mean."

"They want to destroy us. But they want to do it in a very specific way."

"And that is . . . ?"

"By helping us destroy ourselves. That's the mission they were given."

"By whom?"

The young man just shrugged. "The Dark Bringer, Baphomet, Lucifer, Old Scratch . . . whatever you want to call it."

Lori thought about it. "Okay. Slow down. You're telling me you guys are from . . . ?"

"We're the good guys . . . what can I tell ya? The Company by any other name is still the Company."

"May I ask just exactly who this character with the sword and the Prince Valiant hair is?"

"He's the head archy."

"Archy as in . . . ?"

"Archangel, Lori—look him up, Google him, Michael the Archangel, a really cool dude, but with a killer schedule—you ought to see his calendar. He gets all the emergency calls from all the best exorcists— and he likes you, too. And when the boss likes you, you're golden."

Lori exhaled a pained sigh. "How did I get myself into this?"

Nick looked away. "Actually that's kinda-sorta my fault."

Lori looked at him. "Pardon?"

He swallowed hard, then looked at her. "I put the door in your dreams."

For a moment, Lori processed this silently, staring at him. "You what?"

"We're not supposed to recruit people," he said, staring down at the writhe of mist around his lumberjack boots. "But one time I stumbled into one of your dreams."

"I don't—" Lori was starting to say something about not understanding, but when she saw the look on Nick's face she stopped herself. In the gauzy half-light his expression was heart wrenching: a mixture of loneliness, longing, shame, and bone-deep sorrow. But most importantly, Lori recognized something very powerful in the look on his face.

It was like looking into a mirror—a reflection of her *own* deepest feelings of inadequacy.

He looked down at her. "I saw what the divorce did to you. I remember one nightmare you had, you were trying to save your mom from a flood."

She stared at him. "You saw that one?"

He nodded. "I kept going back, I'd see you in these dreams, all alone." He took a step closer, and he reached out and touched her cheek. "So sad. So incredibly sad. I guess I saw myself."

Lori could not move. Something was coming over her, a wave of emotion. Her voice was barely a whisper. "That's how you knew . . ."

He was nodding. "Yeah . . ."

She touched his hand as it softly cupped her cheek. His pale flesh was warm. Lori smiled at him. "You knew I could make it through the door."

"Yeah."

"I'm glad you put it there," Lori said, so softly it was barely a whisper.

He smiled. "Yeah, so am I."

He kissed her.

It didn't begin as anything special. It was just a peck on the cheek, almost platonic, as though he were a brother kissing a sister.

But then . . . Lori felt Nick's arms on the small of her back, and he was hugging her. And it was warm and good. And she felt him pulling her into a tighter embrace . . . and then she was kissing him on the lips.

This kiss meant business. It made Lori's spine tingle and sent electric current coursing down through her. She stroked his hair as she kissed him—hair that she had longed to touch ever since she had laid eyes on it. And she had never really noticed his scent until now, and it was glorious, like woodsmoke, cider, cloves, and old leather. He was strong and he was gentle and he was everything Lori had secretly yearned for over the course of her life.

The kiss went on for one more delicious moment—not nearly long enough. But it was long enough for Lori to feel for the first time in her strange and disorderly life that she was okay, that she was maybe even better than okay . . . and maybe . . . just maybe . . . she had found—

She blinked.

Nick blinked as well, stepping back from her. He turned and gazed around the attic world that was not the attic world anymore.

At first, neither one of them had any idea what they had done. Nor did either realize what happens when two prodigious lucies hook up in REMspace. Nor did either care. All Lori knew at that moment was that the dream world had transformed around them with the subtle abruptness of a quick dissolve in a movie. No longer were they standing in a dank, musty, acrid-smelling attic planet filled with the iconography of childhood fears and forlorn empty spaces.

"This is an interesting turn of events," Lori uttered, gazing up at the tropical sun shining down through rustic palm fronds gently swaying above them.

They stood side by side on the deck of a fully furnished lanai—a sort of outdoor veranda—in some lovely equatorial paradise. Through an arched opening, an azure-blue, cloudless sky rose above a vast white-sand beach the consistency of powdered sugar. The air was as warm as a mother's kiss and smelled of allspice. It wasn't Hawaii exactly . . . nor was it Tahiti . . . nor the Bahamas . . . nor some uncharted fairy-tale atoll in the middle of the Pacific . . . but rather it was *all* these places wrapped up in a beautiful package.

"Come with me," Nick said with a grin. "And don't think about it too hard."

He took her hand and led her across the deck, then through the arched opening of bougainvillea vines and cascading strands of orchids. Nick shed his work shirt and tool belt, and Lori took off her waistcoat, tying it around her waist. The ocean breeze felt delicious on her bare arms and neck. She loosened the tie on her dreads and let her untamed braids flag in the salt-scented gusts. They descended driftwood steps and took off their shoes.

"I heard about stuff like this happening every once in a while," Nick said as he led her by the hand, both of them barefoot, across the beach toward the gentle whitecaps in the distance.

"'*Stuff*'? Stuff like what?" Lori was savoring the soft, warm embrace of the sand on the soles of her feet, the sun on her pale skin, the waves lapping convivially across their path, tickling their toes.

"A collaborative dream."

"A what?"

"Two lucies conjuring a spontaneous wish," he said, shooting a glance at her, smiling.

"I thought we were not supposed to think about it too hard," she wise-cracked, squeezing his hand good-naturedly. She kissed his cheek.

His grin widened. "You got me," he said. "And just for that . . . you get dunked!"

He suddenly scooped her off her feet and lit out in a dead run toward the water. She let out a gleeful little squeal as Nick splashed into the oncoming waves, kicking up foam and sand. The spray felt spectacular on Lori's face, and she giggled hysterically.

But instead of tossing her into the drink, Nick tripped—sort of acci-dentally, sort of on purpose—and they both went down into the crystal-line blue shallows. The waves enrobed them with briny warmth. They clung to each other, laughing like hell, as the water coursed over them, warm and healing and wonderful.

Nick helped Lori to her feet. They both stood there dripping. Their smiles faded. Lori felt heat building within her as she looked up into his sparkling blue eyes. Nick pulled her closer. Their wet skin came together like two circuits firing. Lori closed her eyes as Nick pressed his open mouth down on hers. Her head spun as they explored each other, tasted each other, opened up to each other like flowers blooming.

Lori hardly even noticed that Nick had gently urged her back onto the sand.

Lowering her to the beach, he enveloped her with his body. She lay beneath him, her arms wrapping around him, her nails digging into the rippling musculature of his back. Later, Lori would look back on this moment and think of that corny old flick that her mom had forced her to watch on AMC one time—*From Here to Eternity*—in which a couple of old-school movie stars get down and get funky in the waves washing across their bodies. Lori wondered if Nick had ever seen that movie, and if both he and Lori were re-creating it lucidly somehow. It was impossible to figure this stuff out, of course, and Lori gave up worrying about it.

More importantly, at that moment, as the sun set on their intertwined bodies, and they lay on the warm sand flush from their encounter, and the shadows lengthened and turned purple on the horizon, and the stars ignited overhead and filled the heavens with an endless necklace of diamonds, Lori Blaine fell in love.

She held his face in her hands, his pallid skin almost blue in the moonlight, and she started to tell him, "I think I'm sort of falling in love with—"

A voice, shrill with terror, accompanied by a whoosh of air, suddenly broke the spell: *"DON'T MIND US—WE'RE JUST FIGHTING A WAR OVER HERE!!"*

As though splashed with cold water, Lori and Nick jerked apart, glancing over their shoulders at the source of the voice, which came from the north edge of the beach.

Fifteen feet away, a rip in the night air had formed, almost as though the very dream itself had been unzipped, rent apart, cracked open . . . a razor-thin shaft of light spilling out of the portal.

Lori whirled toward the rip and saw a gaping hole in the dark—like a gigantic wound opening—the flash of mortar fire within it. The noise flooded the dream: the crackle of explosions, the sizzle of radio voices, movement, the blur of combat.

A cold jolt of horror traveled down Lori's spine, every fiber in her being suddenly aligning around the realization that this was very serious.

The archangel's battalion—as Lori came to think of this ragtag collection of dream warriors—had set their front line of defense on a ridge overlooking the vast stone canyon that stretched for miles across

LIMBOworld. In all directions, the dream hive—the endless slopes honeycombed with dark pockets, tunnels, and shadowy cavities—was under siege. Squadrons of massive oily Bogies swirled down from the dark haze in the sky, swarming near the mouths of tunnels leading to innocent dreams. The demons came in waves, constantly replenished and cloned and manufactured by the Demon Queen—a grotesque, giant, winged thing hanging upside down thousands of feet up in the dark heavens—and the invading army looked invincible in both number and ferocity.

From this distance, along the edge of the precipice, it looked as though the beehive were under attack by monstrous prehistoric wasps. The invaders flocked around openings in ghastly undulating clouds, and the only thing keeping the hive safe—at least for the moment—were the bizarre counteroffensives coming off the ridge, which Lori now watched with awe from her position in the shadows behind Nick.

"Forty degrees north, twenty-three degrees west," the older man named Pops was saying into a two-way radio affixed to his battered headpiece, which resembled a holy helmet of carved gold. He strode along the edge of the cliff with infrared-style goggles on and he gazed out at the distant horizon of dream tunnels. "On my mark . . . ready?"

A voice crackled on some remote radio. "Copy that, base, we're standing by."

"Three, two, one . . . and *FIRE!*" Pops said into his radio, and there was a flash that lit up the ridge like a photographer's strobe, which yanked Lori's attention over to the other side of the ridge.

Another holy warrior—maybe fifty yards away, out of earshot, perched on an outcropping of stone—crouched behind a massive exotic gun. A young man in his mid-thirties, with camouflaged pants and giant downy wings folded against his back, he started firing at a trouble spot in the distance—a swarm of black beasts invading the mouth of a dream tunnel.

In the old days they called them "Gatling guns," but this one was different. Made of gilded metal of some sort, the giant revolving chamber held huge loads of holy water. Lori deduced much of this from the crucifix engravings on the casings, as the massive cylinder began to turn and spit out blasts of foamy sacred spray.

Two hundred yards away, the holy water landed on the flock, strafing their wings in puffs of steam, sending the black marauders scattering up into the smoke-stained air. This single "bombing event"—which encompassed mere seconds—was accompanied by a strange whispering litany echoing out over the gorge.

Lori gazed across the ledge and saw the man with the golden hair. Now wearing full battle armor, his chest encased in battered breastplate, his wings open and spanning a width of twenty-five feet, he paced along the plateau with a giant megaphone-shaped instrument to his lips. It too had religious engravings on its bell and its shaft.

The archangel's whisper—calm and steady and confident—leapt out of the megaphone and filled the entire canyon with the rites of exorcism: "*Immunda phasmatis absum—absum in nomen Deus!*"

Lori swallowed a gulp of air as she watched Nick reloading holy water canisters. He worked beside Mrs. Waverly, who was on the radio with some other regiment somewhere, some other battalion, shouting orders.

Nick worked silently, quickly, efficiently, dipping the shell casings into the huge blessed fonts, which stood like a row of birdbaths against the sheer cliff adjacent to the precipice. He didn't notice that Lori was backing away from the action.

A sudden realization flooded her like a million volts of electricity—a white-hot terror so powerful it nearly knocked her over. Nick had said that dreamers from the same general vicinity usually cluster together in here. If Ichabod Kettlekamp's portal was around here . . . then others from Lori's world might be close by.

"Lori?" Nick had glanced up from his work, his face glistening with sweat. "What's the matter?"

She looked at him. "My—"

"What? What is it?"

She barely got the words out. "My mom . . . she dreams a lot . . . she's probably dreaming right now . . . *out there.*"

EIGHTEEN

They had to hold Lori back. It took two of them—Nick and Pops—one on either side of her. Lori wriggled and struggled in their grasp. "They could get to her! Let me go! They could get into her dream!!"

Nick held onto her, whispering tenderly and yet urgently, "Don't worry, Lori, it's okay. Take it easy . . . take it easy . . . take it easy."

"We'll protect your mom," the leader assured her. The man with the Roger Daltrey curls loomed over Lori like a giant, as though he were ten feet tall, with his tranquil blue eyes, his knowing gaze, his broadsword gleaming in the alien light. He had a sad, sympathetic smile on his lips as he reassured her, "It's our job, it's what we do."

"But she's—"

"There's nothing you can do, Lori," the archangel assured her.

"But—"

"I understand," the angel said with a wise and caring nod, his eyes twinkling with something mysterious, something like precognition. Lori had read about religious conversion, moments where people feel the spirit fill them and they find God. Something altogether different was happening to Lori as she looked up into the eyes of the angel and heard the word again. The word reverberated deep in the recesses of Lori's brain like a thought-whisper.

Wild.

"I don't care! I have to be sure!" Lori yelled. She tore herself away from the others, ripping a hank of lacy fabric from her blouse, and she made a mad dash toward the edge of the precipice.

"LORI!" Nick chased after her. He could see her climbing over the ledge, awkwardly sliding down the steep slope of volcanic rock. The demon-clogged sky reacted to the commotion. Black oily wings hastened and changed direction and swooped toward the slope.

"LORI, WAIT!!" Nick, acting on pure instinct, shoved the Gatling gun operator aside. The angel tumbled onto his ass, getting tangled in his flapping wings. Nick grabbed the enormous weapon and ripped it from its moorings, sending sparks and dirt flying.

Lori had already slid halfway down the slope, raising a cloud of black dust.

"WAIT!!" Nick heaved the giant gun—which was the size of a large oil drum in his arms—over the edge of the precipice and down the slope. Fifty feet below him, Lori landed in a pool of stagnant water with a splash.

A Bogy circled overhead, locking its sights on the fleeing girl.

Lori heard the sound before she saw the black vulture diving toward her. She was struggling to her feet as the ragged shriek filled her ears, followed by the drumbeat of oily wings and the shadow engulfing her. She looked up. The thing plunged toward her with jagged mouth opening, revealing a rotting pit of a throat and a serpent's tongue flagging, as long and repulsive as a cancerous vein, tasting the air hungrily, savage and mindless.

Frozen with horror, Lori tried to dodge the thing but it was no use.

The demon reached Lori on a piercing shriek and was one nanosecond away from devouring the girl when a burst of holy water struck the Bogy mid torso, erupting in a cloud of black smoke. More bursts of the sacred liquid flew like streamers of foam, hitting the demon in the head, hitting its soft underbelly, grazing its scaly back.

The creature let out a hellish wail that sounded like a lightning bolt striking high-tension wires. Massive black wings flapped with berserk, directionless panic as the thing careened back up into the sky.

"LORI, THIS WAY!!" Nick's voice pierced the horrible din as the beast vanished up into a cloud of noxious gases above them, sending shock waves across the murky atmosphere. Lori followed the young man.

Nick led her along the edge of the ravine at the bottom of the gorge, hauling the massive weapon and hyperventilating with effort. Lori followed close on his heels, sensing the menacing shadows above them coalescing, reshaping, reforming like living storm clouds, moving over the hive as the demons regrouped for another attack. It was like running through a vast forest that had just recently burned to the ground, the air thick with cinders and ash. Lori could barely breathe. It wasn't just the smoke and the toxic particles in the air. The Bogies permeated the canyon with something stronger than mere pollution—it was a pall of dread that hung in the air and weighed down on every soul present. It was despair and emptiness and misery and anguish and . . . maybe the strongest sensation of them all . . . *hopelessness.*

The black swarm gave off a sense of hopelessness as palpable as rain.

Lori saw Nick—a few paces ahead of her—duck into the mouth of a cave. She followed. Instantly she was plunged into a cold, dark, slimy warren of stone. She could barely see Nick ahead of her, turning a corner and vanishing in the catacomb. She followed him.

A moment later she found Nick in the shadows. He was winded, leaning against the onyx wall of the tunnel to catch his breath "Damn thing is heavy!" he complained, gasping for breath.

She joined him. "I'm sorry I—"

"Don't sweat it. It's okay."

"No, seriously, I—"

"You don't have to explain. You love your mom. I would have done the same thing."

"But how do I—"

"We'll find her, Lori, I promise," Nick said, reaching out and tenderly stroking Lori's hair. Then he reached down to his belt. "Do me a favor. Think about her for a second." Nick pulled an instrument from his tool belt, a small stone the color of milk glass. He held it in his sweaty, trembling hand. The center glowed. Phosphorous yellow light, like fireflies, shone in the stone's core. "Think about your mom, Lori."

Lori closed her eyes and concentrated.

"Oh crap!"

Nick's voice shook Lori out of her daze. She opened her eyes. "What is it?" she asked him, looking around the dark tunnel.

The noise drew her attention back toward the far end of the passageway, the direction in which she and Nick had just come. Fear stabbed at Lori's chest as she saw at least four—maybe five or six—oily black marauders approaching through the shadows.

Their black wings scraped the tunnel walls, their serpentine tongues tasting the air.

"That way, Lori!" Nick waved the stone toward the opposite end of the passage. "Second one from the left! Right before the bend! Hurry! I'll hold them off!"

"But what about—"

"HURRY!!"

Nick tossed the stone. Then he quickly pulled a long metal prod from his belt. The demons approached. Nick thumbed a switch and the prod opened like a switchblade, exposing a gleaming crucifix on the business end. The beautifully ornate toes of Christ were sharpened to a razor's edge.

"HURRY! GO!!"

Lori turned and raced down the narrow tunnel to the second portal on the left.

She found the seam in the stone and pushed it open as though cracking an eggshell.

* * *

Everything changed like a TV program suddenly flickering from color to black and white. Lori found herself climbing into a world of gray tones.

She stepped onto the floor of a dream—she figured out moments later it was the kitchen floor from her house on Monterey Court, nearly unrecognizable in this dreamspace—and she nearly keeled over from the abrupt change in atmosphere. The walls were gray, the ceiling gray, the world outside the window over the sink—the overcast sky, the bare trees—as gray as dirty dishwater.

Lori blinked. The kitchen looked like another surrealist painting—distorted, warped—as though glimpsed through the wrong end of a telescope. The ceiling rose at an angle a hundred feet high. A weird oblong clock on the far wall, the size of a kidney-shaped swimming pool, filled the heavy silence with oppressive ticking.

Allison Blaine sat way at the other end of this gray kitchen world with her back turned. She sat hunched over a wash pail.

Lori lingered at the other end of this bleak dream, unnoticed by her mother. Relieved that the dream was still intact, undisturbed by outside forces—there was no evidence of Bogy intrusion anywhere—Lori was still taken aback by the pervasive sense of loss and desolation in the air. She sensed that there was no food in the fridge, nothing in the pantry, nothing in the plans for dinner, nothing on the horizon. Nothing. She saw her mom compulsively cleaning her wrists with a washcloth, cleaning stains that would not come out. She was as lonely and isolated as a woman had ever been in the history of the universe.

An indescribable sense of despair permeated every inch of this dream.

That's when Lori decided to try something. This was her mother's dream . . . and there was nothing Lori could do about changing it . . . but somehow Lori felt connected to this dream through the umbilical of her own DNA, as though she were part of the fabric of it. And maybe . . . just maybe . . . she had the wherewithal to add a layer to it.

She looked down at the stained floor. In her mind she ordered the linoleum to brighten. It was as if a sheet of color had started to unfurl across the tiles. The true shade of the floor emerged behind the leading edge of Lori's thought-wave. The tiles, bright yellow with blue speckles, were suddenly spotless, radiant. A TV commercial for Mop & Glo floor polish could not have animated it better.

Working silently, unseen by her mother, Lori turned in a slow 180-degree turn. Every inch of the room that crossed her vision suddenly changed, morphed into color. All at once, beams of sunlight filtered through the chintz curtains and the walls straightened, the bizarre bends and distortions returning to normal. The sky outside the window turned as blue as cornflowers.

Lori inhaled a deep breath and focused on a single theme material-izing in a million different forms across her mother's dreamspace: *hope*.

It appeared on the granite countertop in the form of mail from old friends, invitations to parties, and unexpected tax refunds from the IRS. It sprouted in the flowerpots along the windowsill—tiny green shoots of herbs in every pot, promising sweet basil and cilantro and oregano for future meals. It transformed the dreamspace. It drove away the shadows. It bloomed in a rainbow of colors. It lined the shelves with new books to read, new recipes to try, new CDs to listen to, new DVDs to watch.

Hope.

Lori smiled.

It was time to leave.

Lori turned away and found the exit just to the left of the stove, like a seam in the wallpaper.

She got her fingers between the edges and pushed it apart as though opening a huge change purse.

The attack was so sudden, so unexpected, so quick, that Lori barely heard her own startled cry in her ears. The Bogy had been waiting for her outside the portal, coiled like a snake in the haze.

Evidently Nick was occupied elsewhere—drawn away by decoys.

The beast struck with cobra-speed and Lori was thrown backward against the tunnel wall with tremendous force, the air knocked from her lungs.

The demon's tongue lashed out like a bullwhip. Lori screamed. The long black tendril of smoke poured down Lori's throat.

Filling her.

Flooding her.

Possessing her.

NINETEEN

Her eyes popped open. Harsh white light glared in her face. She couldn't move her arms. Her brain wasn't working. Her mind was a jumble of thoughts like a room full of radios all blasting different stations.

Eyes adjusting, she saw that she was sitting on a bare floor in the corner of an empty white room. Dirty white padding lined the walls. Flickering, buzzing fluorescent tubes shone down from the ceiling, flooding the stark area with light. It was so white—so blinding bright—that for a moment, some deeply lodged memory from her childhood, maybe a movie she once saw, told her she was in heaven.

She looked down at herself—*Lori*—that was her name—and she saw her slender form wrapped in a thick, white canvas garment. Her arms, bound and folded against her midsection, were sleeved and tied off behind her. The garment had a steel chain running down through her legs, under her crotch, and around her back.

A straitjacket.

My name is Lori and I'm alone in a padded room in a straitjacket—the sum total of all she knew at the moment—tumbled through her thoughts.

The realization was drowned under a sea of chaotic memories and images: a needle going into her arm; a woman screaming in the room next to her; desperate, scalding tears soaking her mattress; leather restraints cutting into the skin of her ankles and wrists.

She began to wriggle inside the tight confines of the straitjacket.

At first she merely tensed and relaxed, tensed and relaxed, testing the jacket's strength, checking its limits. But the claustrophobic feeling fed her panic. She started jerking, stretching the tight fabric of the girdle. Her brain swam with panic. The terror coursed through her and twitched in her muscles. She started banging the back of her skull against the padded wall behind her.

Falling onto her side, she screamed and rolled. Her mind boiled with rage and confusion. She banged into the opposite corner of the room— the entire padded chamber was less than two hundred square feet and blazing with light—and she cried out, a miserable garbled shriek that sounded like an animal being tortured. Her knotted braids dangled in greasy streamers across her face, adding to the feral, desperate quality of her appearance.

Across the room, a seam in the padding suddenly cracked, and a door swung open.

"Here we go again!" said an orderly in a white coat. He was a beefy man with a thick neck and a crew cut. His horn-rimmed glasses gleamed in the fluorescent light. His face looked familiar for a moment; then the familiarity seemed to drain out of it, and suddenly the man looked as indistinct as a ghost, as though the face had passed under frosted glass. A water hose appeared in his hands.

"Please. I . . . I . . . I need to—" Lori tried to speak, curled on the floor in a fetal position. Her throat raw—probably from screaming—she could now barely produce a sound. She wriggled violently.

Water suddenly erupted from the nozzle in the orderly's grip.

The stream of high-powered water struck Lori in the side of the head. Like a fist, the jet decked her, flipping her over onto her back. She tried to roll away from it but the stream was relentless and brutal. It smacked her in the midsection with the force of a billy club, punched her in the gut, kicked at her legs. Lori began to sob.

Lying on her back now, staring straight up through tears at the dirty, unyielding fluorescent tubes, she cried and trembled in the straitjacket as the waves of voices and unwanted images crashed in her brain.

A new voice suddenly penetrated the horror of the white room. "Enough with the hydrotherapy already!"

The stream died.

The padded walls dripped in the silence. The drone of voices bounced around Lori's skull—a hundred thousand Saturday morning cartoons of gibberish—as she lay on her back, staring at the ceiling, lungs hiccupping with despair. She could barely see the new figure entering the room from the doorway behind the orderly.

"Put it away, Carl, for Chrissake," the figure said. This voice was also familiar somehow. "I'll take over now, you leave us in peace."

"I'll be outside," the orderly said, winding the hose back up.

Lori managed to turn her head. She struggled to focus on the tall, slender man approaching now with a clipboard. A balding man in his fifties, he wore John Lennon glasses and had a security pass clipped to the collar of his nonthreatening sweater vest. He spoke in soft, encouraging tones, like a camp counselor, as he knelt down and cradled Lori's head. "I'm so sorry about that, Lori. They're like a blunt instrument around here sometime."

The school shrink—Lori remembered the man now—was a soft talker. You had to hang on every word to catch what he was saying.

He lifted Lori into a sitting position, gently setting her back against the padding. "I promise you, young lady, we're going to get you back home as soon as possible."

"How did I—" Lori tried to cut through the jangle of noise in her head, but it was impossible.

"Just take a deep breath."

Lori did so. "I n-need to—" Her halting speech resembled a stroke victim. She could not hold on to any one thought. "I'm trying to—"

"You're trying to get a handle on things, I understand. Can you tell me your name?"

"L-Lori."

"That's good, Lori. Can you tell me when you were born?"

"Um . . . y-yes, of course . . . um . . . August. The seventeenth."

"Good. Can you tell me what year?"

"Yes, um, 1999."

"Excellent. Just take deep breaths. Did you have a dream last night, Lori? Is that why you had the incident today? Do you remember the incident?"

"The what?" Lori's brain churned with contrary emotions, fear and urgency. "The incident?"

"You don't remember?" The school shrink let out a weary sigh. "Lori, you attacked some other patients. Practically tried to claw their eyes out . . . ranting the whole time about demons . . . claiming they were possessed . . . screaming 'get out' at them and all manner of things."

"I—w-what?"

Another pained sigh from the therapist. "You tried to claw their eyes out, Lori. I told the administrator it wasn't your fault. I explained that you were probably dreaming again. I told them I would adjust your meds . . . see if we couldn't give you a break from the dreams."

Lori looked up at the doctor. For a single instant it felt to Lori as though she were sinking into the floor, her soul draining out of her. "The dreams?"

The shrink looked nervous all of a sudden. "I don't know if we should get into this—"

"No, please!" Lori tensed in her restraints, grew rigid. "Please tell me what dreams you're referring to."

Another sigh. "Alright. In brief . . . and I don't want to upset you again . . . they're very vivid. Very real. You've related the whole storyline to the group on more than one occasion—"

"The group?"

"The other patients in group therapy. May I ask . . . do you know where you are right now?"

"Um . . . not exactly."

"You're in the River Woods Psychiatric Hospital, in Rockford, Illinois."

Lori closed her eyes and let the pain and despair wash over her. "The dreams. You w-were going to tell me the s-storyline."

The shrink looked at her. "In a nutshell . . . you've been dreaming an elaborate story. It began with a dream of a . . . a session you and I never had."

Lori looked up at him. "What?"

"You dreamt you came to see me and I told you to go through a door in your dreams, and later you went through that door, and you discovered another world. How did you put it?" The shrink reached inside the collar of his sweater vest, pulled a notebook from his breast pocket. He opened it and paged to a key entry. "'A world *behind* the dreams.'"

"Oh wonderful." Lori's voice was breathless, strangled with shock. "Oh God that's just perfect."

The shrink closed the notebook. "Lori, we don't have to do this—"

"Go on, please . . . *please*."

The shrink read on. "You told us about these so-called 'Bogies,' which you describe as demons, and there's a young man in the dreams—what was his name—'Nick'? And there was also an angel."

"Michael."

The shrink looked up from his notebook. "That's right, Lori. The Archangel Michael—roughly the same name as your father—which I have always found very poignant and interesting." The notebook went back into the man's pocket, and then a small pouch came out. From inside the pouch the man produced a prepared syringe. "I'm going to give you something now to help soften things up for a while."

Lori didn't have the energy to put up a fight. She simply watched as the needle pierced the fabric of the jacket and entered her shoulder. She felt the cold pinprick spreading through her.

Her muscles relaxed. "What am I doing here, Doc?" she asked in a weak voice.

The room had gone almost completely gauzy-white all of a sudden, as though the air itself were radiant with angelic light. The shrink rose to his feet and let out a weary, pained sigh.

"We'll get back to that, Lori, don't you worry."

And then he walked out and left her in the luminous white light.

She looked down at the floor . . . crestfallen, crushed . . . but suddenly jerked as something moved in her peripheral vision. She gazed over one shoulder and saw a pink line about two feet long in the white padded wall fading away as though drying under a sunlamp until it completely vanished.

Lori stared and stared at it, as a single tear of blood ran down the padding, then vanished as well into the seams of the floor. Lori shuddered and looked away. She had to be seeing things. She could have sworn she had just caught an image of the wall exhibiting an open wound.

But that would be impossible . . . that would be crazy.

Days passed. Weeks passed. Maybe even months passed. In a blur of medicated routines, and days without end, and nights in the hellish dark, amidst the screams and stench of human decay, Lori lost track of time. Each day, indistinguishable from the one before, lasted an eternity. The drugs kept Lori docile and oblivious to everything but the tedium. She wondered if she was really crazy or if somebody had made a mistake.

She spent her time shuttling between her barren cell of a room and the ancient foul-smelling lounges, where anonymous patients shuffled aimlessly in slippers, muttering and drooling on themselves. Each week, her hair grew more and more tangled and unruly and frizzed at the ends, until she began to resemble some sort of simian creature with a ropy mane of wild mahogany locks.

The hospital had three stories. Lori spent most of her time on the uppermost floor, where a labyrinth of corridors connected huge barracks and activity rooms lined with meshed windows. She sat up there most days, her dreadlocks veiling her miserable face. For hours on end, she would peer through those greasy strands of braids, staring out the reinforced windows at the bare trees that bordered the hospital property. The seasons came and went. Winter rolled in and blanketed the landscape with dirty snow, soot-stained from the runoff of nearby steel mills. At night Lori could hear the crackle and thunder of the mills, melting steel, forging girders and rebar. It made her sick to her stomach. It reminded her of the vacuum in her brain, all sparking synapses leading nowhere, as blank as the snow on a TV screen.

The school shrink—his name was Philburton, Lori learned after staring at the man's security pass one day—made attempts to help her. He would meet privately with Lori in one of the staff meeting rooms. And for a long while Lori believed that the shrink was trying his best to help.

The shrink seemed fond of Lori, or maybe felt sorry for the poor girl, and worked hard to unravel the mystery of the dreams. For weeks he scrawled chalk diagrams across a forty-foot-wide blackboard at one end of a meeting room. Lines and arrows connected the names of imaginary people like Nick Ballas with various settings and plots manufactured in Lori's dreams. After a while the blackboard started looking like an elaborate calculus equation.

The mathematics of Lori's hallucinatory world, in the words of Dr. Philburton, was as rich and complex as quantum physics. Wish fulfillment, conflict resolution, repressed memories, buried trauma, abandonment issues, latent homosexuality, codependency, self-medication—all of it morphed into one of the most intricate, detailed, convoluted recurring dreams ever recorded in the annals of psychology. Philburton decided to write a book about it.

That's when Lori started doubting the shrink's sincerity. Lori felt eyes on her sometimes—behind mirrors, late at night, through the lenses of security cameras—and she started feeling like the two-headed calf at the Oddities Emporium freak show. She was the Girl in the Bubble. She was a lab rat. She was a brain floating in a fluid-filled glass container.

Winter gave way to spring, which gave way to summer, which gave way to autumn, and finally the passage of time became moot, meaningless, shapeless.

At some point they put Lori back in the straitjacket for good. They said they were worried she would hurt herself—if not others—if they allowed her to wander freely. This made no sense to Lori, as she was a lifelong pacifist and wouldn't harm a bug and had no recollection of trying to hurt one of her fellow patients. They kept Lori in the padded room around the clock now and fed her three times a day. They fed her nasty crap that looked like cat food, spooning it into her dry, cracked mouth, as one would feed a baby.

Lori began to lose so much weight she literally started to waste away—becoming a skeleton of a person. Time continued to crawl. She actually wondered what it would be like to kill herself. But that was impossible with her restraints. She considered holding her breath until she expired—but that's a lot more difficult than it sounds—or she could crack her skull against the wall, but the padding got in the way of that little plan. She would think of something.

One day she was alone in the padded cell, on the floor in her restraints, when she heard the strangest noise. It came from the padded wall to her left. It sounded like a balloon stretching—that strange rubbery creak that precedes a blowout—and Lori's head lolled toward the noise.

At first she saw the incredible sight without even recognizing it.

The wall was bulging.

It looked like a bubble forming in a soufflé. The bulge grew. It looked as if something was forcing its way into the room from the very fabric of the padding. Lori blinked and tried to focus on it.

She figured it was simply another hallucination. She had been having the most horrific visions during her stay here—ugly demonic faces gaping at her from every dark corner—but the more she stared at the bulge, the more she realized this was different than her other visions.

This was real.

The bulge was shaped like a person. It stretched and protruded like a pregnant belly about to give birth, the rubbery creaking noise filling the air. Lori swallowed dryly and blinked and tried to comprehend what she was seeing. Her brain raced.

The bulge finally burst with a wet pop.

Nick Ballas tumbled into the padded cell, falling onto his hands and knees, one of his tools slipping off his belt and rolling across the floor. "Damn these things!" he commented irritably.

"You clear?" a voice called out behind him.

"All clear!" he replied as he struggled to his feet, scooping up the tool. It was a length of cable wound into a tight coil.

Lori felt an icy paralysis spreading through her, almost like an invisible weight. She tried to say something but she had turned to stone.

"Coming in!" the voice announced, and another figure pushed its way into the room.

It was the Archangel Michael, dressed in his battle garb, his long curls flopping with the effort. His wings had released, the multifaceted feathers spanning half the length of the padded room.

Deep inside her soul, Lori felt herself splitting into two equal and opposite parts.

One part of her had never been happier to see two souls in her life.

Another part of her let out a piercing, bone-chilling wail of contempt.

TWENTY

"You're gonna be okay, Lori . . . just hang in there." Nick spoke in hushed whispers as he unwound the cable. He was obviously trying to maintain his professional distance, but his eyes burned with emotion as he prepared to cleanse her. "I promise we'll get that thing out of you in a jiff."

Lori felt something jolt through her, like electric current. It straightened her spine and made her head whiplash back against the padding.

"Ready?" the archangel asked Nick. He had drawn his magnificent broadsword from its scabbard. His face was a mask of concentration. His wings tensed and scraped the ceiling, as though twitching with the synapses of his musculature.

"All set," Nick replied, unfurling the coil of cable as though shaking open a sheet on laundry day. The cable spread into a net. It looked like a metal fishing net one might use to trawl for lobster.

"On my signal," the archangel said, moving around Lori to the other side of the room. The gleaming point of the sword dripped a tear of holy water. It shimmered in the dim light like a diamond.

Lori's mouth yawned open and a voice she had no control over burst out of her on a dry wheeze. "PETO ABYSSUS!! ABYSSSSSSSSUSS!"

The archangel calmly raised the sword. "Three, two, one, and ... GO!"

On the archangel's order, Nick suddenly raised the netting and called out—in unison with the archangel's clear, steady voice—the sacred Latin chant that had survived the centuries in primeval texts: "*In Nomen a Patris—Solvo Puer!*"

Lori felt herself levitate. It was not a gentle, buoyant feeling, either—as a magician might raise a volunteer from the audience off the floor in some Vegas lounge act. On the contrary, this was a sudden and violent lurch upward, as though Lori were caught in the whirlwind of a tornado.

"*IN NOMEN A PATRIS—SOLVO PUER!*" Both voices called out in unison, accompanied by a flinging of holy water across Lori's face.

Lori slammed backward against the wall as though pulled on guide wires. The impact knocked the breath out of her. Roman candles streaked across her blurred vision.

"ABYSSSSSOOOOOSSSSSSSSSS!!" the demon voice roared out of her.

"*IN NOMEN A PATRIS—SOLVO PUER!*"

Another thin tendril of sacred fluid spattered Lori's face as she hung in midair, five feet off the floor, pinned to the wall like a bug in an exhibit. The water burned her skin like acid.

"*IN NOMEN A PATRIS—SOLVO PUER!*"

Lori slid to the floor in agony, still wrapped in the straitjacket, landing on her tailbone. Something rose up her gorge.

"*IN NOMEN A PATRIS—SOLVO PUER!*"

At first Lori thought she was about to vomit, but this was a thousand times worse, because this was a living thing wriggling out of her. It felt like a toilet plunger thrusting up her esophagus and out her throat.

"*IN NOMEN A PATRIS—SOLVO PUER!*"

The black thing burst out of Lori's mouth like a living column of smoke.

Lori saw it through watering eyes as she jerked against the wall, lungs heaving, body folding up and collapsing into a heap on the floor. It was as though she had coughed up a gigantic black smoke ring that swirled out of her and filled the room.

The Bogy materialized between Lori and the net with ghastly detail.

Lori could see every vein in the flesh of its leathery, black wings as they spread to their full span—at least twenty feet—its head tossing wildly with its terrible scales and reptilian yellow eyes.

"NOW, NICK!"

Several things happened very quickly then, almost too quickly for Lori to follow. Nick swiftly and professionally tossed the metal net over the demon, which let out a hideous roar—a keening noise like two glaciers scraping—and then the Archangel Michael moved in, raising his broadsword with a flourish over his head, his movements preternaturally skilled, his wings flexing backward like pinions on a catapult.

The tip of the sword pierced the net and ran through the demon's midsection.

Lori cringed at the noise. It crashed off the walls of the padded room, vibrating the floor with the force of an earthquake. It was a chorus of voices, many different voices, each of them shrieking in a different key, as the thing in the net writhed in spasms of pain. The flesh of the Bogy seemed to disintegrate around the edges of the sword as the archangel pulled it free.

Over the space of an instant the thing in the net dissolved. Like black ice melting in a furnace, the beast shrank and sizzled and withered. The voices receded, as if echoing across an invisible chasm, as the net collapsed.

The thing under the net bubbled in a puddle of black goo for a moment, and then the black goo itself dried and flaked away with time-lapse speed.

The silence that followed was like a sledgehammer blow to Lori's skull. Her ears rang. She struggled to sit up, and realized all at once that she no longer wore the straitjacket. She looked down and saw that she was back in her cable-knit sweater and ripped denim, and the room had changed.

"I'm really sorry you had to go through that, Lori." Nick reached down and grabbed the edges of the metal netting. He lifted it off the floor and shook the debris from it. He worked with the unfussy efficiency of a hotel maid making the bed.

Lori rubbed her eyes. Her lanky arms, freed from their restraints, felt numb and stiff. She no longer huddled in a padded cell. Her braided hair had returned to its customary length. The harsh white light had given way, almost as though somebody had flipped a switch, to the gloomy light of the dream tunnels. The aftershocks of the battle still crackled somewhere faraway.

Looking around the narrow passageway, Lori realized she was back in the hive, sitting on the stone floor just outside the portal to her mother's dream, the exact place where she had been attacked. She stared at the slimy walls of the stone catacombs. "Oh my God," she uttered under her breath, trying to sort it out.

"I know," the archangel said softly, sliding the broadsword back into its sheath. The angel came over and knelt next to Lori. Dull light glimmered on the folded wings behind him, which refracted the light in their silvery convolutions. "It's a little jarring." He pulled a penlight from his belt and checked Lori's eyes. "How are you feeling, Lori?"

"I'm . . . not quite certain. Ask me later."

Nick was coiling the net. "Whole thing was my fault, the whole mess. I got a little tied up when I should have been guarding the mother's portal."

"I'm not mentally ill," Lori uttered, still a little groggy and dazed.

"Not any more than the rest of us around here," Nick said, kneeling on the other side of her, putting the coil back on his belt. He gently stroked her shoulder. His eyes filled up, glinting with emotion. He hugged her. And she hugged him back. And he fought the tears as he said, "What's the old saying? 'You don't have to be crazy to work here but it sure helps'?"

Lori tried to say something else but the emotion got the better of her. She put her head on Nick's shoulder and she started to cry. Softly, shoulders trembling, she wept into the nape of his neck. Her tears soaked his shirt.

"It's okay," Nick said softly, holding her. He kissed her forehead. "Everything's gonna be okay now."

Lori got herself under control. She looked up at Nick, then over at the archangel. "Wait a minute. Wait. How long was I—"

She stopped herself because she noticed Nick and the angel exchanging another glance. The way they looked at each other sent a trickle of gooseflesh down Lori's back. Battle sounds echoed like heat thunder outside the tunnels. "Don't tell me," she said, her heart sinking. "My time ran out."

Another furtive glance between the angel and Nick. What the hell was the matter with them? Lori's stomach clenched with dread.

"I'm stuck here now? Is that how it is—a vegetable somewhere on life support?"

"Lori, this is probably gonna come as a little bit of a shock," Nick finally said.

"Whatever it is, Nick, tell me, please, just tell me the truth."

The archangel softly interjected: "Lori, you remember the night you went to St. Louis?"

"You mean Carlinville? The nursing home? The facility where Nick is—"

"That's right . . . the same night you encountered the farm boy on the highway?"

She looked at the floor and shuddered. "How could I forget?"

The archangel glanced at Nick, then back at Lori. "And you remember when you returned home?"

"Yes."

"And your mom made you the banana pudding?"

Lori had to think about that little detail. This was over a year ago. At least she thought it was over a year ago. The demon had done some rewiring in her head. "Well . . . yeah," she finally said.

"And the last thing you did before you went to bed was translate the Latin that the farm boy had cried out on the highway?"

"How do you know all this?" Lori asked.

The archangel gave her that enigmatic smile. "As I said, it's what I do. It's my job."

"Plus," Nick piped in, "you told me about it that night in the haunted house. Remember?"

Lori admitted that she did indeed remember. "But what does this have to do with how long I was—" She stopped herself, the truth beginning to dawn on her.

"Lori, here's the thing." Nick took a deep breath, gently holding her by the shoulders and looking deep into her eyes. "It's still that night, Lori."

"What?"

He nodded. "In your world, it's still the wee hours of that night."

"How did—"

He was still nodding. "Only a few hours of WAKEworld time have passed."

It took a while for Lori to absorb this. While she was wrapping her head around it, the archangel gave Nick a nod. Nick reached down to his belt and grabbed the little metal prod—the wake-up Taser. "You have to go back, Lori," he said, and something in his voice worried her.

"Wait a minute—"

Nick thumbed the switch on the prod and two little antennae popped out. "There's work to be done in the real world," he said and raised the prod.

"Wait. Give me a second here." Lori looked into Nick's eyes, then she looked at the angel. "What are you referring to when you say there's *work* to be done?"

The archangel took a step closer, meeting Lori's gaze. "The farm boy, Lori."

"Ichabod?"

The archangel nodded. "Turns out he's a conduit just like you."

She stared. "A conduit between the two worlds?"

Another grave nod from the archangel. "That's right. Only this farm boy is a conduit for the *Bogies*, and he's about to rip a hole in the waking world through which the forces of darkness can pass."

Lori got very still. "Which means?"

The archangel sighed. "Oh, let's see . . . Armageddon . . . the Apocalypse . . . rivers running with blood, plagues of death, disease, that kind of thing."

Lori thought about it and thought about it, until Nick softly said, "Time's running out, Lori. Gonna have to zap you back."

"Okay, wait!" She raised her hand, the idea percolating in her brain. "Let me ask you something else." She looked at the angel. "If I get him back here, can you cleanse him like you cleansed me?"

Another loaded glance was exchanged between Nick and the archangel. At last the golden-haired man nodded. "That we can," he said.

"I have an idea," Lori said then. "A way to get him back here. But I need to know one more thing."

The archangel waited with an enigmatic smile on his handsome face.

Lori licked her dry lips. "You keep saying I'm a '*wild* one,' I'm *wild*. What does that mean?"

The archangel's smile lost some of its bliss. "Alas, Lori, you have to discover this for yourself."

Nick added, "Look into your gift, Lori. Look into yourself."

"What do you mean, *gift*? You mean being lucid?"

"You can do what *they* do."

"What?! What does that mean?! Nick, wait! What do you mean by '*what they do*'?!"

"Good luck, my love," Nick said and gently pressed the tip of the prod against her temple.

TWENTY-ONE

Lori awoke in the darkness of her bedroom on Monterey Court amidst the Bob Marley posters and incense candles and wadded dirty clothes. This time, she did not jerk awake. She did not come back to the real world with a convulsive start, as she usually did, almost as though bursting up and out of a stormy sea gasping for air. She simply sat up in a tangle of blankets and looked around the dark. Her eyes, sticky from all the crying in her sleep, searched the room.

The luminous digits of the clock on her bedside table said 3:47 A.M. She made note of this with a sigh. They were right. Only a few hours had passed since she had turned in on the evening of her confrontation with Ichabod.

Lori thought of Ebenezer Scrooge. She thought of that scene when the old miser awakes on Christmas morning, relieved that the spirits had done their number on him in a single evening. At the moment, though, Lori didn't feel even remotely as revitalized as Scrooge. She would not be buying any turkeys this morning.

She inspected her legs, which were still emaciated and sore. In a strange way, however, they felt as though they were on the mend, stronger than she remembered.

She moved to the edge of the bed and swung her legs over the side. The hardwood felt cool on the soles of her bare feet. She stood. Clad only in her tattered leggings and a Ramones T-shirt, she shivered. Her slender legs, as narrow as pipe stems, felt weak but serviceable.

She noticed her crutches across the room, leaning against her cluttered desk where she had left them. She also noticed the laptop still open, powered up, its screen sleeping. She saw the hastily scrawled notes next to the computer—the translation of Ichabod's creepy litany delivered on the hood of a hurling Chevy Geo.

You will not stop us, it is too late, we are legion.

It seemed like a hundred years ago. But Lori realized she had logged onto that translation site only a few hours earlier *on this very night.* It was such a huge gulp to swallow it almost made her dizzy . . . but it didn't. It didn't because she stood there thinking, thinking about what the archangel had said.

Lori sat down at the desk, lifted the laptop's lid, and got back online.

Fingers busily tapping, she had an idea. She remembered researching lucid dreamers. Many months ago, before the coma, before Ichabod, before the strange events at the imaginary madhouse, Lori had done a cursory search on the subject. A little Google here, a little Wikipedia there, and she had come up with the basics of lucid dreaming.

She hadn't dug very deep—if she were honest with herself, she would have to admit she had no patience for research—but now she had a nagging feeling there was something important there.

Something she had missed.

She watched the screen flash and fill with the royal blue bars and squares of the Psychology101.com home page. She scrolled down the topic panel—she remembered doing this that first time, but she had logged off before she got to the submenu under lucid dreaming—and now she clicked the link for HOW LUCID DREAMS BEGIN.

She found herself leaning closer to the screen as she scanned the page. The text informed her that a lucid dream can begin in three ways.

Three?

She couldn't remember reading about three ways to bring on the phenomenon. She remembered the first one, which was when the dreamer, while in the middle of a dream, simply concludes that she's dreaming. Scientists call this dream-initiated lucid dreaming, or DILD for short.

The second method involved the conscious use of a device called a "mnemonic," which Lori understood as a memory tool, not unlike the mental crutches she used when struggling to remember the capital of Paraguay or the formula for mass times the speed of light. A city called Asunción was the capital of Paraguay, and Lori would never forget that fact because she thought of herself as an Asshole Shunned by her peers.

Asshole Shunned was her mnemonic for *Asuncion*, which led her to Asunción.

And MILD was the acronym for mnemonic-initiated lucid dreaming.

Now Lori leaned closer. She gaped. The cathode light from the laptop made her eyes burn as she stared at the tiny block of text explaining the third method for kick-starting a lucid dream:

This phenomenon occurs when the dreamer goes from a normal waking state directly into a lucid dream state with no apparent lapse in consciousness—not unlike a supercharged daydream.

Lori swallowed hard, a gulp that felt like a peach pit in her throat. She stared and stared at the acronym for this method.

They called it wake-initiated lucid dreaming.

WILD.

She got dressed. She pulled on her black leggings, laced up her Doc Martens boots, and pulled on a faded gray sweater. She found an old pocketknife in her desk junk drawer. The size of a small banana, with an imitation tree bark handle, it wouldn't be much good in a fight—especially with a denizen from hell—but it was all Lori could come up with in the way of a weapon. She put the knife and her keys in a small leather pack that she belted around the waist of her black leggings.

The house was as dark as the inside of a cast-iron pot as Lori crept across the deserted living room. She could hear the furnace ticking. She could hear her own heart beating. And maybe, outside the walls of the settling house, the far-off screech of a barn owl. Lori decided to check on her mom before she made any rash decisions.

Allison's bedroom was on the other side of the house, her door slightly ajar, her room dark and silent. It was 4:21 A.M. when Lori peered through the gap and saw something that gave her an idea. In the shadows of the modest little bedroom, with its Laura Ashley curtains and family photos on every surface, Allison Blaine slumbered soundly. She had the coverlet pulled up to her neck, her face turned toward the door, her eyes closed, the pupils at rest under their lids. The slightest wisp of a smile showed on her narrow face.

Mission accomplished, Lori thought, the idea occurring to her then on the sudden spark of a synapse way in the back of her brain.

My mom's deeper than stage five right now, deeper than REM, deeper . . .

Lori turned away from the room and went back into her bedroom. She found her iPhone lying on her bedside table, picked it up, and dialed Hugo's number. It rang and rang before Hugo's scratchy, groggy, Kermit-the-Frog-on-NyQuil voice crackled in the earpiece. "Lori? What the fuck? You have any idea what time it is?"

"I know, I know . . . I'm sorry." She spoke softly, slowly closing her door, careful not to awaken her mom. "Listen, I need a favor."

"Dude . . . at like a quarter past insane o'clock in the morning?"

Lori gripped the iPhone tighter. "I know it sounds crazy . . . but you're the only person who can help me."

"What could this possibly involve that could not wait until a civilized hour?"

"Do you still have that phone number for that dude downtown, runs around with Simmons and Jamie and that weird bunch?"

After a rusty, clogged coughing sound, Hugo's voice returned. "Who?"

"You know . . . that skanky dude from Heritage Hill, supposedly deals various and sundry illegal substances."

"The meth head? Scofield?"

"Yes! Yes!" Lori paced in a nervous little circle, the soles of her Doc Martens threatening to wear a rut in the carpet. "That's the guy. Do you by any chance have an up-to-date phone number for that guy?"

More rustling noise from the other end. "Jesus . . . hold on." A faint beeping noise. "Gimme a second." More rustling. "Here it is. I'll text it to you."

"Hugo, thanks. You're a lifesaver." The sound of his text came whooshing into Lori's device. "I am so sorry I woke you up."

"Wait!"

Lori frowned. "What—what is it?"

Hugo's voice lost some of its bleary quality, got a little sharper, more serious. "Lori . . . you're not going on some sort of crazy bender, are you?"

Lori sighed. "Nope."

"Then what are you doing calling a drug dealer in the middle of the night?"

She thought about it. "Fixing things, Hugo. Once and for all." Pause. "I'm sorry I woke you up."

She hung up.

On her way out she grabbed her black waistcoat and put it on. A quick glance in the floor-length mirror by the front door gave her a start. She hadn't looked at her own face for what seemed an eternity. She looked drained, malnourished, maybe even a little nuts. Her eyes, sunken in a pale mask of grim determination, stared back at her with sullen regard. She looked like a nineteenth-century opium addict. Which was ironic, since she was about to employ narcotics for a very specific and strange purpose. "Wild my ass," she muttered to herself.

Then she slipped out, careful not to slam the screen or descend the porch steps too loudly.

The windshield of Allison's Buick LeSabre kept fogging up as Lori backed the rusty ocean liner down the drive, applied the brakes, then put it into gear and slowly pulled away from her house.

The car's interior smelled of stale coffee and Nicorette gum—Allison had been trying to quit her half-pack-a-day habit for as long as Lori could remember—and the draft through the open vent made Lori shiver. It was still early autumn in west-central Illinois, but the nights had already turned bitter—especially *this* time of night, when the sky was pregnant with dawn.

If Lori's memory served, Allison had mentioned something about taking a sabbatical from work. This was good, since Lori needed as much time as possible this morning. On a typical workday, Allison would be up and about by 8:00 A.M., dressed and caffeinated by 8:30, and likely to notice Lori and the car missing before 9:00. But perhaps *this* morning her tendency to sleep in would buy Lori more time.

The entrance to Highway 27 loomed in the headlights, and Lori took the north ramp.

She noticed the western horizon starting to glow a dull sapphire blue behind the tree line as she pushed the car past fifty-five, past sixty, and held it at sixty-five. The faint smell of manure coming through the vent mingled with the grassy stench of the country air. Everything had an eerie, luminous cast to it now as daybreak threatened.

Lori checked the dashboard clock. It was already past five.

She took the War Memorial Drive exit and made her way through the drab, industrial outskirts toward the business district. At this hour, the low-slung office parks and warehouses along Thirty-Second Street had a third world air about them. She zoomed past flaming oil drums and stray dogs slumbering on top of Dumpsters. Shadows clung to the garbage-strewn alleys, and sodium-vapor lights sent pools of yellow down on deserted street corners.

Up ahead, she saw the silhouette of a scarecrow-thin man in leathers leaning against the outer door of a shabby transient hotel building. Peter Scofield looked like central casting for a drug dealer—a Valesburg Central High School dropout who had become legend for making a fortune in Vegas and returning to Valesburg to invest his winnings in the nonprescription pharmaceutical biz.

"Keep driving, for fuck's sake," he murmured angrily as Lori naively pulled up to the curb in front of him, rolling down her window as though about to order the six-piece Chicken McNuggets Happy Meal. "Park that piece of shit at the end of the fucking street," he instructed helpfully. "And don't be waving your fucking money around like a stupid fucking tourist when you come back on foot."

She did as she was told, parking the Buick out of sight, climbing out of the car and lifting the collar of her waistcoat to ward off the chill as she casually strode back toward the drug dealer. She pretended not to be shaking as she said, "You remember what we talked about on the phone?"

Scofield moved a toothpick thoughtfully around his smirking mouth. "Seem to recall something about roofies?"

"No." She clenched her fists. "I don't want roofies. What I need is something very specific for a very specific purpose."

Scofield gave her a look, his creepy smile widening. "Lady . . . they're always for a specific purpose."

TWENTY-TWO

The Kettlekamp farm sat like a giant barnacle on a barren stretch of land in the northeast corner of the county. The fields hadn't been tended for years, and the once-thriving dairy business had long passed into bankruptcy. Ichabod's father, Earl-Jay Kettlekamp, had succumbed to emphysema years ago, and the mother, Arlene, had allegedly run off to Davenport with an encyclopedia salesman. Now, as far as Lori knew, the only two souls still residing in the ugly, squat farmhouse—with its boarded windows and peeling wood siding—were Ichabod and his senile grandmother.

By the time Lori made it out there and saw the broken-down fence marking the southernmost edge of the Kettlekamp property coming into view up ahead, it was getting light out. Magic hour, some folks called it—that time when everything hushes. Crickets fall silent. The air goes still, and the shadows turn purple and indigo against the lightening sky, the trees like black lace stitched against a jewel.

Lori pulled off the highway well before she reached the ramshackle wooden gate at the end of the Kettlekamp's drive. She didn't want to give herself away, in case . . . well, *just in case*. She turned the car off, and the engine dieseled for a moment, then gave up the ghost.

The silence made Lori's ears ring. She tensed her legs against the steering wheel. They felt strong enough to get her where she wanted to go. Maybe not strong enough to win a race. But strong enough. She carefully clicked open the door and got out, careful to close it as quietly as possible. She hobbled around the back of the car. Inside the trunk she found a tire iron in the shape of a crossbar with sockets of different sizes on each end . . . *just in case.*

On her way to the front gate, she saw the first rays of the morning sun peeking through the unincorporated woods to the west. The beams of light, cutting through the early morning mist, looked positively Arthurian—primordial, mystical, like those of a fairy tale. A distant freight train, wending its way south to Carbondale or Memphis, shooshed in the morning air somewhere, its mournful, moaning horn rising up into the cobalt heavens over the river.

The gate squeaked when Lori pushed it aside. She glanced up at the meager house. No lights. No sign of life. Ichabod's truck was gone. Lori didn't know if grandma still drove or owned a car. But one thing was certain: the place looked as dead as a blown fuse.

The crunch of Lori's footsteps on the gravel drive shattered the stillness.

Behind the house she found rusty farm implements lying half buried in the crabgrass. An old truck chassis sat on blocks near a dilapidated toolshed, looking like a fossilized velociraptor, the sun's early vectors shining through its dew-spangled cobwebs.

Lori wasn't sure if she should break into the place or ring the bell or call the police for backup. She wasn't sure *what* she should do. She only knew she should do *something.* She decided to peer through a window.

The casement next to the rusty screen door rose about five feet off the weed-infested foundation. Lori had to boost herself up on a rust-flecked tractor wheel to see through the dirty glass. She got schmootz and grime on her leggings, her arm, and along the sides of her Doc Martens, but she barely noticed. With the cuff of her blouse sleeve she wiped the grime off the greasy pane, craning her neck to see inside.

What Lori saw got her heart going. In the shadows of the Kettlekamp's kitchen, broken crockery lay strewn across the floor. Words and symbols were scrawled on the cabinet facing in a black, sticky substance that may or may not have been dried blood. The carcass of an animal—probably one of Ichabod's hunting dogs—lay in a pool of blood.

The refrigerator door was open. The tiny bulb inside it illuminated overturned Tupperware containers, broken bottles, and oozing trails of unidentified leftovers. But the worst part, the part that sent a cold current down Lori's spine and got her moving, was the dark object on the fridge's center shelf, wedged between a carton of orange juice and a shriveled cantaloupe.

The severed head of Ichabod Kettlekamp's flea-ridden hunting dog stared blankly out from the cold light of the fridge.

Pure instinct was driving Lori Blaine now. Ichabod Kettlekamp was Lori's responsibility. The back door was unlocked.

Lori went inside.

The place was as silent and still as a mausoleum, the air putrid with mold and metallic grime, like an old penny that had been handled by many dirty fingers. A clock ticked somewhere. The flesh on the back of Lori's neck prickled as she crept across the blood-spackled linoleum floor of the kitchen. The soles of her jackboots snapped and crackled.

Overturned chairs and broken glass littered the Kettlekamp's living room. Pictures of Jesus lay ripped and torn on the floor. Grandma's doilies, soaked in a deep scarlet, lay strewn across the bloodstained braided rugs. Bloody graffiti covered the plaster walls, the same phrase over and over, in different permutations: *Nos Es Legio, Nos Es Legio, NOS es LEGIO, noseslegionoseslegio, noseslegioNOSESLEGIO, noseslegioLEGIOLEGIO-LEGIO L E G I O—*

Lori could see a cluttered hallway to her left. Three open doorways beckoned to her. Although Lori had never set foot in this modest little house, she had a feeling these were the bedrooms.

She took a deep breath, her sweaty grip tightening on the tire iron, and started across the living room toward the hallway.

The first door was a bathroom. A quick glance confirmed nothing out of the ordinary. The farm boy and his grandmother were not exactly diligent housekeepers—the toilet bowl was green with mold, filthy towels were bunched on the floor in one corner, the mirror was cracked down the middle—but no clues jumped out at Lori.

Further down the hallway was a bedroom, its door ajar. Lori peered in and saw the unmade bed, an antique bureau cluttered with pill bottles and ointments, a small space heater by an aluminum foil–covered window. Obviously the room of an elderly person. Again, Lori was expecting to see more carnage—perhaps Grandma trussed up like a turkey in the closet—but nothing unusual caught her eye.

The house *felt* abandoned, tossed away like the shell of an old, brittle cicada. Lori's grip on the tire iron turned oily with sweat as she continued down the hallway. The last door on the left—also ajar—offered Lori an unobstructed view of the pigsty that was Ichabod Kettlekamp's bedroom.

At first glance it looked like a cabin on a ship that had capsized. The unmade bed, its yellowed mattress blotted with stains, sat at an angle against the back wall. Posters for the World Wrestling Federation and Pinkney County tractor pulls hung in shreds, partially torn off the cracked plaster walls. The dresser lay on its side, dirty clothing spilled across the mud-soiled carpet. A lampshade emblazoned with pictures of Pamela Anderson lay overturned on the floor.

Upon closer scrutiny Lori saw the newer stains—still fresh, still gleaming in the dim light—smeared across practically every surface. Blood marks can look almost black in the gloomy light of dawn, like oil or dark chocolate. Lori recognized the magic words from the living room. The "penmanship" had deteriorated here, though, suggesting a chronology of the previous night.

Ichabod had apparently returned from the showdown on the highway full of madness and messages to communicate. He had come in and attacked the living room first. Then he made his way down the hall to this room, where he had commenced with the ransacking of his things. But why? Was he looking for something? And what about Grandma? Had she been home at the time? She must have been home. She was like a hundred years old . . .

Lori was imagining where in God's name Granny Kettlekamp could have been last night when she saw the closet gaping open across the room, its folding door hanging by a thread. But it wasn't the spray of clothing lying at the foot of the closet that grabbed Lori's attention.

What caught Lori's eye was a litter of boxes in the shadows of the closet.

She went over and knelt to take a closer look. At least a dozen or more cartons—each one the size of a brick—lay in disarray on the floor, telling the tale of a hasty rummaging and even hastier departure. Some of the boxes were flattened, some were torn—but all had been emptied in a hurry.

At first, somewhat incongruously, Lori thought they might be for some kind of male toiletry or cologne. The graphic on the side of each box—two big, flaming Day-Glo words with a big X drawn in lightning bolts—proclaimed the contents to be *EXTREME SHOCK*. What the hell *was* Extreme Shock—condoms? Mouth spray? Energy drinks? Lori picked up an empty carton and read the small print.

Gooseflesh rashed her arms and back as she read the smaller line of print beneath the trademark: *Tungsten-NyTrilium Slugs, 12 Gauge, 2¾ in, 25 grain, 2020 fps, Match Grade Anti-terrorist Munitions.* And below this, in attractive script, as though extolling the product's natural organic freshness: *The World's Most Advanced Ammunition.*

Lori sprang to her feet. She dropped the tire iron. The thing made a thud that seemed to rattle the entire house. Lori clenched her fists, turning this discovery over and over in her head.

Like dominoes falling, the circuits of her brain computed what a bunch of empty shotgun shell cartons in Ichabod Kettlekamp's closet actually meant.

The realization glued Lori to the carpet for a moment . . . until she registered the fact that she was hearing a noise—a new noise—coming from somewhere else in the house. Throat drying with panic, she cocked her head and listened closely. It was coming from beneath the floor.

It was coming from the cellar.

Every fiber of her being told her not to go down those rickety wooden steps behind the laundry room. Every cell in her brain told her not to venture down into that profound darkness. But she knew she had no choice. She *had* to investigate the strange, hollow thumping noises that now emanated from the shadows of the Kettlekamp cellar.

It sounded almost like Morse code being tapped out on a hollow log. And as Lori descended each creaking step, her tire iron ridiculously poised for battle—as if a tire iron would suffice in a dustup with the supernatural—the thumping sound became clearer and clearer. It had a random sound to it. And yet . . .

At the bottom of the steps a pull-string dangled from a bare light bulb. Lori yanked it. The dull glow of incandescent light burst open the darkness, and the thumping noise ceased.

The mess screamed at Lori. If Ichabod's bedroom was an overturned boat, the basement was a ship rent apart by a hurricane. Weight-bearing wooden pillars, cracked and chewed up, looked as though someone had taken a chain saw to them. The floor, made of crumbling pavers, gleamed with blood puddles and shrapnel from an exploded oil furnace. Pipes and ancient air ducts hung down from the ceiling joists, torn from their moorings and dripping black fluid.

Lori took a step away from the stairs, her hand welded to the iron cross.

As though peering through the vines of a petrified jungle, Lori gazed through the foliage of dangling pipes and chains and insulated cords. In the dim reach of the single bare bulb, she saw the other side of the cellar—a scattering of paint buckets, rusty cans, bent heating ducts, and broken mason jars drifted against the brick wall—bathed in shadows and a proliferation of blood writing.

Lori saw the source of the thumping noise, and the sight of it jump-started her pulse again.

Legend had it that Davy "Ichabod" Kettlekamp had a *pair* of hunting dogs. Mutts, basically, with a pinch of bloodhound. Mostly what the dogs hunted were scraps from the garbage, but once in a great while, according to rumor, Ichabod would take the dogs coon hunting. Western Illinois had always been lousy with raccoons, and they were easy pickings for a farm kid with a 12-gauge and two hungry hounds. But over the years, the dogs had gotten lazy, and Ichabod had lost interest. The larger of the two mongrels—Lori had no idea what their names were, or even if they *had* names—was at this moment upstairs, staring out at the world from behind a half gallon of sour milk.

The second dog, the smaller of the two, hung by the neck from the cellar ceiling.

The strangest part wasn't the pool of blood, still sticky, that had spread across the scabrous floor under the animal. Nor was it the deep gash visible in the fur of the hound's slender neck, as though the dog had been "bled" for some time in some unspeakable ritual. The strangest part was what Lori saw flopping against the adjacent wooden pillar.

The dog was wagging its tail.

Clearly dead, as dead as a dog can get.

And thumping its tail against the wooden post.

TWENTY-THREE

Had it not been for the video camera, Lori would have gotten out of there right then. The fear had tightened her midsection like a vise, and a sense of horrible black doom had come over her, worse than her hallucination in the lunatic asylum, worse than anything she could remember, as she backed toward the foot of the stairs, her eyes bugging, gaping out from behind strands of black-dyed hair. A dead mutt was bad enough. A dead mutt wagging its tail was too much.

Fortunately, Lori was beginning to understand the intersection between dreams and reality a little better with each cycle in and out of REMspace. If she was as "WILD" as the archangel claimed, she had powers in both realms, which could come in handy if the Bogies were as disconnected from either world as they seemed. It was dawning on Lori that the Bogies were un-manipulatable because they were distinct beings that existed outside any known realm, and they had untold demonic powers. They could alter time and space. They could tap into a person's fears. They could whip up hallucinations. And they could make dead dogs wag their grotesque tails. But Lori had some tricks of her own up her ragged, thrift-shop sleeves. She took a deep breath and clenched her fists, and she felt that faint tremor of electricity travel up her spine.

She was beginning to realize that *time* was her medium, her canvas upon which to paint new scenarios. She breathed deeply and heard the tapping of the tail slow down, retarding with the slowing of elapsed time, until it sounded like a low, dripping faucet. *"You can do what they do,"* Nick had said. Another deep breath and Lori looked around the cellar.

That was when she noticed the tripod in the corner. Had it been anything other than a video camera—one with its battery light still glowing, no less—Lori probably would have ignored it and bailed. But this was important. Somehow Lori knew this deep in her churning gut.

She had to investigate.

Pushing the hanging debris aside, Lori crossed the dark basement, giving the reanimated dog plenty of room, avoiding eye contact with it. Cinders crunched under her boots as she approached the camera—that horrible, slow-motion *thump-thump-thump* the only sound in the stillness of the cellar. Lori kept her gaze glued to the camera.

The thing had a small outboard monitor the size of a cigarette pack. Lori set the tire iron down and stood in front of the camera—it was aimed out at the dog—and she carefully rotated the tiny screen with trembling hands so that she could see what was on it. The screen was black.

Lori found the PLAY button on top of the camera housing and pressed it. Nothing but electronic snow filled the tiny screen.

She found the REVIEW button and held it down. All at once a blurry, out-of-focus image flickered on the miniature monitor: a poorly framed close-up of Ichabod Kettlekamp staring right into the lens— only his chin, his lips, and a portion of the left side of his face visible— jerking and twitching in fast-reverse motion. The farm boy was saying something into the camera.

Lori pressed PLAY.

"Rehhhsssss-PEEEESAY-post-tay," snarled the farm boy, speaking perfect church Latin in that hideous, baritone growl that Lori had first heard in a moonlit cornfield—now slowed down to a belching demon's wheeze.

Lori fumbled for her iPhone—now fully charged—and pressed a sweat-slick finger down on the Siri icon. The auto-translator kicked in with a beep.

On the video, the farm boy's ghastly lips undulated around the words. "*Respice post te . . .* respice post *TE!*"

Lori looked at her phone. The translator wheel was turning, still booting up.

Meanwhile, blackened lips, glistening with drool, repeated the string of words into the camera lens. Sounding like the lowest chamber of a pipe organ from hell, the voice rumbled with hatred and contempt for these seemingly innocuous words: "Rehhhssss-PEEEESAY-post-tay!"

Lori stared at the phone, waiting, then looked back up at the video as the farm boy enunciated each word with devilish relish.

"Respice post TE!"

Lori blinked. Once. Twice. The English translation had appeared on the iPhone's tiny screen. Lori's spine went cold as she read the words.

LOOK BEHIND YOU

All at once she whirled around just in time to see a figure standing in the shadows behind her.

Lori let out a scream as the figure draped in faded denim overalls showed its teeth in either a smile or a grimace—it was hard to tell which—and Lori tried to say the boy's name but couldn't make her voice work.

Ichabod Kettlekamp raised the Remington 12-gauge shotgun at her. Lori jerked backward. Ichabod squeezed the trigger.

Lori saw a huge flash of magnesium-white light that blinded her.

The basement foundation rattled with the extraordinary noise of the blast.

PART THREE

WILD

"Evil comes at leisure like a disease.
Good comes in a hurry like the doctor."
—Gilbert Chesterton

TWENTY-FOUR

Anyone familiar with the concussion of sound waves that accompanies the discharge of a Remington Model 870 tactical shotgun knows how enormously noisy the blast can be—*especially indoors*. Most sportsmen who use the gun legally to kill ducks and geese prefer to wear protective apparatus over their ears. Tonight, however, in the Kettlekamp cellar, the roar of the blast took Lori by surprise. She flinched back so abruptly that she bit down on the back of her tongue hard enough to draw blood. But at the same time, she had managed—somehow—to instinctively grab the hot steel barrel in the moment before the gun was fired. Perhaps it was her burgeoning skill at manipulating time and space, or maybe she was just lucky, but she managed to avert the muzzle just enough—maybe a half a centimeter—to send the roar of the blast off into the wall.

The sabot slug drilled into the insulation, sending a rosette of feathery dust into the air. Lori reared backward, ears ringing. She tripped over her own feet and fell to the moldy cement floor.

In that scintilla of time it took Ichabod Kettlekamp to pump another shell into the chamber, he looked down at Lori with the insect-like fascination of a praying mantis taking measure of its prey, his gangly body towering over her, his wheat-straw hair prickling out like metal shavings under a magnet. He was fully under the influence of a Bogie now, and the parasitic entity showed itself in the egg-white film over his eyes and the black gelatinous rot between his teeth as he grinned lasciviously down at her. He aimed the weapon at her face and hummed an atonal sound in the back of his throat.

"Davy, NO—WAIT!" Lori made her second instinctive move at that point and drove her steel-toed Doc Martens boot up into his groin with the force of a battering ram. The impact practically sent his testicles up into his midsection, and his body convulsed backward, a gasp of air issuing from his lungs. The diversion gave Lori enough time to roll out of the line of fire an instant before he squeezed off another shot.

The blast chewed a divot in the cement and sent particles flying in every direction.

At this point, Lori was gasping for breath, trying to scuttle across the floor toward the stairs. Ichabod tossed the empty weapon aside and lunged toward her. Lori let out another keening yelp as Ichabod pounced on her with the full force of his weight. It felt to Lori as if a steamer trunk had fallen on her—that is, a steamer trunk with noxious breath and vise-grip fingers.

Supernaturally strong and fast clawlike hands dug into her coat.

She tried to roll away again but the unyielding grip had her by the collar and was pushing her back down. Ichabod growled something in Latin and banged her head on the floor. Again and again. Lori saw stars with each impact. The pain thrummed in her skull, threatened to crack her head open, and squeezed all the breath from her throat. She couldn't even let out a scream now. All she could do was gasp every time her head smacked against the hard, cold floor. She gazed up through watery, wooly eyes, and even in her agony noticed several troubling things about Ichabod's face.

The skin around his eyes and mouth had darkened as if charred, and most of the flesh covering his skull had stretched taut like a drumhead, almost as though the bones underneath were rearranging themselves and bloating with the infectious parasite inside him. His nose bore the demonic cleft down its middle now, but the eyes—buried in dark flesh, lupine, phosphorous, a hideous icy white around the yellow iris—were the worst parts.

Those eyes radiated the kind of contempt that Nick had alluded to earlier: *They want to destroy us.* In all their radiant ugliness, those eyes told the story of a hundred thousand years of genetic programming—the compulsion to hate, to dominate, to brutalize—all of it glowing now within the slits of two narrow yellow irises. Here was the dark underbelly of human history. Here was pure evil, incubated in the nightmares of ordinary people, spreading like plague throughout the world. From the banal to the profound . . . from cheating on income tax returns to perpetrating genocide on the world . . . here was the incarnate of darkness.

But Lori had no chance to ponder such things because right then she felt something pressing down on her throat, a tremendous pressure on her trachea. She tried to speak, tried to plead with him, tried to find the real Davy Kettlekamp behind those wolf-like yellow eyes, but she could not utter a sound, could not breathe. The farm boy's hands were tightening around her throat with the force of a boa constrictor.

"N-nn-o . . . NN-NO—NNNGGNH!"

Her choked gasp came out on a breathless grunt as she stared into those incandescent eyes. The two faces were now inches apart, but Lori could barely see—a red shade drawing down across her vision—as the hulking farm boy strangled her. She could feel her flesh going livid as the blood flow and air were completely cut off.

Manual strangulation can be fatal if not interrupted within twenty to thirty seconds. The first sign of trouble is an increasingly hypoxic state of the brain, which commonly results in dizziness followed by hallucination. Lori's vision blurred as her body convulsed in the farm boy's unrelenting grip, the dizziness coursing through her. The next sign of grave physical danger is a disruption of blood flow. Ichabod's huge, calloused hands were compressing Lori's carotid artery so severely that she felt the cold hypovolemic shock washing over her as she saw snowflakes begin to float down through the dank atmosphere of the cellar.

But even amidst the terror of strangulation, Lori knew something that Davy "Ichabod" Kettlekamp did not know. In fact, she knew something that the entity inside him did not even know, despite the fact that such beings are often thought to be prescient and telepathic. In this case, only Lori knew that she had a trump card in the form of a cold, hard, plastic object in her right hand.

Something changed suddenly on Ichabod's face. His simian features tightened, his chromium-yellow eyes widening, a tendril of drool looping out of his snarling mouth. Lori felt the blessed loosening of his massive fingers on her throat, and she gasped and coughed and her lungs heaved for air, replenishing her oxygen-starved brain. It felt as though she had been drowning and finally surfaced, sucking lungs full of air. In her right hand, the hypodermic needle remained buried to the hilt in the thick muscle of Ichabod's thigh.

The farm boy blinked and teetered as though suddenly inebriated.

Lori managed to roll away, still gasping and coughing and struggling to see through her traumatized, watery eyes. She had released her grip on the needle, and now, gasping for breath, ten feet away, she threw a glance back at the farm boy, who had fallen to his hands and knees as though exhausted at the end of a marathon race. From the look on his face, the thing inside him was just now realizing what had happened. The hypodermic still stuck out of his jeans just above his hip bone. From the way he was pitching and yawing back and forth, Lori realized that she must have gotten lucky and the needle must have hit his femoral artery.

Ichabod Kettlekamp collapsed to the cement floor of the basement, out cold, already starting to snore. The ketamine that Lori had purchased from the skuzzy drug dealer earlier that morning came with its own injector. Commonly known as horse tranquilizer, Lori had learned on the Internet that ketamine was one of the only controlled substances that she could get her hands on that would put a person to sleep within a minute or so, even faster if you hit a vein or an artery.

Now Lori had one last dose to administer before it was too late.

She crawled across the cold, paint-chipped cement to the point at which the farm boy now lie slumbering noisily. Working quickly—she figured she only had a minute or so before Ichabod reached the REM state—she pulled the needle clear of his leg and saw that a small amount of colorless, odorless fluid remained in the receptacle.

Lying down next to the overgrown farm boy, she plunged the needle into her own arm, hitting a vein and sending liquid sleep into her marrow.

TWENTY-FIVE

Less than a minute later, the basement floor softened, and then liquefied, as though made of candle wax, turning into a gelatinous substance through which Lori and Ichabod began to slowly sink.

The sound faded away as they sank deeper and deeper into the darkness below the basement, and Lori felt as though they were both settling into the earth like rain. Eventually every last shred of sensory information was muffled and then obliterated by the primordial darkness. It was the dark found only inside a cave under the sea in the deepest part of the Mariana trench. It was the black void at the beginning of the universe—the darkness of the singularity—and it engulfed the two of them like a womb.

At some point—it was impossible to know when or how or why—Lori felt as though she had landed on a spongy, granular surface. As if a rheostat dial had suddenly begun to turn, her closed eyelids began to flicker with an orange glow—faintly at first, but getting brighter and brighter with each passing second—until she realized that firelight was burning somewhere nearby.

She flicked her eyes open. It took her a moment to focus on her surroundings. Everything around her was a blur—huge stationary shapes that she couldn't begin to identify—and she was still lying on her back as she had when she fell asleep in the Kettlekamp basement only moments ago—or was it hours ago? Or perhaps days ago? She was still groggy and bleary and not even certain about where she was or how the hell she had gotten there. What happened to Ichabod? How did he simply vanish into thin air?

At first all she could register was the fact that she lay alone, outdoors, smack dab in the middle of a wasted landscape of volcanic rock formations reaching as far as the eye could see. She gazed up at the sky. It was neither day nor night. The sky had that piss-yellow cast that it gets before a storm. Very dark, but again, not completely night. It was the color of a bad liver. The sickest kind of yellowish-gray one could imagine, and gilded with very faint veins of lightning that pulsed and stitched through the atmosphere. Thirteen suns blazed wanly down on the blasted terrain, and soon other things were making themselves known to Lori.

From somewhere in the gloomy middle distance came the crackle of voices, reminding Lori of police radios or the chatter of airline pilots. The sound caused her to widen her eyes and blink some more, as her pupils began to dilate and adjust. Was she dead? Was she hallucinating? Was any of this real? She could barely draw a breath. She swallowed the coppery taste of panic.

She knew in the back of her mind where she was. She was not religious, but if there was a real hell, this was it, this was definitely it, terrible in its dark, industrial vividness. The air was like the inside of a coal furnace, thick with smoke and grainy with acrid particulate matter. The more she looked at it, the more she realized the topography of this place resembled a barren, war-torn desert littered with garbage that stretched beyond the desolate horizon, its ground a dirty shade of gray, almost mildew colored, stirring and shifting in the intermittent whirls of wind. Primitive roads, fossilized into the ground like scars, scattered with detritus, crisscrossed the land. Gargantuan heaps—which Lori first misidentified as trash—lay on the edges of embankments.

On the distant horizon rose great and ugly towers belching black smoke and flame. Some of them sprouted girders that dipped and bobbed with the irregular pulse of oil derricks. Innumerable lights shone in the hills, perhaps the infrastructure of ramshackle cities, some of the lights arcing with the brilliance of spot welders. The silhouettes of immense wheels and millstones and generators turned languidly against the putrid sky.

Pupils fully dilated now, adjusting to the stagnant dusk, Lori managed to rise to her feet and suddenly realized something . . . something which sent feverish chills down the length of her body. The dark, ragged objects, which she first misidentified as garbage and wreckage—on the ground, in the ditches, and along the crests of hills—were *human souls*. Passing in and out of shadows, as indistinct as ghosts, they were tattered spirits trudging aimlessly, talking to themselves, answering some inaudible inquisitor.

Closer observation revealed tangles of writhing bodies in ditches and moraines, some of them clawing at each other, biting each other, chewing on each other's flesh with the feral hunger of rabid dogs. They had an unreal quality, like half-formed figures in a faded photograph. The light passed through some of the bodies with the watery, ethereal gleam of daylight shining through gauzy, threadbare curtains.

All at once Lori realized that *this* was where the Bogies lurked when not possessing humans—a place as horrible as hell and as palpable as the glassy volcanic rock crackling beneath Lori's feet as she ventured forward a step at a time. And these were the poor dreamers who had been possessed like puppets, earmarked to wreak havoc on the waking world, an army of possessed souls.

As she walked, Lori studied the multitude of lost souls—their number impossible to calculate—all milling about this bleak industrial wilderness in varying stages of malnourishment, deterioration, and madness. Ichabod was out there somewhere, among their number, wandering aimlessly, just waiting to unleash evil upon the real world, helpless to resist the parasitic entity smoldering within him.

Light flickered suddenly from a geyser of yellow flames, spewing sparks and smoke up on a ridge nearby. Other vent holes pocked the distant berms and shadowy crevasses. Another one shot up into the air with an oily gasp twenty-five feet away from Lori, a fountain of flame, as if the very ground was belching fire. The dazzling light made Lori start. She took a deep breath.

"Get your shit together," she admonished herself, the sound of her hoarse, weak voice like a bee buzzing in her ear.

As if in answer to this sudden verbal scolding, a noise echoed from far away—a jet-engine sound, which rose and swelled—raising hackles on her neck as she gazed off in the direction of the commotion.

In the distance, maybe half a mile away, a brilliant, luminous, crackling, superheated shaft of light, as wide as a river, was coming her way.

It was so mesmerizing, so ethereal, so otherworldly, that Lori could not help but stare—despite the pangs of fear suddenly bolting down her solar plexus. Paralyzed with awe and confusion, horror-struck in her raw, panicky state, she allowed the flaming thing to close the distance. A hundred yards away, the wave of fire—which seemed to have a mind of its own—changed its course slightly. It charged like a rolling supernova toward Lori and began to transform. Lori began stupidly backing away.

The ribbon of fire began to fork at one end, opening with the suddenness of a cobra's mouth, parting and vomiting out a passenger. Then another. And another. Until a battalion of enormous, arachnid-like creatures the color of black mold came charging toward Lori. She instantly recognized the immense size of the things, the oblong, hairless skulls, the cloven noses sniffing at the air like giant boars nuzzling truffles in a vast dung heap. If the centaur of Greek myth were allowed to age and dissipate and die and rot and then bloat with the noxious gases of the grave, one might approach the gruesome sight of these things.

Bogies.

The worst parts were the *eyes*. The magnesium-yellow eyes. Like twin pilot lights coming at her, they grew more and more prominent and luminous with each enormous stride of the creatures' simian haunches. And the closer they loomed, the colder the terror coursed through Lori's veins, until she finally found her legs and turned and began to flee.

She ran and ran across the leprous sands, heading toward the distant hillocks of volcanic ash, the drumming of hoof-like feet on the ground behind her closing in. She could almost feel the slimy, baleful gazes of the demons on the back of her neck like a clammy draft encircling her as she fled.

In the distance she saw a familiar figure running up ahead of her, running in the same direction, intermittently glancing over his shoulder at the demons. Dressed in faded overalls, sweat-damp chambray shirt, and clodhopper boots, he looked like what he was: *an overgrown child running from a monster.* From the farm boy's awkward strides and gasping breaths, it was clear to Lori—even amidst her terror—that Ichabod Kettlekamp was no longer in the thrall of a demonic spirit. He was as petrified as she, and he was helpless in this netherworld—powerless in the face of the Bogies' black magic.

Up ahead, Ichabod tripped and fell, going face-first into the grainy lunar surface.

Trembling with fear, sobbing uncontrollably, he began to crawl. He looked like a massive baby, as though he had wet himself with fear, his face covered with snot. As Lori approached, something strange flowed through her with the suddenness of a coronary attack. Her heart tightened in her chest as she watched the enormous, sun-weathered farm boy crawling frantically through the sand, trying in vain to flee the oncoming brigade of evil. Something very close to sympathy—maybe even *empathy*—coursed through Lori as she reached the farm boy. David "Ichabod" Kettlekamp had a lot more in common with Lori Blaine than most kids—social outsider status, loneliness, the product of a broken home—and she felt somehow responsible for him right now.

"Davy?" She nearly stumbled to the ground herself as she slammed on her brakes and knelt down by the sniveling shell of a human being in overalls. She didn't care that the demons were closing in, their evil stench like a furnace on the back of her neck. "Davy, don't worry . . . I'm with you now . . . I won't let them harm you."

The farm boy managed to look up at her through teary, hound-dog eyes. "Blaine?"

She nodded. "That's right, Davy . . . it's Lori Blaine. I'm with you now."

He cocked his head at her. "What the hell are you doing in my dream?"

Something clicked in Lori's head suddenly—snapping down with the abruptness of a guillotine switch—and she straightened bolt upright.

The earth around them—in fact, the entire landscape—began to change.

Lori sucked in a breath.

The air went still.

TWENTY-SIX

It began—as seismic shifts often do—with the faintest tremor. Lori looked down. Three or four feet from where Ichabod lay in the granules of ashy gray earth, an invisible finger traced a simple declarative sentence, as a child might scrawl a message on a deserted, uncharted beach, and Lori stared and stared and stared at it, absorbing it on a cellular level—

THIS IS A DREAM

—and at first she didn't notice the entire battalion of Bogies skidding to a halt behind her, almost like a pack of attack dogs suddenly sensing danger, perhaps smelling a larger, more deadly predator in their midst. Nor did Lori notice the way the very atmosphere around her seemed to prickle and crackle with static electricity, the air pressure suddenly spiking as though the entire world had begun to spin on a centrifuge. Nor did she notice Ichabod's shocked expression as he scanned the territory around them.

All that Lori could compute at that moment were the myriad signs popping into view all around her. THIS IS A DREAM proclaimed a road sign sprouting out of the earth like a time-lapse film of a seedling growing. THIS IS A DREAM declared a row of neon letters materializing on the side of a tree. THIS IS A DREAM announced a billboard on the side of a bridge trestle in the distance.

Over and over again the news flickered at her from unlikely places.

She heard a noise in the sky and looked up and saw a small propeller-driven biplane scuttling across the jaundiced clouds, tugging an enormous advertising banner imprinted with the words *THIS IS A DREAM*. She heard a papery rustling noise and looked down and saw a stray page of newsprint all wadded and torn, tossing like a tumbleweed across her feet, until it landed flat against a nearby fence post, its facing page emblazoned with the headline in 72-point font:

EXTRA! EXTRA! READ ALL ABOUT IT!

THIS IS A DREAM!

Something broke loose inside Lori as she slowly turned and saw sign after sign popping into existence out of thin air—in blinking lights, in Day-Glo colors, in graffiti, in cursive, in bold whitewash paint strokes across rustic surfaces, in enormous carved stone-block letters like great monoliths that had existed for centuries across the horizon—informing her that she was indeed having a dream.

Right then she whirled and saw the contingent of Bogies like a firing squad, standing in a semicircle fifty feet away, frozen in collective shock, staring at her with awe in their serpentine yellow eyes.

"Leave him alone," she said softly to the creatures, not even sure they could understand English. "Stop tormenting him and leave him alone!"

One of the Bogies lifted its oblong face to the gray heavens and let out a caterwaul of such piercing sharpness that the scream shattered glass bulbs in distant streetlights in tiny sequential explosions that seemed to go on for an eternity. The other demons started inching toward Lori, grimacing, menacingly showing their piranha-like fangs, which lined their moldering black gums. The chorus of growls was like a great rusty turbine starting up.

Standing her ground, her hands on her hips now, Lori could feel her blood almost fizzing in her veins with galvanic, supercharged energy. She decided to speak in Latin, because she was a lucid dreamer and this was a dream and she could do anything she damn well pleased now.

"*Dimittite eum!*" she barked at them, ordering them out of Ichabod's dreams. Then she told them to get out of every dream of every human. "*Dimittite TOTUM!*"

The air buzzed and crackled with electricity as the Bogies gaped at her.

Lori smiled coldly. Then she added one last line in old-school church Latin so she was sure they understood. "Veni, et educ me si globi!"

Come and get me if you got the stones.

They came at her all at once from all directions, like a riptide of black storm waters engulfing a shore. Some of them unhinged their enormous jaws, showing their jagged razor-sharp teeth as they went for her jugular. Others reached for her with impossibly long arms, clawing at the air with ivory talons as sharp as daggers. Still others lashed out with long, slimy, forked tongues shooting out of their gaping mouths and flagging at her as though poised to sting or poison or perform some other hideous obscenity on her. Lori did not back down, did not budge from her position in front of Ichabod, who still lay on the ground behind her, huddling in terror and shielding his face. In that incredible nanosecond before the first Bogie struck, Lori blinked.

Over the space of a synapse sparking, she willed changes in the fabric of time and space.

The earth beneath her positively quaked with the sudden shift in the dream universe. She let out a battle cry that vibrated the air and sounded like a vast knife-edge scraping the sky. At the same time, she opened her arms as though welcoming the demons into a maternal embrace. Her flesh turned to steel, her tendons elongating magically, her arms becoming twin sabers so long and sharp they looked as though they could cut through cities.

The first Bogie to reach her tried to sink its teeth into her jugular but instead lost its left arm and shoulder in one clean slice. Blood the color and consistency of motor oil spurted from the demon's wound. Lori spun gracefully away from it, her magical bladed arms gleaming in the yellow light as more of the monsters pounced.

Her left arm decapitated another demon with the ease of cutting through smoke, the monstrous head jettisoning up into the air with a frozen look of shock on its lupine features, a contrail of black blood-mist flagging after it. Another spin, and her right arm went right through the midsection of a third Bogie, causing it to convulse in paroxysms of pain and surprise, tossing its oblong, hairless skull backward as a bucking horse might try to escape the bit. Lori let out another yawp as she spun away.

She had only moments before another pair of Bogies reached her, each one coming from an opposite direction, so she willed time to slow down. The two demons suddenly decelerated as if a cosmic projector had shifted into slow motion, their baleful, glaring, yellow eyes only ten feet away from Lori, but filled with helpless anger, watering with poisonous rage, their movements retarding into suspended animation. Lori turned away from them.

At first she figured she would need a flat surface upon which to project the secret weapon. She saw a gnarled, bare tree about fifty yards away but it seemed too narrow. She saw a rocky precipice about a hundred yards down a winding path but it seemed too distant.

It would be too difficult to get Ichabod in his current condition all the way over there in time.

Throughout this strange lull in the action, as the demons closed in on Lori in syrupy, super-slow motion, Ichabod huddled on the ground behind the girl, transfixed by it all, watching with eyes nearly as wide as saucers. He could not believe what he was seeing—even in a dream—this Amazon with the dreadlocks, this antisocial chick from his English class, now wiping the floor with these beasts.

At that moment, Lori latched onto a location at which to conjure the secret weapon.

It was a good thing she finally thought of it then, too, because the slow-motion demons had arrived. She could smell them closing in, feel the putrid, greasy aura of their evil filling the air. She spun around just in time to see their horrible piranha teeth and luminous eyes—now only inches away from her.

Acting purely on instinct, she ducked down into a crouch as the Bogies soared at her. She slammed her eyes shut once, twice, and then willed the passage of time to speed back up, removing the slow-motion spell.

The Bogies collided with each other, the impact knocking each of them momentarily insensate. Stringers of black drool flung off in all directions as the massive creatures collapsed to the ground with a pair of thuds.

Lori rose back to her full height and was about to conjure the secret countermeasure when she heard a thrumming of wings behind her, and a roar of watery white noise, and she spun around in time to see Ichabod screaming.

The assault was so sudden and violent that Lori's brain seized up for a moment.

They were carrying him away. They were scooping Ichabod up and he was screaming, and they were carrying him away to parts unknown.

That was when Lori started screaming herself.

TWENTY-SEVEN

In the 1950s, a Dutch neuroscientist named Heinrich Slauz published a series of papers on dream mechanics. In addition to his findings that the neurological makeup of a dream is almost identical to the brain's state during wakeful daydreaming, he also discovered that neurotransmitters work overtime during a particularly vivid nightmare, to the point of being exactly the same—biologically speaking—as real-life experience. In his paper titled "The Black Balloon: A Neural Substrate for Cognitive Experience During the Common Nightmare," he hypothesized that the intermittent bursts of neuropeptides during a bad dream can explain why certain symbols or situations—when taken at face value by a non-dreamer—might seem trivial, random, or banal at first glance. But for the dreamer, these symbols have inordinate power and emotional context and . . . well . . . *creepiness*.

At the moment, in fact, Lori Blaine was discovering this the hard way as she dropped to her knees and reverted back to her early childhood and shrieked uncontrollably as the impossibly vast flock of winged creatures swarmed down on the writhing body of Ichabod Kettlekamp. With their tufted, scab-colored fur, pointed ears, pug-dog faces, and enormous, translucent leathery wings flapping like dervishes, the flying monkeys lifted the gangly farm boy by the nape of his neck. Ichabod was keening and flailing as though caught in a threshing machine. The simian creatures made a collective noise that brought to mind a hive of wasps as they lifted the boy by the shoulder straps of his tattered overalls and began hauling him up into the hellish amber sky.

Lori rose to her feet and gawked at the heavens. She felt her guts tighten and go cold with terror as she watched the perfect reenact-ment of the flying monkey attack from *The Wizard of Oz*, a scene that had played over and over in her mind's eye as a child after her mother had shown her the movie on an MGM Sixtieth Anniver-sary DVD, an iconic image that had haunted her dreams from that moment on.

To this day, she had trouble with bats because of those damn flying monkeys—a phobia as real as a case of hives or shingles.

Now the demons were hooking into the main circuit of Lori's fears.

"C'mon, focus!" she told herself as she clenched her fists and watched the sky fill with dark, hirsute, winged vermin carrying Ichabod away. She willed herself to grow wings, and the flesh between her shoulder blades tingled and burned for a moment, and then the cold sensation of vestigial flesh sprouting from her back sent chills down her spine. In her peripheral vision she saw her great angelic wings unfolding, casting shadows on the wasted earth around her. "C'mon, c'mon . . . they're getting away . . . COME ON!!"

She felt the wind of her flapping wings levitating her off the ground.

The sensation was incredible—almost like being attached to invisible bungee cords—as she launched herself into flight. It took a little effort but she got the hang of it quickly, madly flapping her wings as she steered a course toward those ink blots on the horizon, and that single flailing human in their grasp.

The fetid wind coursed around her like a clammy blanket as she soared after them, and she smelled brimstone and char in her nostrils. Her eyes burned. The ground below—at least a thousand feet down—rushed beneath her like black river rapids. But she kept her gaze latched onto the swarm of flying monkeys in the distance, and she kept girding herself by repeating the mantra, "One way out . . . just one way out . . . if you can just make it before—"

In the distance, the vast flock of monsters was soaring over a scorched mountain range with Ichabod writhing in their grasp like a worm on a hook. Below them, the cathedral of jagged, black summits formed a crude demarcation line between two separate territories of the dreamscape. Beyond the craggy peaks stretched a primordial land of active volcanoes, lava flows, steam vents, and noxious clouds of low-lying methane that flickered and streaked with static electricity. This was Hell's armpit, and for some reason, Lori realized right that instant that the monkeys were taking Ichabod into the territory of the Queen.

It was a certainty found only in dreams: Lori knew—she just innately *knew*—that this was the most dangerous part of the Bogies' homeland. It was as if the fact were lodged in her back-brain and had been lodged there all her life—that *this* was the realm of the Dark Queen—the closest thing to a feminine version of Satan the universe had yet created. Or perhaps it *was* the Devil—maybe the Devil was a woman—Lori wasn't sure. All she knew for sure was that she now found herself careening down through toxic clouds toward rivers of fire burning like cancerous arteries, black cliffs moldering with ancient decay, and an infinite number of craters and holes pocking the vast and leprous volcanic terrain.

A half a mile ahead of her, the black flock suddenly made a sharp turn.

Lori flew after the careering swarm as they lurched into a dive—thousands of them—diving in formation—plummeting down through the poisonous clouds—leading Lori down, down, down, down, down—and Lori felt the cold, fetid air rushing against her skin as she plummeted—and she blinked the tears from her eyes as she plunged faster and faster—and she saw the monkeys pouring into a gargantuan hole in the ground—a mine shaft—a tunnel—a black hole—a vortex—and Lori shrieked as she dove toward the gaping maw.

For a moment—in dreamtime it could have been a single millisecond or it could have been eight hours—Lori felt herself plummeting down through the black void of a narrow shaft.

Completely blind in the dark, she felt the gravitational forces threatening to rip her guts out through the soles of her feet as she dropped at a rate of descent comparable to a space capsule reentering the earth's atmosphere. The sound of her own scream formed an icy cocoon around her, echoing down the shaft as though greasing her descent, until she dropped out the bottom.

She splashed down in a black, oily, underground reservoir, landing with such force that her back molars cracked and her internal organs slammed against the carapace of her bones as she plunged momentarily into the silent cold blackness under the surface.

In a dream, especially one that involves falling, one rarely lands. In a falling dream, one usually wakes up right before landing. In fact, according to folklore, if one lands in a falling dream, one dies in real life. Lori was about to learn how the Bogies' dreamscape adhered to its own set of rules. She struggled back to the surface and burst her head out of the mire, gasping for breath.

That was when she saw Ichabod lying on the charred stone banks of the reservoir maybe ten or fifteen feet away. He looked as though he were having seizures or convulsions of some kind, lying in a fetal position in the acrid fog, jerking with tics and grunts and eyes slamming open and shut, open and shut, open and shut.

"Davy! It's okay! I'm here!"

Lori climbed out of the muck and rose to her full height on the stone floor of the mysterious cavern. She could feel an earthquake coming. It vibrated the floor beneath her, traveling up her tendons, growing more and more intense. The air hummed like a tuning fork. She took a step toward Ichabod and the farm boy suddenly rose up on gangly legs and clodhopper boots, snarling and spitting at her in Latin. The demon was inside him again.

Suddenly paralyzed with fear, blinking fitfully, Lori froze in her tracks when she saw the cables. Thin, metal guide wires were attached to Davy Kettlekamp's shoulders, to his arms and knees and feet. Puppet strings glistening dimly in the gloom, the lines ran upward into the shadows of the cavern ceiling, their ends looping around a primitive wooden crossbar about the size of a chandelier.

Lori gazed up and felt her blood turn to ice water in her veins.

The Dark Queen, a humanoid thing at least fifteen feet tall, her face made of smoke, jerked the crossbar with a flourish and grinned down at Lori—it was the grin of a Venus flytrap opening, the smile of a corpse with clown white on its face—and in the midst of all of it, in the waves of horrible black dread radiating off that smile, Lori Blaine did not back down, did not shrink away.

Standing face-to-face with the source of so much misery and mayhem, Lori realized that she had one last card to play, just one . . .

One way out . . .

TWENTY-EIGHT

At that moment, two things happened almost simultaneously. In fact, if one could measure such things with any degree of accuracy, one would find that the two equal and opposite actions that occurred next transpired within one millionth of a nanosecond of each other. Far more important, however, was the fact that one of the two things that followed—according to precise measurement—occurred one scintilla of an instant *sooner* than the other, which in dreamtime provided enough of a margin to trump the other event.

Lori sprang into action first—although to the casual dreamer it would have appeared as though she leapt at the same moment the Queen lashed out. In Lori's mind a switch was flipped as she lunged toward Ichabod, slowing down dreamtime to its molasses-slow essence, her arms reaching out and grabbing the farm boy by the collar.

One millionth of a nanosecond later, the Queen lunged forward on her gigantic haunches, her glistening, poisonous tongue shooting out of her jagged sharklike mouth toward Lori. The tip of the serpentine tongue drilled through the air with alarming precision, heading straight for Lori's neck, taking on a quality—in the extreme slow motion of the dream—of a needle pushing through a bloodstream, all of this in time-lapse slowness, the bifurcated tip of the tongue penetrating the space so forcefully it appeared to send ripples of transparent currents in its wake

But while all this was going on, of course, Lori had already darted out of the line of fire, grabbed Ichabod by the nape of his overalls, and was yanking the enormous farm boy toward the far wall of the cavern.

Unbeknown to either Ichabod or the Queen, Lori had made an important decision only moments earlier. Out of the corner of her eye, she had glimpsed the smooth, onyx, glassy surface of the wall to her right, and she realized all at once that the uniform, polished stone was perfect—an ideal canvas upon which to project her secret weapon—and now she executed this Hail Mary move at the last possible instant.

Behind her, the Queen was rearing backward in shock, sucking her tongue back in her maw, the slow-motion spell faltering slightly, the elapsing of time beginning to return to normal. At that moment, the expression on the Queen's cadaverous face pinched and contracted into an utterly ghastly grimace of pure, unadulterated evil and hatred, the yellow-eyed gaze turning to a spot welder, fixing its flame on Lori, the Queen's black lips peeling away from countless crooked, exposed fangs.

The Queen then executed one last attempt to destroy this carpet-bagger, this intruder, this interloper.

Across the stone chamber, Lori had already begun the process of escape when she felt the sharp, invisible hooks of the guide wires striking her in the back, the barbed ends sinking into her flesh. In less than two seconds, the Queen would reel her in like a fish on a hook, possess her, turn her into a puppet, vanquish her to wander this hellscape for eternity, but Lori would not allow that to happen. She had one last move to make, one last chance . . . *one way out.*

Lori felt the slimy, acrid, prickly heat of the Queen's breath on the back of her neck as she focused her attention on the wall, and the secret weapon, and the last thing she must now conjure. *You have the power to change things,* her shrink had told her so many months ago. *You can do what they do,* Nick had urged her, and now, over the space of a single fraction of an instant, a soupçon of time, she made her brain imagine the object that had brought her to this place, the thing that had beckoned to her from the very beginning, the object of her desire, the key to everything.

It started as a single crack in the wall, as though it were a glacial spit of land cleaving down the middle, and in no time at all the crack was forming a rectangle as though some unseen scrivener were etching a beveled outline of a ten-foot-high box in the obsidian stone wall.

The Queen began to pull Lori backward, tugging every fiber of Lori's being back toward the darkness, toward oblivion, toward endless pain and misery, as thin razors of light began to seep out of the cracks in the wall. The ghost of a knob materialized about waist high, the colors now filling in as though an invisible paintbrush were shellacking the thing with deep shades of brown and indigo and gray. Panels formed next, rotting wooden panels with holes and scars, a shriveled corsage of funeral flowers positioned near the crown, at the top, under the lintel.

That Which I Should Have Done I Did Not Do (The Door) had been the official title of the Ivan Albright painting Lori had first seen at the Art Institute of Chicago so many years ago—a locked door, painted in deep blues, gangrenous greens, and moldy browns, at least ten feet high, with long, blackened, charred panels like burnt strips of skin, and an ancient brass knob that was old and tarnished and as dull as a rotten tooth. And there, in the dream, right now, *right this instant*, was the *keyhole*, through which that dim strand of light spilled out at her like a finger.

The Queen let out a skull-fracturing shriek that shook the cavern floor as Lori quickly opened the door, pushed Ichabod through the gap, lunged through the opening herself, and slammed the door behind them.

* * *

"Good Lord, it's about time," a voice rang out of the shadows to Lori's immediate left. Lori had tripped over her own feet crossing over the threshold from the Bogie's dreamspace to the narrow catacombs of BACKworld. Now she rose to her knees and gazed around the rusty girders and reinforced tunnels of the In-Between.

Next to her, Ichabod Kettlekamp lay writhing on the floor, his dirty fingers curled into claws and his lanky body tensing and convulsing as though it were being electrocuted. His face was a mask of agony.

The old woman rolled out of the shadows in her wheelchair with her headset on. "I thought you were gonna keep us waiting until next year's hemlines came out!"

"Go easy on the girl, Mrs. W," another voice piped in from Lori's immediate right. The Archangel Michael stepped into view with his doctor's bag in one hand and his chain-mail exorcism net draped over a shoulder. He looked like some kind of mythical shaman or seventeenth-century priest preparing to swing some badass incense. He dropped the net over Ichabod. "He's fighting the residue left inside of him," the angel commented, kneeling down by the squirming farm boy. "You did well, Lori," Michael said, turning to her, proffering the warmest, sweetest smile Lori had ever seen, a smile for wounded soldiers and lost children. "We'll take it from here." Then, almost as an afterthought, the angel said, "Nick!"

From the far reaches of the corridor walked the young man with the bed-head hair and the Johnny Depp smirk. He carried the golden cattle prod in one hand. "I think there's a future for you in this crazy racket," he joked as he came over to Lori and knelt down beside her. "I'd be lying if I said I wasn't totally proud of you."

She smiled back at him, and then laid her head on his shoulder. "God, I'm tired."

"Understandable." He kissed her hair and stroked her matted dreadlocks that lay against her sweaty neck. "We have to get you back. You're bumping up against a time crunch." He armed the prod and looked at her. "Then you can have a nice long nap—off the clock."

She looked up at him. "Thank you."

"For what?"

"I don't know." She shrugged. "For being so cute."

He grinned. "Anytime."

"I'm ready."

She closed her eyes as he touched the tip of the prod to her brow.

TWENTY-NINE

When she opened her eyes she was back on the squalid cement floor of the Kettlekamp cellar, and someone was aiming a penlight in her eyes.

"Yep, she's coming around." The voice was male, a slight Southern accent, hovering over her numb body. Lori could feel a second pair of hands cradling the back of her head but her eyesight was still too bleary to identify anybody. The crackle of a radio voice sent chills down her flesh as she blinked and focused.

"Thank God, thank God," the female voice said on the other side of her. Lori recognized her mother's voice and blinked and blinked until she could make out Allison Blaine's drawn, wrinkled eyes, a down coat draped over the woman's shoulders. "I don't know how many more of these episodes I can take."

"M-mom, I . . . I . . . I think everything's gonna be fine." Lori's voice seemed to startle everybody in the room—a crowd which included a paramedic (the one with the Southern drawl), a female forensic lab worker in a white coat, two uniformed police officers, and a pair of plain-clothes detectives—all of whom snapped to attention at the sound of her groggy, sleep-caked voice. Ichabod Kettlekamp lay next to her, snoring fitfully, face flicking with the undertow of REM sleep. Something about the way the lab assistant went back to her dusting of the bullet holes in the wall bothered Lori. How long had she been out this time?

"Let's get you checked out, sweetie." Allison Blaine exchanged glances with the cops and the medical personnel. On cue, the paramedic, a middle-aged black man who looked like a soap opera actor, pulled a stethoscope and started checking Lori's vitals.

There was one other person in the room whom Lori hadn't noticed at first. He came reluctantly forward now from a shadowy corner, and as he skulked into view, Lori's vision sharpened until she was able to identify the young man's shopworn hoodie, long dyed hair, and elfin manner. Hugo Stipple looked rattled as he forced a smile. "You freaked us all out, dude . . . once again."

Allison spoke up. "If it weren't for Hugo, sweetie, we never would have found you."

"Oh yeah?" Lori shared a loaded glance with Hugo. "I don't remember telling him anything about—"

"He was the one who thought of checking the Kettlekamp place. I thought he was crazy."

The paramedic looked up with a strange expression on his face.

Allison looked at the medic. "What's the matter?"

The medic sighed. "No matter how hard I try, I can't find anything wrong with her. She's dehydrated, and maybe needs a little IV glucose to stabilize her, but other than a few bumps and bruises she's totally fine."

"Listen to the man, Mom," Lori joked as she sat up against the bare insulation of the wall. "And stop trying to find something wrong with me."

Allison stared at the medic. "Two weeks she's missing, and that's all you can say?"

Lori looked at her mom. "Two weeks?" She took a deep breath, and then let out a long sigh and brushed a strand of dreadlock from her eye. "At least *this* time I don't have a year's worth of homework to make up."

Nobody in that reeking cellar found Lori's joke the least bit amusing.

Except Lori.

She laughed and laughed at her own joke, after a while not even certain what exactly she was laughing at.

On the long drive home—Allison had been forced to rent a car during Lori's disappearance—the two Blaine girls talked of the past, present, and future. They spoke of dreams and good and evil and how long a person can go without food and water. They stopped at a burger joint to have lunch—a meal which Lori consumed with ravenous hunger, despite the medic's cautions to take food and water gradually. They took the scenic route back to Monterey Court, enjoying the lovely Indian summer that had been bestowed on northern Illinois that week. Lori felt an unexpected calm. There would be many meetings with the police in her future—most cops want to know why a person breaks into another person's home, causes gunplay in the basement, and then drugs both intruder and intrudee—but for now, everything seemed right with the world.

By the time they turned the corner at the top of their street, Lori was talking about maybe taking a little nap. Despite the fact that she had been in a drug-induced coma for two weeks, she really could use some shut-eye. Allison marveled at this as she turned into their drive, pulled the rental to a stop, put it in park, and let it idle for a moment as she stared at her daughter. "I would think that sleep would be the last thing you'd want to do."

Lori shrugged. "You would think so . . . but there it is."

"Whatever you say, honey," Allison said, turning the car off with a sigh. Then she looked at Lori with a strange expression on her face, the faintest hint of a smile, colored by the sadness of parental regret glistening in her eyes. "You know something, though . . . I don't think I've ever seen you like this."

"Like what?"

"Almost like . . . for the first time in your life you're looking forward to going to sleep."

Lori thought about that for a long moment, the late afternoon sun warming the air, dappling the front of the house with filigrees of light filtering through the leaves. "Yeah," she said with a nod, getting out of the car, stretching her weary bones. "You could say that . . . yeah."

They went inside.

Lori didn't even bother changing into her sleepwear. She sprawled onto her bed in her waistcoat and leggings, and was practically sound asleep before her head hit the pillow . . .

. . . unafraid for the first time in as long as she could remember of what she would find in her dreams.

EPILOGUE

THE MYSTERIOUS OTHER MIKE

"Yesterday is but today's memory, tomorrow is but today's dream."
—Kahlil Gibran

On the other side of the door Lori hurried through the darkness. She used instinct to navigate. When she reached a bend in a tunnel, she would close her eyes and call upon her skill to make the correct turn. It took her a while. But something beckoned. Like a homing device in her head. Something reached out to her from the labyrinth of darkness.

She made one last turn and saw the passageway ahead of her widen. Through the distant opening, she saw the black, volcanic cliffs rising up like massive rib cages. She could see the countless holes in the crags, the portals to dreams, obscured behind ghostly blankets of vapor. She advanced through the shadows and came to the edge of a precipice.

Pausing to catch her breath, she saw movement way in the distance, at least a hundred yards away.

Three figures loitered outside the threshold of a familiar dream portal: an old woman in a wheelchair, a tall gray-haired gentleman, and a scruffy-cool young man. They looked like expectant family members killing time in the waiting room of a maternity ward. Silhouetted in the eerie magenta light, the young man puffed on a cigarette as he paced across the mouth of the portal. Lori had never seen Nick Ballas smoking before.

It was a little disconcerting.

She rushed down the slope, kicking up black dust as she went. Then she made her way along the cinder-strewn ravine toward her friends. As she approached, Nick glanced up and signaled with a wave.

"That's a nasty habit," Lori said to Nick as she trotted up to the group.

"What—*this?*" Indicating the smoldering cigarette between his fingers, he gave a shrug. "That's the beauty of BACKworld." He dropped the butt, snubbed it out with his combat boot, and gave an enigmatic grin. "Everything's guilt-free."

"Look what the monkeys dragged in," Mrs. Waverly said, showing her dentures in a cockeyed smile. She thumbed the switch on her armrest, and her chair whirred toward Lori.

"It's actually kind of wonderful to see you guys," Lori said, her gaze lingering on Nick. She yearned to touch his hair, to feel his strong arms around her. "Would it be totally corny of me to say that I missed you?"

"Isn't that precious, she missed us," Mrs. Waverly commented wryly.

"I think she's referring to me," Nick said with a smidgen of defiance in his voice. His gaze had not wavered from Lori's since she had arrived.

Lori grinned at him. "You are correct," she said. "As usual."

Nick nodded toward the portal. "Shouldn't be long now, we got the Shadow out of him . . . just cleaning up the mess in there."

"That's great."

Another awkward moment of silence, and finally Lori gave in to her impulse. She reached out to Nick, pulled him into an unyielding embrace, and laid her head on his shoulder. The old woman looked away.

"Thank you . . . *thank you*," Lori uttered softly into his ear, so softly it took a moment to register on Nick. "Before I met you I was—"

"Hey," a voice said from behind Lori. She felt something bump her rear end.

Lori and Nick kept hugging each other.

"Hey," repeated the voice, the wheelchair bumping Lori's behind again and again.

Lori and Nick finally loosened their clinch, and Lori turned toward Mrs. Waverly.

The old woman reached out and gave Lori a good-natured punch in the arm. "I was wrong about you," she said. "You did good."

"Thanks, I guess, I—" Lori started to say when another voice broke in. "All done!"

The words—delivered in a clear, melodious, authoritative tone—came from Lori's immediate right, commanding her attention. The archangel's voice was accompanied by a puff of air that sounded like the seal on a jar cracking open.

Lori whirled toward the portal just in time to see the Archangel Michael emerging from Ichabod's REMspace. The golden-haired super-being, clad in battered armor, had a satisfied gleam in his eyes as he pushed through the membrane and rose to his full six-foot-plus height. It was the expression of a surgeon after a long procedure to remove a cancerous tumor. It was the look of success that said, *Yeah, we got it all out, the biopsy's clean, the boy's going to live to be a hundred, go ahead and visit him.*

"There she is," the archangel said with a warm nod as he wiped the soot from his hands with a towel, fixing his opal-blue gaze on Lori.

"Hello, sir."

"Such manners," the angel marveled. "Call me Mike."

Lori nodded. "That was my father's name, actually. Full name, Michelangelo, from Montego Bay, Jamaica."

"Yes it was," the angel said, and then gave Lori a puzzling little glance. "As a matter of fact, I've been meaning to talk to you about that."

"You have?" Lori looked at the angel, then looked at Nick, then looked back at the angel. "You've been meaning to talk to me about my dad?"

"Don't worry about it, they'll be plenty of time for that," the angel told her after a moment's hesitation. "That was a brilliant move with that tranquilizer, Lori. It kept him in REM indefinitely, where we could work on him. You want to see him?"

Lori looked at Nick again, then looked back at the angel. "Ichabod?"

The angel nodded.

With a shrug Lori said, "Why not?"

The archangel made a grand gesture toward the portal that reminded Lori of a bellhop in a fancy hotel gesturing toward a luxury suite.

* * *

The backyard of the Kettlekamp farmhouse had transformed, expanded by half in each direction, the brown, bald lawn now lush with a thick carpet of Kentucky bluegrass, the sky high and blue, the sun-washed air sweet with clover. No more man-eating weeds, no more anxiety. In fact, Lori found the yard to be strangely familiar and unfamiliar at the same time, as though it had morphed into *every* good backyard behind *every* good house in the world.

The entire extended Kettlekamp family sat at a long table in the shade of a hundred-year-old oak. Cousins, aunts, uncles, neighbors—all chowing down on a feast of roast pig, slaw, watermelon, potato salad, baked beans, beer, shaved ice, strawberry shortcake, and sweet-tea. Ichabod's mom, back from her decade-long affair, sat at the head of the table, next to her husband, Ichabod's dad, a weathered old guy in a straw hat, returned from the grave, his arm around his beloved original wife— as though her infidelity, not to mention his death, had never happened.

"Blaine!"

Lori heard a familiar gravelly voice and spun toward a folding chair under the tree, on which Davy "Ichabod" Kettlekamp sat blissfully spitting watermelon seeds and moving a lump of Red Man chewing tobacco around his bulging mouth. The gangly farm kid had never looked happier. Hell, Lori had never even seen him crack a smile, and now the kid was grinning a slimy brown grin at Lori like it was Christmas morning.

"Hey, Davy," Lori said, walking over to the tree. "How do you feel?"

"Not half bad," the rangy boy said, spitting another seed. "Tell ya the truth, I ain't felt this good in a coon's age."

"That's great."

"Blaine, yer somewhat of a deep thinker, ain't ya?"

Lori looked at him. "What do you mean?"

"Wrap yer head 'round this one," the farm kid said. "You think a person can split into halves?"

Lori gave him a shrug. "I don't know . . . maybe."

The farm kid spat. "Fella came here a minute ago, took the bad part outta me."

Lori nodded. "That's good, Davy."

"Felt like I was upchuckin' half a horse, but it felt damn good gettin' rid of that thing." Ichabod reached for his chunk of watermelon, slurping another bite out of it. "Looked like a country singer, this fella," the kid mumbled with his mouth full. "Real good-lookin' fella."

"Like Roger Daltrey," Lori mused.

"Who?"

"That's right." Lori nodded. "From the Who."

Ichabod looked puzzled. "The what?"

"The band? The Who?" Lori saw that the farm kid was completely vexed. "Never mind. It doesn't matter."

The farm boy spat another seed. "This fella said his name was Mitchell . . . no, that ain't right . . . *Michael*. That was it. Name of Michael."

Lori nodded, said nothing.

"Funny thing, too," Ichabod added. "We got another Mike hangin' around here somewhere."

Lori felt a tingle at the base of her spine. "Pardon?"

"There's another fella," Ichabod said, jacking a thumb toward the long table across the yard. "He ain't family. Nice enough fella, though. Name's Mike, too. Real egghead, this guy. Black fella." Ichabod chuckled, the pink juice dripping down his scruffy chin. "Ain't that a kick? Place is crawlin' with Mikes."

Lori could barely hear Ichabod's voice now.

She was too busy searching the picnic table for this mysterious *other* Mike.

The English professor and acclaimed poet, Michelangelo Blaine, sat at the far end of the table. A handsome, compact man, with caramel skin and dark, curly hair just beginning to pepper with gray, he wore his customary tweed sport coat, the fabric dusty with chalk from his daily dissertations at the blackboard. His round tortoise-shell eyeglasses gave him the air of a nineteenth-century composer.

"Hey, my little girly-girl!" the professor called out in his lilting island accent, after glancing up from his sweet tea and potato salad, noticing Lori under the adjacent oak tree.

"Dad?" Lori approached slowly through the festive smoke of roasting pig. "What are you—"

"Look at you," Mike Blaine enthused, standing up, wiping his mouth with a napkin. "You've grown up on me, girly. Come here, Lor."

The two of them stood facing each other at the end of the table, while the Kettlekamp clan went about their business of feasting and chattering and laughing. Lori could not figure out what to do with her hands. Emotion rising in her gut, welling up in her eyes, she wondered if she should give her dad a hug. "It's good to see you, Dad," Lori said finally.

"C'mere, you sweet thing," the professor said with a grin, and pulled the girl into a bear hug.

Of all the things Lori had enjoyed over the last year in REMspace— endless supplies of double-chocolate fudge pudding, infinite cable channels, and even a burgeoning romance with Nick Ballas—nothing compared to being hugged by her absent father. All the resentment and contempt and anger that had been festering inside Lori for so many years melted away in that single embrace.

"How did you get here?" Lori asked the professor after the two of them had finally released each other from their desperate hug.

"Long story," Mike Blaine said with a wink.

"Where have I heard that before?"

"We're in what you might call a hybrid," the professor explained. "Your REMspace is melding with Ichabod's."

Lori stared at her father, thinking it over. "Wait a minute, wait . . . how do *you* know this?"

Mike took a deep breath. "Ah, child . . . therein lies the rub."

"Am I like *manufacturing* you?"

"Not exactly."

"Then you're real?" Lori's heart chugged in her chest. "You're really here?"

"Well, see, the thing is . . ." He paused and scratched his chin (he pronounced "thing" like "ting"). "That's going to take a while to explain."

Lori took a deep breath and gazed across the horizon to the south.

The Kettlekamp acreage had never looked so green, so lush. The sea of cornflowers danced in the breeze. Puffy clouds hung in the azure sky. The smoke from pig spit curled up and scented the wind with savory, salty pork fat. Lori noticed a trail winding off into the back forty. She turned to her father and gestured toward the footpath. "We got time, Dad, if you want to take a walk."

The professor smiled. "You know what? A walk sounds pretty nice right about now."

Lori grinned. "After you."

They turned and strolled across the luxuriant carpet of freshly mowed grass to the edge of the property, where an excellent old split-rail fence ran along the edge of the cornfield. The trailhead was groomed and trimmed with gravel, and the twosome—father and daughter—started along the path, side by side, talking softly.

"Girly-girl . . . with me it started the same way it did with you," the older man was saying as they vanished around the edge of the cornstalks. "It started with a door in my dreams . . ."

The wind kicked up, and soon their voices faded into the soft, hushed whisper of tassels swaying.

The Kettlekamp reunion continued unabated. And soon the two dreams gently disengaged with each other, like yolks separating from whites, until there was only a tranquil afternoon on a farm . . .

. . . and somewhere in the distance, a young woman coming to terms with her secret legacy.